STATUS RED

Book Three in The Ascent Trilogy

Clive Hawkswood

There can be no covenants between men and lions, wolves and lambs can never be of one mind, but hate each other out and out and through. Therefore, there can be no understanding between you and me, nor may there be any covenants between us, till one or other shall fall and glut grim Aries with his life's blood.

Homer. The Iliad, Scroll 22, line 232

And the wolf will dwell with the lamb, and the leopard will lie down with the kid, and the calf and the young lion and the fatling together; and a little boy will lead them.

Isaiah 11:6

CONTENTS

PREFACE

STATUS GREEN

Extinction event theoretically
possible, but unlikely

STATUS AMBER

Extinction even threat
identified and verifiable

STATUS RED

Extinction event imminent

PROLOGUE

In the distance the thrum of a low flying aircraft echoed off the barren slopes of the Moroccan Atlas Mountains. The one hundred and sixteen villagers of Amekoura paid it little attention. The men of working age were busy tending to their crops in the stepped hillside below the small community. Everyone else, especially the children, was more interested in the old Range Rover that was bouncing down the single road that was their sole artery to the outside world.

When the car came to a halt a small army of well-wishers gathered around it. Dr Zarif Tobji from the University of Rabat had become something of a local celebrity since first coming to them a month earlier. They didn't really understand the research project he was working on, although the village elders pretended that they did. What really mattered to them was that he was a doctor who was more than happy to treat them free of charge and with no obligations attached.

The nearest hospital was in Er Rachidia, which was nearly 100km away. For the people of Amekoura it was as familiar to them as the far side of the moon. They were accustomed to caring for themselves. They looked after their own, but their pride did not stop them accepting help when it was offered. From his base of medical generosity, Tobji had quickly won them over.

They had become accustomed to his visits. While there he had managed to speak to every single villager. Any suspicions about the stranger had faded away as quickly as the thin morning clouds that regularly skittered across the distant peaks. His care for their welfare was genuine. The young women said that such sincerity could not be faked. The older women laughed and told them that handsome men had a way of making you believe in them.

The fathers kept a close watch on all the women when Tobji was around. That was to be expected of them. After all, he was not one of them and they had a duty to protect their womenfolk. However, even the staunchest traditionalists among them gradually warmed to him. He was equally comfortable sitting and drinking tea with the greybeards as he was talking about farming to the hard men who grew food in the unforgiving soil. And he never tired of quizzing them about their health, and what illnesses they had suffered from. Whatever their replies he would offer help or advice. The men never said that they agreed with the young women about Tobji's sincerity. They did not need to. Their actions demonstrated the respect they had for him. Whether it was an invitation to break bread or take a smoke with them, each in its way was a clear signal of his acceptance.

Today was different. He had told them he would be bringing a colleague and, sure enough, this time he had a companion in the car with him. As Tobji got out he waved at the crowd of children who were scurrying towards him. He slammed the door of the battered Range Rover to make sure it would shut properly. It caused a plume of dust to sprout from the roof. He skipped around and opened the passenger door.

A woman stepped out. She was wearing khaki trousers and a white blouse. A silk scarf with a floral pattern was tied about her head. Sunglasses concealed her pale blue eyes. She reminded Tobji of Hollywood stars from the Fifties, like Bette Davis and Joan Crawford. Even out here in this arid good for nothing spot that didn't even appear on road maps, she maintained an ageless grace and style. She didn't flinch as she surrendered the cool air-conditioned environment of the car for the scorching sun, and ninety-degree temperature.

Tobji had prepared her for the behaviour of the locals, and she held her ground as the children rushed forward with the froth and vigour of a breaking wave. Some pointed at her and waved to their mothers as if they were personally responsible for uncovering this pale creature who had arrived in their midst. Others hopped up and down. They squealed and called out to get her attention.

A slight boy who barely came up to her waist reached out to take her hand. Tobji had given her a few words of Arabic to use, and she smiled back at the children, saying *marhaban, marhaban.* They responded with the same word of welcome and a gush of other words that she did not understand. With her free hand she reached into a pocket and took out boiled sweets which she quickly passed around. It took a second dip to get enough out for all of them. As the other children tore at the wrappers, one set of small fingers tightened on her own. She looked down at the boy who was holding her hand. Abject woe had replaced the excitement on his face. He was the only child not to have received a treat. She patted her pocket. It was empty. The boy saw her gesture and his mouth sagged further. She crouched down so that her eyes were level with his. With a flourish she produced a silver pen that had been clipped to her belt. She handed it to him and made some gestures which persuaded him that it was a present for him to keep.

He was a polite child and remembered to say *shukran* before raising the pen as if it was some sporting trophy before running back through the gaggle of youngsters to show off his new prized possession.

Tobji growled playfully at the tots, and they scattered as if chased by some mythical desert monster. Then he acknowledged the smiles and chuckles of the adults who were watching on. He spied an elderly man leaning against one of the small houses and called out to say he would be along shortly to look at his knee again. The man, all leathery skin and wrinkles, raised a gnarled hand in agreement.

Tobji turned to his guest and said, 'is it not as I described it, Virginia?'

Virginia Brightwell took in the yellowing squat buildings of the village, the stream that was its life blood, the walnut trees that lined its banks, and the paltry mixed crops beyond that of potatoes, melons, peas and peppers. They were of no account to her. She focussed instead on the people. In the small fields dark shapes were toiling to produce enough to survive. In the village the older women wore hajibs. The younger ones tended to be bareheaded. The men who weren't working wore woollen djellabas or loose-fitting cotton shirts and trousers. The children were dressed in an array of ill-fitting track suits, replica soccer shirts, and faded dresses.

Down the street she saw the boy with the pen showing it proudly to two women who were sitting on boxes and sipping at the heavily sweetened tea that was a staple in the region. The smell of slow-cooked tajines drifted from the three-room brick house behind them. Brightwell's hyper-sensitive nose bristled as the mix of cooked spices reached it.

Brightwell said, 'you chose well, Zarif. It's exactly as the photographs and maps depicted it.'

Beneath his well-trimmed moustached, his white teeth flashed in appreciation. He said, 'I can put names to each of them. Most do not have formal medical records, but I have accessed those that do and compiled additional data from my conversations with the rest. Offering free medical treatment and medicines enabled me to examine many of them too. I have uploaded all the results.'

Brightwell already knew all of that. Tobji was nervous and talking just for the sake of hearing his own voice. It was forgivable. He was loyal and had done all that was asked of him. She would not berate him for his passing weakness.

The sound of the plane grew louder.

Brightwell checked her wristwatch. She said, 'it's on time. Fetch me the binoculars.'

The boy with the pen skipped across the narrow, rutted road to show his treasure to somebody else. He called happily to her. She gave him her broadest smile and a mock salute which made him even happier.

Tobji leaned into the car. His weight caused more red dust to detach itself from the roof and hood. He came back with the high powered, military standard, binoculars and gave them to Brightwell. She used them to scan the horizon to the west. After finding the dot when it passed over the last of the mountains, she tracked it as it flew low over the hilltops.

Without lowering the binoculars, she said, 'activate the cameras now, Zarif. I will want to review the experiment in detail.'

He did not question her orders. That was something he would never do. He pulled a hand-sized tablet from his cargo pants and opened the app that allowed him to control the video cameras that he had so carefully secreted around the village on his two most recent trips. One was on the roof of the sole two-storey building in the village. It was where they pooled and stored their crops. Its sweep covered the road and every building along it. Others covered the outskirts of the village and the nearby fields. Between them they could see everyone in Amekoura. The sole exceptions were those who were indoors, but at this time of day there would be few of those.

As the plane got closer more of the villagers looked skyward. It was unusual for aircraft to approach the village and it was even rarer for one to be coming in so close to the ground.

With the advantage of the binoculars and with prior knowledge of its approach path, Brightwell got a good look at it long before any of villagers did. She also had the benefit of having seen it before.

The brightly coloured yellow and red PZL-106 stood out against the vividly blue sky.

The squat single-seat monoplane had a four-bladed propeller and was powered by a single radial engine. Behind the engine was a 1300-litre container that could carry whatever was needed for spraying, crop-dusting or firefighting. It was a slow and noisy plane. It was designed for functionality and not stealth. It was a workhorse and not a warrior.

As the plane bore down on Amekoura, everyone stopped what they were doing to stare up. The children chattered and whooped. Even the boy with the pen was distracted by the roaring engine and the flash of exotic colours rushing towards them.

Brightwell put the binoculars down and took out a stopwatch from the trouser pocket that had not held sweets.

The plane that had seemed to take an age to reach them now raced overhead. The children covered their ears to block out the sound of the racing engine. The down draft from the propeller churned up dirt and grit. The PZL-106 was so low that they could easily make out the face of the pilot, but they could not see the release button that he punched. A fine mist descended on them.

Brightwell started the stopwatch.

The plane shot across their heads in parallel with the road and then banked steeply. The engines became even louder. It went out for about half a mile, finished its turn, and then swept across the fields. For the second time the pilot released the mist to float down on the farmers.

Brightwell did not bother watching the aerobatics. It was the people of Amekoura that continued to demand her attention. A girl, no more than three or four years old, was the first to scream. Her pathetic wails caused everyone to look towards her in time to see her drop to the ground.

Brightwell clicked the stopwatch to stop it. Seventy-two seconds had elapsed since the mist had descended.

The silence that followed was momentary. Around the village people of all ages were shrieking and collapsing. They twitched and rolled in the dirt as if their souls were desperate to escape their tortured bodies.

Others acted instinctively or quickly shrugged off the shock and dashed to comfort the fallen. Mothers clutched their dead or dying children and bellowed in agony as if their beating hearts were being torn from their chests.

Nobody had time to watch the plane disappearing back over the hills.

Tobji glanced fearfully at Brightwell. He said, 'the success rate can't be more than fifty percent.'

'I've got eyes, Zarif. I can see that as well as you can,' she snapped at him.

'I am sorry, Virginia.'

She sighed and reassuringly patted his arm. She said, 'no, you must forgive me, Zarif, it's not your fault. It's disappointing that's all... disappointing.'

Instead of going to help the villagers, the only doctor within 20 km climbed disconsolately back into the Range Rover. Without another word Virginia Brightwell joined him and they drove off.

Behind them the boy who had held her hand was now a contorted corpse splayed out in the road. The silver pen was still gripped tight in his lifeless fingers.

CHAPTER ONE

Alan Harman sipped his Americano coffee. He was sitting at a window seat of Koko's Koffee Kafe in Palo Alto. In the gathering darkness of the evening its welcoming atmosphere and subdued neon lighting fused with the aroma of coffee beans to create a relaxing haven for the patrons.

He had never been to California before and had so far seen very little of it apart from this urban patch that was within the orbit of Stanford University. He was on a stakeout. He thought of it that way because that was how it was described on every cop series he had ever seen on television. And he had watched countless hours of those during the long nights when everyone else slept. It was only very recently that he had learned why he needed so little sleep.

It was not the first stakeout he had been on. Far from it, although those had been while he was on duty. He supposed that technically he was still a Detective Sergeant in the British Ministry of Defence police force, but he had left that life far behind him and would never be returning to it. In fact, his whole life had condensed into the pursuit of a single purpose.

He could not afford to be distracted by thoughts of what he would do after that. Which was why he was avoiding eye contact with the other customers and focussing solely on the apartment block opposite.

He was on a quest to find Virginia Brightwell. A man who lived in one of those apartments would be the launching pad for that. When the man returned home, and the lights went on, Harman would pay him a visit. One way or another he would get the information he needed. The threat presented by Brightwell and her cohort of Ascendants was too dreadful to allow for any weakness on his part. Not anymore. They might be an evolved form of humanity, but no matter how genuine their fears for survival were, it could never justify the eradication of lesser mortals.

For too long he had harboured doubts about whether he and the Normals, that she so despised, had the ability to stop her. That was before she tried to kill him and had instead inadvertently triggered a change that had burned through his mind and body. Dormant DNA had sprung painfully to life. He became one of them. Now he too was an Ascendant. He was still learning what that meant. Coping with the enhanced sensory inputs was gradually becoming easier and he used every spare moment to try and master them. It still left him feeling like a toddler who had stood and taken its first steps, but who, so far, had no concept of what running would be like.

Some of the chains that bound him to his past life had been ripped apart. Others he had consciously escaped from. His ex-wife was dead. Brightwell had caused Carol King, his best friend, to be murdered. Peter Salt, the man he had subconsci ously come to see as his mentor and navigator around all things Ascendant, had been killed by someone acting under Brightwell's control. Those links to his past could never be mended. His solace, such as it was, came from the pursuit of revenge for their loss.

That was why Harman had distanced himself from his erstwhile employers at The Department of Emerging Threats, ET1. Their efforts to combat the Ascendant threat would never be good enough. They would only get under his feet. He had chosen to hunt alone and that was what he would do.

Or so he thought.

He had been concentrating so hard on watching the apartment block that he did not sense or see the man approach him.

'Would you mind if I joined you,' the newcomer said gently. He was holding a Koko's branded mug. Steam swirled from it.

Harman's lean face turned towards him and took in the bald pate, the moustache and goatee beard, the light-reactive glasses, the chinos and the black t-shirt which had printed on it, *I don't digibyte.* He was maybe mid-thirties and was not untypical of Koko's clientele from what Harman had observed since arriving.

Harman said, 'I'm waiting for a friend. I'm sure you can find an empty table somewhere else.'

The man shuffled uncomfortably and smiled uncertainly at him. He said, 'that didn't go as planned. I suppose that's what comes when I try to ad lib rather than stick to the script. Let me try again.'

Harman tensed as it became clear this was not some chance encounter.

The man cleared his throat and said, 'my name is Charles Hope. Peter Salt sent me. So, for the second time, would you mind if I joined you?'

Harman opened his ears to every conversation in the café, and re-inspected everyone who was there. None of them seemed out of place. Hope appeared to be alone.

'It's just me, all on my lonesome,' Hope said, 'here to help.'

Harman did not want to attract any viewers to the scene that was being played out and so nodded at the chair across from him. Hope gratefully accepted the invitation and placed his mug on the table. He said, 'that's a relief, it was getting embarrassing. I was afraid people would think I was trying to pick you up.'

Harman brushed aside the newcomer's lame attempt at levity and said, making it sound like an accusation, 'you say that Peter sent you?'

'That's right, he....'

Harman raised a hand to stop him talking and said, 'care to tell me how he did that when he's been dead for four days?'

Hope's eyelids flickered and he tugged nervously at his beard. After a few seconds he took a deep breath and said in a low voice, 'I assumed as much, but hearing you confirm it is a kick to the guts. I thought I was prepared for it, but wow it really takes some processing. I'm glad you let me sit down before telling me.'

Harman assessed every twitch of Hope's changing facial expression and every change in the intonation of his words. If Hope was feigning surprise and sadness, he was doing a good job of it. Then again that proved nothing. Some people were simply incredibly good actors. It would take a lot more than tears, crocodile or otherwise, for Harman to drop his guard.

He said, 'that's as maybe, but you haven't answered my question.'

Hope focussed again on Harman as if he had for a second forgotten who he was. He said, 'what? Oh yes, how did I know that I should come find you? It's no great mystery. Peter would message me every two days and said if he ever failed to report in then I should find you and offer whatever small help I could. When I didn't get the last scheduled message, I knew something bad must have happened. I suppose I

15

didn't want it to be as bad as you've told me. Peter gone? I can't get my head around it.'

Harman set his jaw as he chose his next question. If it came off like he was conducting an interrogation, then so be it. He had come too far and there was too much still to play for to be hampered by the constraints of politeness. Hope would have to do a lot more persuading if he wanted to be believed.

Cutting to the tender heart of it, Harman said, 'Peter never mentioned you. So why should I trust you?'

'You know him, I mean knew him – he never gave away more than he had to. His whole life was a secret. It must be that way for the likes of us. He probably thought he was protecting me,' Hope said and then paused. It was his turn to reflect on the man he was talking to. Then he added, posing it as a challenge, 'and he told me that you were a Normal, but you're one of us, aren't you?'

Harman did not deny it and nor did he tell Hope that, while Salt had been there to witness the outcome of his transformation, he had been shot dead very soon afterwards. Instead, he said, 'this will work better if I ask the questions and you answer them. All I'm convinced of so far is that you knew Peter Salt or had been told about him. That's not nearly enough. Give me something that you would only know if Peter had shared it with you.'

'Yes, yes, I can. I can. Sorry, I'm gabbling. I know I am. I get like that when I'm nervous. I'm not used to all this skulking about. Is skulking even the right word? This isn't how I imagined it would be. I made a promise to Peter, and I'll keep it. I have to, don't I? It's just...'

'Charles,' Harman interrupted him, 'or whoever you are, concentrate and answer my question.'

'What? Your question? Yes, yes, sorry again. Peter gave you a list. A list of Ascendants for you to track down if anything happened to him,' Hope said expectantly as if it was a magic spell like *open sesame* that would give him access to Harman's trust.

Harman did not react. Salt had given him the list for exactly that reason, and he had shown it to nobody before tearing it into shreds and flushing the pieces down a toilet at The Denver Health Medical Centre. It was a tick in the credibility box for Hope, but it would take more than one of those for him to pass muster.

'Did Peter show you the list, Charles?'

'No, I've never seen it.'

'That's odd, isn't it, if he wanted you to help me?'

'Peter never did anything without a good reason. If he chose to pass it to you then he must have believed you were the one to put it to good use.'

'As you said, until the end he thought I

was a Normal. Wouldn't it have made more sense to give it to an Ascendant like you? Wouldn't you be better equipped to make use of it?'

Hope looked lost and covered his hesitancy by slurping from his Koko mug. When he was ready, he put it back on the table and said, 'I can't speak for him. Perhaps he sensed something in you even if he wasn't consciously aware of it.'

'And that's all you can come up with?'

Hope ran a hand across his scalp as if patting down some non-existent strands of hair. He leaned back in his chair and with a half-hearted attempt at defiance said, 'look at me and look at you. In his shoes which of us would you have faith in to hunt them down? Peter was a good friend to me and never asked for anything in return until this. Do you know why? It's because I had nothing to offer him. All I ever wanted was a quiet life and he never once criticized me for that. The world will turn, and evolution will not go any faster or slower because I choose not to put my shoulder to its wheel. I'm no fighter. I don't know how many are on that list of yours or who they all are, but that still wouldn't have prevented me or Peter knowing that any one of them could probably chew me up and spit me out. Are you happy now?'

'Happy isn't how I would describe my

current emotional state. Happiness and I haven't been acquainted for some time,' Harman said, visibly unmoved by Hope's soul searching. 'If you're being truthful, and that's still a big if, why did he think you would be of any use to me at all?'

Hope pointed to himself and then to Harman as he said, 'Ascendant...Normal. Or so Peter thought when he put me up to this. I'd be a poor substitute for him. I admit that. He will still have seen one of us being of value to one of you.'

'By your own account, wouldn't you have been a poor choice for that role?'

Hope laughed uncomfortably at that. He said, 'what makes you think he had many alternatives? If you're assuming that I've been selling myself short and that only modesty prevents me from acclaiming myself as one of the great Ascendants like Peter, then you couldn't be more wrong. I am what I am, but Peter never had cause to doubt my loyalty. Over the years that particular pigeon-hole of Peter's has shrunk further and further. I can't put it any other way – you got me because I'm all he had.'

Like any good inquisitor, Harman knew when to back off as well as he did when to press hard. He changed the subject and asked, 'is Hope really your name?'

Hope shrugged and said, 'it's not the one I was born with. Peter must have explained that longevity makes it hard to live our lives with just one identity. That's something else you will have to get accustomed to.'

'You selected it for yourself. Does that reflect your general sense of optimism or are you a massive Bob Hope fan?'

'A bit of both. It's hard to watch Hope and Crosby on the big screen and not feel more positive about life. It is a non-descript name for the non-descript life I wanted. Let's say that it fits me well.'

From the corner of an eye that less than a week ago would have been incapable of noticing it, Harman saw a subdued yellow seep through the blinds of the apartment across the road. The first person on the list had come home.

Harman fixed Hope with an unwavering glare and said, 'I must go now, Charles. You can stay here and wait for me to return, or you can go back to wherever it is you came from, but do not under any circumstances follow me. Are we understood?'

As Harman rose, Hope said eagerly, 'I can help you. You've only recently activated your new talents. If Peter was here, he would have guided you in their use. He would have answered all the questions you must have. I could do that. That I could do. Yes, yes, I could.'

Harman stared down at him and for the first time relented slightly. He said, 'you're gabbling again, Charles. Wait here and maybe we could talk about it some more.'

Hope began to stand. Harman told him to sit down again. Hope did so. He was always willing to follow orders if they came from the right source.

As Harman pushed his way out through the glass doors, Hope allowed himself a small smile. He had seen the first chink in Harman's armour of suspicion. He was sure that if he continued to push at it, he would break through and win Harman's acceptance. Sitting there with his cooling mug, it was all he wanted.

*

Harman could well have done without the unexpected appearance of Charles Hope. He was surrounded by imponderables and one more was an unwelcome addition to the plates he was spinning in his mind. The first test was to see if Hope could do as he was told.

After skipping around the criss-crossing traffic, Harman hopped on to the sidewalk across from Koko's Koffee Kafe. He ducked into the dark recess of a closed store and looked back the way he had come. He waited there for a few minutes until he was sure that he was not being tracked by anyone, and that included Hope.

When he was satisfied, he moved quickly up the street to the small apartment block. The main doors were locked. No surprise there. Access could only be gained by putting the right four number sequence into the keypad on the wall, or by buzzing the apartment you wanted to ask them to let you in. The man he wanted would not be that obliging, and if he tried buzzing people randomly one of them was likely to call the police. Nobody in their right mind would admit him simply because he concocted a stale story about having a delivery for them. That happened in the movies and nowhere else. In real life, people were too crime conscious for that.

He had scouted out the building earlier in the day and had identified a more anonymous entry point. As it was that time of the evening when a lot of people would be coming home from work, he did not anticipate having to wait for long. He walked down the side of the building and out on to the small road at the rear which led to the block's underground car park. Light streamed out through the metal shutters that barred access to it.

Harman edged back to the corner and took up station there. He took out a phone that he had bought downtown a few hours ago. He held it at the ready. The street was quiet but if anyone saw him, he would pretend to be making a call. He wasn't sure what the average mugger or burglar was expected to look like in that part of town, but he was sure that he did not meet the profile that would make any passers-by immediately suspicious of him. If challenged, he would use his British accent to good effect and play the lost tourist. If that failed, he would have to resort to influencing them.

He was a novice at the manipulation technique that seemed to be commonplace amongst Ascendants. It was a skill, a power, that he needed to train. Peter Salt would have helped him, he knew that. Without him, Harman was teaching himself and he could not know whether he was a good pupil or not. Until then he had used it to facilitate travel without documents or payment. His conscience had not balked at the petty larceny. It was almost a victimless crime and he had committed it for the greater good and not for personal gain. What bothered him much more was using men and women against their will, or at least without their willing consent. He had seen people commit murder under Virginia Brightwell's influence and those images would never leave him. That was bad enough, but his reluctance stemmed from somewhere deeper within him. He could not escape the feeling that by influencing a person he was somehow violating them. He had tried rationalising it with the excuse of cowards throughout history, that the ends justify the means. He had quickly discovered that such thinking did not cut it in his own personal court of morality. It was plain wrong. There was no getting away from that. Which meant he was going against himself and his own core values when he influenced anyone. Not that he would allow his personal sensibilities to stop him when the crunch came. If it left a bad taste in his mouth, he would find a way to swallow it and move on. Nothing mattered more than stopping Brightwell. Nothing. Under a week ago, although it seemed longer, he had killed a man for the first time. It wasn't something he ever wanted to do again, but he would if he had to.

On reflection, it struck him as odd that it had been so easy to reconcile the necessary death of an evil man, when he found it so hard to accept the relatively small abuse of an innocent one. All he really took from that moment of introspection was that Ascendants, assuming he was not atypical of them, found it as hard to manage their emotions as the Normals did.

Within ten minutes a car pulled up at the garage. The driver used a remote- control device to activate the gates. They rattled leisurely upwards. When they stopped the car entered. Harman sprinted forward as soon as the gates began their clanking descent. He got there just in time to throw himself to the ground and roll underneath them before they could snap shut. He crouched behind a pillar until the car was parked. From the clicking of heels on the concrete he knew it was a woman who had got out. He had no wish to scare her and so stayed where he was until she had entered the elevator and its doors had slid together behind her.

When all was still, he went to the stairs. He reasoned that there was less chance of running into anyone if he went that way. He came out on the third floor and went to apartment thirteen. Harman was not a superstitious man. It did not prevent him from wondering if that number would be unlucky for him or the man inside. Then he smirked to himself. He would not have gone there if he wasn't already sure of the outcome.

There was a doorbell, but he chose to knock instead. It was more visceral and abrupt. That always made it more unexpected and unnerving for the person in their home. If you're seeking to question a suspect or arrest them, it helps if you can put them on the back foot from the outset. He had been told that on a training course way back when. He hadn't been persuaded of it then and nothing had changed, but what did he have to lose? As the instructor had said, try to seek every small advantage – it might only take one to make all the difference.

Harman could hear music from inside. Something classical. Something he didn't recognise. Culture and the arts had played no part in Harman's life, and it seemed that becoming an Ascendant had not changed his tastes. He had learnt something else about himself. The volume was lowered. He detected a flicker of movement on the other side of the spyhole and knew he was being watched.

'Mr Blanc,' he said, 'my name is Alan Harman, and I would like to speak with you.'

Harman made it sound professional and non-threatening. He had frequently told his old friend Detective Inspector Carol King that you catch more flies with honey than with vinegar. Not that she believed him. She had her own style. If she was there now, she would be pushing him aside and be kicking the door in. The memory of her saving his life and then dying in his arms was still fresh and raw. It made what he had to do personal. Harman was not lacking in motivation.

A muffled voice from inside the apartment asked who he was and what he wanted.

'I'd like to talk to you about Virginia Brightwell.'

'Are you alone?'

'More alone than you could know,' Harman said.

The door opened a couple of inches. It was as far as it would go with the chain on. Blanc looked him up and down and then checked to see if anyone else was in the corridor.

'May I come in?' Harman asked, in the same tone as he might if asking a maître d' whether the restaurant had any tables available.

'Who are you?' Blanc said, sounding a bit bolder.

'I did say. My name is Alan Harman.

Here's the thing, Thibault, you must have known that me or someone like me would come along sooner or later. You've chosen to hide in plain sight, which is not really hiding at all is it?'

'Where did you get my name? Who is this Virginia Brightwell you mentioned?'

Harman sighed and said, 'we are both grown men, Thibault. We're too old for playing games. I got your name from Peter Salt. I know you've been helping Brightwell. All I want is a bit of information and then I will be out of your hair. I'm not here to hurt you or disrupt your life. Then again, if you choose not to co-operate, I could pass your details on to, let's say, the Department for Homeland Security. One call from me and they could be here before that music you are enjoying has come to an end. They're still smarting from missing out on Brightwell in Colorado. I'm sure they'd love to get their hands on you and, when they do, you can kiss goodbye to whatever life you've made for yourself here. So, what will it be, Thibault?'

Blanc's mouth hardened. His lips took on the appearance of pink corrugated iron. Then he relented and the French Canadian said, '*merde.*'

The oath was directed at the Fates rather than to Harman.

He unchained the door and stepped away, leaving Harman to let himself in.

The unheralded visitor took in the studded leather sofa and chairs, the antique bookcases and the leather-bound volumes that populated them, and the oil paintings that hung on the walls. As with the music, Harman didn't have a clue whether the collections were of real quality or not. Many of the book titles were in French and his basic schoolboy knowledge of the language gave him no help in identifying them.

As Harman closed the door, Blanc went to a drinks tray and poured himself a glass of Rémy Martin XO from a cut glass decanter. He didn't offer one to his unwanted guest. He knocked it back in one go and then refilled his glass. He said, 'I had hoped it would take longer before someone came knocking on my door. How did you find me?'

'Peter Salt, who I'm assuming you've heard of, gave me four names. Surprise, surprise, after Brightwell escaped from us in Colorado, three of them suddenly left their posts at various academic institutions. You on the other hand chose to stay beavering away at the Department of Genetics, at Stanford University School of Medicine. The internet is a wonderful thing for finding people and it wasn't hard to find you. Which makes me worried.'

'Why is that?' Blanc asked on cue. He held the glass of cognac beneath his nose. A body language expert might suggest he was hiding behind it.

'It struck me that maybe you're the tethered goat who has been left in the clearing to draw the tiger out.'

Blanc laughed mirthlessly and said, 'and that would presumably make you the tiger? You do have a high opinion of yourself, don't you?'

'Brightwell hasn't mentioned me to you?'

'Whoever you are, you are so far below her that she wouldn't be able to see you if she used a microscope. If your name ever did come up, it wasn't important enough for me to remember it.'

Harman wasn't sure that he believed him. It didn't matter. He said, 'tell me where Brightwell has gone, and I will leave you in peace. It's as simple as that.'

'I can't do that.'

'Try harder.'

'No, you misunderstand, Mr Harman. I do not know where she is and no amount of persuasion by you or Homeland Security will change that simple fact. Ginny got quite the scare at the 191 Ranch. She didn't tell me exactly what happened, but her reaction spoke more eloquently than words. She triggered an agreed security protocol. We moved away from a committee structure to a cell structure, although we are individuals rather than cells. Each of us maintains contact with the person above and below us in the chain. Unfortunately for you I am at the bottom of that chain and probably lucky to still be on it at all. You see, Ginny has concluded that only a traitor in her ranks could have led to her being traced to that small mine in the Colorado mountains. As I helped to outfit her laboratory there, suspicion, like you, has darkened my door. I have been abandoned.'

Harman sensed no artifice in Blanc. As the Ascendant sipped again at his cognac, Harman instead felt waves of resignation and resentment washing towards him. Blanc had fallen from grace through no fault of his own and he was as alone as Harman was.

'Things are tough all round,' Harman said, deliberately making it sound harsh. If this fool thought he was worthy of any sympathy, he could not have been more wrong. 'If I must go through every link in your chain, then I will. Tell me who's above you and where they are. If you've really been abandoned, then you owe them nothing.'

The alcohol inspired self-pity that had infused Blanc was fleetingly replaced with malice as he said, 'it won't do you any good. You won't get to Ginny in time.'

'Then you've nothing to lose by giving up your friend. Who is it? Osterfeld, Chen, Hagihara or somebody else?'

'Salt really did give you some names, didn't he? I had wondered whether you were bluffing or not.'

Harman said, 'I have no need to bluff. And that scare that Brightwell got at the ranch, well that was me.'

Blanc blinked rapidly and drained what

was left in his glass. He placed it down on a leather coaster. Harman saw the faintest quivering of the Canadian's hand.

Blanc said, 'I find that hard to believe.'

Harman raised an eyebrow and said, 'the tremor in your voice and that twitch of your fingers betray you.'

Blanc snorted and said, 'only one of Us would have noticed. All that tells me is that you are an Ascendant with some talent...and that you're a traitor. But you're still a pup and Virginia would lose no sleep over the likes of you.'

Harman knew better. He did not have to say so. He crossed to the nearest row of books and took one out. The binding was old, the paper was thin, the typeface was delicate. He said, 'have you read this?'

Blanc took a step towards him. The fear in his eye was unmistakeable. He said, 'please be careful with that. It's very rare.'

Harman hefted the book in his hand as if it was a baseball that he was preparing to throw. The anguish that his small action caused in Blanc was as tangible as that of a mother dreading that somebody was about to drop her newborn babe on to the floor.

He said, 'you didn't answer my question.'

'Damn you, of course I have read it, now please put it back.'

'Do you remember every word of it? Did

you grasp every theme?'

'It is a work of beauty, to be savoured and enjoyed. It is complex and marvellous. It is not a cheap script to be learned by heart.'

Harman made as if to toss it over to Blanc. The Canadian did more than flinch. He looked to be on the verge of a heart attack. Harman gently returned the tome to its place on the bookshelf and said, 'I wouldn't understand any of it so I will have to take your word for that. My point is that you've read that book from cover to cover, probably several times, and yet you seem to think you know me better than you do it even though we met barely moments ago. For a man in your position, I'd say that was unwise. I confronted Virginia Brightwell and lived to tell the tale, as they say. If nothing else, that might suggest it would be wise for you to co-operate with me.'

Blanc inserted himself between Harman and his beloved book collection and said, 'I still have no reason to believe you.'

'Maybe so, Thibault, maybe so. Let me be more direct then. It strikes me that you have much to lose. Things rather than people, but obviously things that are precious to you. It doesn't take an Ascendant to guess that you haven't gone into hiding like the rest because you couldn't bear to be parted from those precious things. You made that choice once. All I'm asking you to do is to make the same choice again. You give me a name and location and I will be gone. You will never hear from me again. Maybe Homeland Security or someone else will eventually come knocking at your door again. There's nothing I can do about that, but if they do it won't be because ten seconds after leaving here empty handed, I've called them and given you up. What's it to be?'

'You know the answer. You knew it before you knocked on my door. You're right. It remains to be seen whether my decision was correct or not, but I've made it and there's no reason to change it now.'

Harman felt as much as saw the odd mixture of resentment and surrender that lay behind Blanc's words. He didn't dwell on it. He hadn't come there to be Blanc's new best buddy or psychologist. He was a means to an end, no more or less than that.

Harman said, 'name and location then, Thibault, that's your ticket to getting rid of me, but don't try lying. Unless I get killed going wherever it is you send me, if it's a false path I will make sure you end up spending the rest of your long Ascendant life in a padded cell with not a single luxury to savour and more pain than you can imagine.'

'Your point is made, your threats are redundant,' Blanc said. 'The person above me in the chain is Daiyu Chen. She is on your list, I believe?'

33

'I already have her name, what I need is to be able to find her.'

With his books no longer at risk, Blanc returned to the decanter and refilled his glass. He sipped at the amber liquid and said, 'she is in Gran Canaria. She has taken refuge at a farmhouse up in the mountains. It is about two miles north of the village of Fataga. It's called the Finca Klausen. You will find it easily enough. She wanted me to join her there. Said she could protect me.'

'Were you tempted?'

'Not in the slightest. Daiyu is not my friend. I doubt that she has any of those. If she wanted me there it would have been because she had some use for me and I'm tired of being used. You see, she wants to be Virginia. She wants to sit on top of the pack and every one of us she adds to the tally of those who are beholden to her makes that more possible. I expect she will be glad to see you once she learns that it's Virginia you are after and not her. She will like nothing better than for you to do her dirty work and get Virginia out of the way.'

With his nerves twitching like antennae at the prospect of hidden danger, Harman took a moment to reflect. It was all feeling too easy. He couldn't afford to let his hunger to reach Virginia Brightwell blind him to traps along the way. He said, 'if she wants to be shot of the top dog, why doesn't she do it herself?'

Blanc chuckled. It sounded more like choking than laughter. He said, 'she is ambitious, not reckless. If they went toe to toe, Virginia would destroy her. As a frontal assault would not work, she prefers to chip away at the foundations of Virginia's authority.'

'Brightwell must know that. Why does she tolerate her?'

'That is a question I have asked of her. All she said was that Daiyu had her uses. I suppose there has been some truth in that...'

'I get the impression that her explanation didn't satisfy you?'

'Explanation? Ginny doesn't really do those,' Blanc said, 'but since you ask, I suspect the real reason is that she feels stronger for knowing there is someone who will keep her on her toes. But I'm only guessing. Who really knows what is going on in her head?'

'Yet you chose to follow her? Why?'

'She is the solution. Surely that's obvious. She will stop the Normals from destroying us.'

'As simple as that?'

Blanc looked at him anew, as if realising that he was talking to the dumbest kid in school. He said, 'yes...as...simple...as...that.'

'If you're so committed to the cause then I don't understand your willingness to help me stop her.'

Blanc laughed out loud, the alcohol in his system triggering the exaggerated outburst.

With his voice reaching a crescendo, he said, 'you are as priceless as, as...I can't think what. You surely don't believe you can stop her, do you? She is a force of nature. She will sweep you away. You are a fool. I'm telling you what you wanted to get rid of you. I'm not betraying Ginny. I'm serving you up to her. My young tiger, you think you are the cat, but you are really the mouse.'

Harman took no offence. There was a fragility about Blanc that meant he didn't merit such a personal reaction. Whatever he might say, to Harman he remained no more than a step to be trodden on as he climbed the stairs towards Brightwell. After waiting for the laughter to subside, Harman said, 'what's the timetable for her to deploy the weapon?'

Blanc considered his now empty glass and put it down without topping it up again. The humour drained from him as quickly as the cognac had drained from the glass.

'Who knows, as I said I'm out of the loop.'

'You must have some idea,' Harman pressed him, 'it is not that long since you were her bag carrier.'

'She's a perfectionist. She will want to test it before using it fully. That will take as long as it takes. She will not be dragging her feet though. You should scurry away after her, little mouse, time is not on your side.'

Harman allowed the sad attempt at last minute defiance to pass without comment.

Whatever Blanc had once been, he had become no more than an abandoned soldier left behind with no orders to follow and with no purpose in his life. His world had shrunk to his work at the University and the few crumbs of comfort in his apartment. The old Alan Harman might have pitied him. The new Alan Harman silently damned him to whatever lonely and ignominious future awaited him.

Harman said in a neutral tone, 'I will give your best wishes to Daiyu Chen.'

Then he left.

*

Harman had been concentrating on Thibault Blanc and had given no further thought to Charles Hope until he had left the apartment block, this time via the front doors, and was heading back to Koko's Koffee Kafe. The nervous bookworm was not what he expected of an Ascendant, although as to his knowledge he had only ever spoken to three of them the small sample size meant he could easily be mistaken. He had refused to let the unexpected encounter distract him from the pending confrontation with Blanc. With that behind him he would have to decide quickly what to do about Hope.

While he mulled it over, he used his phone to go online and check out the routes to Gran Canaria. A couple of minutes of clicking and scrolling and he had the information he wanted.

Something told him that when he got back to the café, Hope would still be waiting exactly where he had left him like a quivering puppy who wasn't sure whether it had been abandoned by its new owner. With Chen's whereabouts at his fingertips, Harman would soon be jetting off to the Spanish island in the Atlantic. He did not have the luxury of putting Hope through some impromptu tests to judge his worthiness. The man had the potential to either be an anchor that would drag him down or manna from Heaven. Harman had to choose which it was.

Hope was an unknown quantity and that in itself made him dangerous at a time when Harman was finding it hard to trust anyone. Even if his story was taken at face value, it was impossible to know how much of an asset he might be. On brief acquaintance his temperament was fragile, and he seemed an unlikely candidate for recruitment to the war against Brightwell and her people. Then again, Peter Salt would not have sent him if he was incapable of giving Harman the help he might need. Which meant that any decision about him really rested on the reliability of Salt's judgement and whether, as Hope claimed, Salt was responsible for sending him in the first place.

Harman spooled back through their

earlier conversation. Harman had sought to prove his *bona fides* by asserting his knowledge of the list of Ascendants that Salt had provided. Who else could have known of that? There was Daiyu Chen who had originally given the list to Salt, but she would have had no knowledge that Harman even existed. Certainly, nobody had been present when Salt had given him the list so that ruled anybody else out. Which left Sebastian Kent. The head of ET1 had been told about the list, but the man was as likely to talk as a clam whose two halves had been superglued together. Then again, it might suit Kent's purposes to have someone attach themselves to Harman in order to spy on him and report back. That was very easy to believe. What was infinitely harder to accept was that Kent would trust any Ascendant enough to send them on such a mission. It all pointed to Hope having been sent by Salt, just as he had claimed.

Which meant that, as Harman approached the Koffee Kafe's doors, he was left still deciding how much faith he could place in Salt's thinking. That one was much easier to weigh in the balance. Fair enough, Salt may not have been spoilt for choice when identifying a guardian angel for Harman, but he would not have persuaded Hope to take the part if he was not up to it.

A nagging reluctance to accept any help still told Harman to ditch Hope and go it alone.

He had been relishing the short-lived freedom of being unshackled from the strictures of ET1 and did not want to be saddled by the company of anyone else. The mere idea of it made him feel heavier and sluggish. And that was without the added burden of not knowing how far he could rely on Hope or the story he had trotted out.

The counterbalance to that was the rational voice in his head which told him he needed someone to hold his hand while he came to terms with being an Ascendant. There was still so much he did not know. He was like an orphan cast adrift into a world that he did not understand. Worse still, it was somewhere that his enemies called home. The likes of Brightwell, Blanc and Chen had been born Ascendants. Their journeys may not have been easy, but at least they had had lifetimes to understand what they were capable of and to cope with their differences. What if Blanc's barbed arrow had been well aimed? What if he really was the mouse and not the cat?

His ignorance was not bliss. It seemed to taunt him from behind a veil which was just thick enough to let him see that something was there without him being able to divine precisely what it was. If Hope could provide a pool of knowledge, no matter how shallow, could he really afford not to sip from it?

Harman stepped aside to let a couple of departing customers out of the café and nipped back through the closing door into the wrap around warmth of the room and the tempting scents of various types of coffee beans.

The table where he had been sitting was populated with a small bowl containing sugars, sweeteners, and wooden stirring sticks, and a single mug. His stomach lurched slightly as he registered Hope's absence. That reaction told him what his decision was about the unimpressive, bespectacled, bald man that he had left there not so long ago. However, it was a moot point given that Hope's trepidation appeared to have got the better of him.

Harman's disappointment was very short lived. Hope came out of the men's room. His head was down. When he raised his chin and saw Harman his face lit up like a miser who had lost a dime and found a dollar. The tinted glasses that shaded his eyes did nothing to conceal his pleasure.

He hurried to Harman and said, 'I didn't expect you to come back.'

'Why did you wait then?'

'One has to live in hope,' Hope said brightly, 'or what's the point of living at all? Did everything whatever everything is in this case, go well?'

Harman wasn't yet ready to share any confidences and so restricted himself to saying, 'if I take you along with me, are you ready to do what you're told when you're told?'

Hope's happiness evaporated. He swallowed hard before replying, 'within reason.'

'Alright then. Here's the deal. You can string along doing exactly what Peter asked of you for as long as you're useful to me or until you quit.'

'Are you always so blunt, Mr Harman?'

'I would say it's not in my nature, Charles, but as of this minute I can't be sure of that anymore.'

Hope nodded approvingly, 'honesty is good. I can be more help to you if you are honest with me.'

'You're in then?'

Hope adjusted his spectacles and said, 'if I'm being honest, that prospect makes me more than a little scared, but I will honour my promise to Peter.'

Harman checked out the room again. Nobody was paying them any attention. Satisfied with that, he said, 'do you want another coffee?'

Bishop grimaced and patted his stomach. He said, 'the second cup made me queasy. I've been in that rest room for a while. I dread to imagine what a third cup might do to me.'

'Alright let's get out of here.'

'Where are we going?'

'First off, we'll get a good night's sleep. Then I will meet you at the airport tomorrow morning at 8.30.' Harman took a paper napkin from the counter and scribbled his phone number on it. He handed it to Hope and said, 'any problems, call me.'

Hope carefully folded the paper and stored it in a pocket. He said, 'where are we going?'

'Have you ever been to the Canary Islands? Lovely scenery, great weather and full to the gills of German and British holidaymakers.'

'I'm not sure I could point to it on a map, but it sounds very nice. Are there any direct flights?'

'No, we will go via Scotland.'

'Is that really the quickest route?'

'Well, it's not the slowest and there's somebody there that I'd like to speak to while I have the chance.'

Hope scratched his chin. As his fingernails scrabbled through his goatee beard, Harman could hear the ruffling of hairs as surely as he used to do when combing his hair. He had quickly adjusted to the improved ability of his ears, but every now and then there were sharp reminders, like this, that made him appreciate how deep a transformation he was undertaking.

Hope said, 'I believe I have surprised myself. I feel...energised.'

'Good for you,' Harman said, 'but keep it under control or you will find yourself rushing off to the men's room again.'

*

Ernst Mannson could mask his presence from other Ascendants. He did not attribute it to some evolutionary blip. He knew with utter certainty that it was a gift from God. It was one of many that had been bestowed upon him so that he could be equipped to fulfil his mission. The Ascendants were abominations. They had no place on God's Earth. Man was made in God's image. The Ascendants were deceivers. They were intruders. They were demons made in Satan's image. And he was the tip of the spear with which God would smite them.

The thoughts emboldened him as he walked along the quiet streets outside Thibault Blanc's apartment. The shops were closed, and most of the locals were in their beds. The early hours were Mannson's favourite time of the day. For that brief span of time this tainted Eden felt a little cleaner, a little less polluted by the ungodly.

As a boy growing up on the family farm near Hanover in Pennsylvania he had been immersed in the community of believers. Those of German stock held on tightly to the brand of Protestantism that their forebearers had brought with them over a hundred and fifty years before. It was pure and unyielding. He wasn't sure at what age he realised that he was different. Maybe it was in his first year at elementary school. For a brief period, he had enjoyed being the cleverest, fastest, strongest child. He remembered as if it was yesterday getting the results of those first tests and running all the way home to tell his father. His delight did not last long. His father had dragged him out behind the barn and whipped him with a belt for being so prideful. It was a sin, and the young Ernst soon learned the price of committing it. When his mother found him curled up and crying in the dust, she had not embraced him. She had instead prayed over him and asked for God's forgiveness, not for her husband but for her son.

At first it made no sense to him. Pride might be a sin, but there was no denying that he was simply better in every way than his peers. The teachers knew it and so did the older kids who baited him. Instead of it making him popular, his otherness alienated them. By the third term of that first year, he was deliberately putting wrong answers in tests, asked fewer questions in class, and withdrew as much as he could from sports. He slept less than everyone else and so used his extra time to study the Bible. He had been taught that it contained the word of God. That being so, he contended that only an imbecile would not strive to understand the wisdom that it must contain. At dawn each day he would be settled in that same spot behind the barn waiting for first light so that he could dive deep into the sacred words before taking his solitary walk to school.

Their pastor, who also happened to be his Uncle Gerd, said in a sermon that God had a purpose for everyone. That resonated with the young Ernst. Somewhere within the Bible he would discover what his purpose was to be. After all, God would not have made him different for no good reason.

When he was fourteen, he went to High School. Halfway through the year their history teacher took the class on a field trip to Pittsburgh. It was about thirty miles from Hanover, but he had never been there or to any other big city before. His father had been reluctant to give his permission for the visit. As he saw it, the farm and the Good Book gave them everything they needed. To want more was to exhibit greed. It was Ernst's Uncle Gerd who proved to be the unlikeliest ally of all. He had argued that if good men did not witness sin, then how could they be expected to guard against it and, when all was said and done, it was no more than a day trip. His father eventually relented, but grudgingly said to his son, *on your own head be it.*

It was while visiting the Fort Pitt Block House that young Ernst met the woman who would change his life. The tour guide was in her forties and unremarkable in every facet of her being. He traipsed around at the back of the class, bored with the banality of the guide's talk and irritated by the flippant chatter of the other kids. Their next stop was due to be the Heinz Memorial Chapel and to him the sooner they got there the better.

When the tour finished, they were told by their teacher that they had half an hour to explore independently and to pick up any souvenirs if they wanted them. On no circumstances were they to leave the premises. While their history teacher took a well-earned break, the children broke up into their little gangs of three or four and darted off in different directions. All except Ernst, who leaned against the nearest window and stared at the park outside. None of the other schoolchildren invited him to go with them. At the age of twelve he had learned that if he spoke to people in a certain way, they would do what he wanted. When he did that, he left them feeling happy about it. That was best. So as his classmates split off around the historic site none of them ignored him out of spite or indifference. They left him where he was because without knowing why they were sure it was the right thing to do.

He only turned back into the room when he felt the guide approach. She had not made any sound, but he knew she was there as surely as if she had tapped him on the shoulder.

She asked if he had enjoyed the tour. He said it had been fine. They both knew he was lying. Then she had introduced herself as Emily Fisher and asked his name. There was something about her that made him uncomfortable. He provided his own name but nothing else in the hope that would encourage her to move on. Instead, she moved closer and the blandness that had characterised her was replaced with a stare that could cut through iron. She had a presence that he could not describe. She was unlike anyone he had ever met. It made him nauseous. He told her to go away, not angrily or impolitely, but calmly as he did when wanting people to do what he wanted.

Emily Fisher did not budge, nor did she show any flicker of hesitation or confusion. He had come across the less easily influenced before and knew that trying harder would quickly shape them to his will. It was what he always did with his Uncle Gerd. What he had not faced until then was someone who was completely unaffected. It was unsettling and he hated it.

For some reason he could remember the conversation that followed, not as fragments or as impressions, but literally word for word.

She said, 'it's not easy being different, is it?'

'I don't know what you mean.'

'You do, Ernst, you do. It shines from you. We are the same, it's nothing to be frightened of. Do you know anyone else like you? Do you have someone to talk to?'

She smiled. There was compassion in her eyes. Ernst could not see that. All he could see was a witch who could see through him and to his every secret.

'You should go away,' he said, straining for her to do what he wanted.

Her smile became even more fixed as she said, 'we can't do that to each other, only to the Normals.'

'The who?' he asked, not sure he had heard her correctly.

'Normals,' she said pleasantly and waved an encompassing hand towards everyone else in the large room, 'the ones you hide from because you know it wouldn't be safe if they really knew what you are capable of. It must have been lonely for you thinking that you were alone. You're really not. We Ascendants are few in number, but it's a growing number. You can be yourself with us.'

Whatever was going on, Ernst was not enjoying it. He felt naked in front of this stranger. He blurted out, 'I can be myself before God. That is all I need.'

'Dear, dear, dear. You really are in need of some guidance if you think any God is responsible for us. We are the product of evolution. It is the age for mankind to progress again and we are the first flowering of that. Nothing could be more natural.'

His fresh face went red and hardened. Sounding even younger than he was, he said, 'that's blasphemy. There's no such thing as evolution.'

'Oh, what rot. Who's been filling your head with rubbish like that,' she said, gently teasing rather than chiding him.

Sounding even more like a petulant child, he shot back with, 'My uncle Gerd. He's our pastor and he would not lie. It's in the Bible and that doesn't lie either.'

She sighed and stroked his hair. He didn't like that either.

She said, 'let me ask you this then: can Adam, Eve or anyone else in the Bible do what you can do? What I and the others like us can do? Who in that book of books can hide like we do, be as smart as we are, be as healthy as we are, and who can make most people do what we want by merely directing them to? I know it's a lot to absorb. We all go through it. All I'm asking of you is to think about those questions and then, if you want or need to, come seek me out again. I'm here most days. And remember, you are not alone.'

She smoothed his hair like a loving mother and left him with his thoughts.

For a long moment he could not take his eyes off her and then he ran, faster than anyone had seen a boy of his age run and sped from the blockhouse and out into the park. He was vaguely aware of his teacher shrieking at him to come back. It didn't matter. When Ernst returned, he would make the educator forget all about it.

The next two weeks were the most tortuous of his life. He spent every spare second reading and re-reading biblical passages. Then after Friday dinner when his uncle had joined them to break bread and pray, he managed to get the pastor alone and they walked around some fields because Ernst had told him that it would help with his digestion. Uncle Gerd hadn't considered the idea before but suddenly it was a perfect idea to him.

As they strolled along, Ernst had put the question to him exactly as Emily Fisher had phrased it. Pastor Gerd was a diligent man who gave no religious advice lightly. On the second lap of the fields, with his feet starting to ache, he eventually said, 'there have been many men who were different, as you put it. Think of the plagues brought down by Moses. Lazarus rising from the dead. Then there's Enoch and his son Methusaleh, who both lived for hundreds of years. Yes, there are plentiful examples of men who were different from the normal. What I can't think of is anyone who hid himself among the flock so to speak, and who used some special power to bend people to his will. It seems to me that we are all guided by God's Will and anyone seeking to subvert that cannot, by definition, be godly. I will ponder the issue further, but there is a parallel that comes to mind.'

Ernst had already reached a conclusion of

his own and was desperate for his Uncle Gerd to offer him a believable alternative. He had to know what the pastor was thinking and so with no little reluctance pleaded with him to say it.

Gerd checked over his shoulder as if fearing that somebody was listening to them and said, 'it does not do to talk of such things.'

He spoke with a finality that Ernst could not accept. Ernst told him in that special manner of his to carry on.

Gerd said, 'I suppose you are old enough to discuss such things sensibly. What you have described is reminiscent to me of the behaviour of Satan and his demons. They hide among us, do they not? They seek to make us all believe that they do not exist, and yet they exist solely to lead us from the path of God. Is Satan not the Great Deceiver? Do he and his minions not put thoughts in our heads that should not be there? They are not mortal men such as you and I, so why wouldn't they live longer than us, be immune to disease, and be stronger in every aspect save for the absence of souls and the love of God. I tell you, Ernst, I wish with all my heart that it was not true, but if they did not exist then why would God and the Bible warn us against them?'

'Then how would we know them? And if we do not know that, then how can they be stopped?'

Gerd looked appreciatively at his nephew

and said, 'sometimes you are wise beyond your years, Ernst. They will know each other, I am sure of that, because the legions of Hell are as one. For us, we can only know them by their deeds and actions. And, more importantly than anything, trust in our Lord and Saviour to protect us from them.'

It was as Ernst had thought. His dread fears had been confirmed. When it was dark and the house was silent, he climbed from his bedroom window and went to the barn. The sky was clear. He had never seen so many stars, but it was too dark to read and, besides, the Bible had revealed all that it could to him. If he was a demon, then he deserved to die and he would happily do so if that was God's wish. He lay flat on the straw ridden ground and stared up. Then he closed his eyes and prayed. If God did not answer, then he would be forlorn. If that be so, he had already chosen the cross beam in the barn from which he would hang himself at first light. If God did answer, it would be to tell him what plan he had in store for him, and Ernst would follow it unto his dying breath. All was in God's hands.

At some point during the night, he fell asleep. That was when God spoke to him. He awoke blessed. He had peace of mind and God's work to do. It was glorious.

The next day he skipped school, put a few things in a rucksack, and with his meagre savings bought a ticket to Pittsburgh.

The morning after that, early visitors to the Fort Pitt Block House found it closed and cordoned off by police cars. The very first among them would just have been in time to see the body of Emily Fisher dangling from a window by the rope that was knotted fast around her neck. It was the rope that Ernst had brought from the barn. He had killed his first demon.

As long as it didn't interfere with his work, Ernst Mannson often thought back to that most beautiful of days. He had been serving God ever since. Finding other Ascendants to dispose of was never an easy task, but at the hospital in Denver he had overheard Harman telling Sebastian Kent about the list. He had gone there to kill Harman and instead had come away with the promise of many more. All he had to do was follow Harman while he did the hard work of locating the Ascendants on that list. Harman, like a fine dessert, would be left until the end.

Mannson could hear a few cars still travelling through Palo Alto. Everything else remained still. The last light went out in the apartment block. Mannson gave it another fifteen minutes before going to the front doors. He had watched with amusement earlier in the evening when Harman had made such a dramatic entrance to the building. He really was still a babe in arms as far as being an Ascendant was concerned. Much easier surely was to do as he had done, which was to watch the entrance safely from a distance during the daytime and see what numbers residents inputted to the keypad.

He tapped in 2554 as he had seen others do. There was a dry click as the lock opened. He closed the door quietly behind him and advanced up the stairwell. A demon was awaiting God's justice at Mannson's hand in apartment thirteen.

CHAPTER TWO

Edinburgh Castle is a stone monolith perched high above the city on the plug of an extinct volcano. From that towering defensive vantage point, it is hard to look in any direction without seeing some well-respected centre of academia or research. Many dated back to the Sixteenth Century, others were newer. One of those, almost in the shadow of the great castle, was the Institute for Defence and Security. It was there that the taxi from the airport dropped off Alan Harman and a visibly excited Charles Hope.

The glass entranceway was familiar to Harman. He had been there once before, and it was not that long ago. On that occasion he had ostensibly been there to investigate a burglary, although it was technically no more than a break-in because nothing had been stolen. Instead, something had been left. It was the late Peter Salt's business card, although he had been very much alive when he had planted it in the office of the renowned weapons theorist, Dr Sidney Grosschild. That was when Salt, in his own roundabout way, had been trying to educate Harman and ET1 about the existence of Ascendants and the real threat posed by Virginia Brightwell.

Harman said, 'okay, Charles, it will be simpler if I do this alone. It shouldn't take too long.'

Hope shivered and zipped up his grey hoodie. He said, 'I wish I'd brought a coat with me, but never mind. I can't believe I'm here. What a place, what history. I love it.'

'Go see the sights then, but don't get lost. I aim to be on that afternoon Ryanair flight to Gran Canaria. I will meet you back here in two hours. Be on time because if you're not I will go without you.'

'Should be long enough for me to hop on one of those open top tour buses that I saw when we drove in.'

'You sound like a tourist. I thought you'd hitched a ride with me to help, not to see the world.'

'Is this man you've come to see an Ascendant?'

'I've no reason to think he is,' Harman said, not knowing why that possibility had failed to occur to him before.

'Then you don't need my help right now, do you?'

'Tell me one thing then, Charles. Peter told me that Ascendants can normally sense other Ascendants. Is that true? Will I know whether he is one or not?'

Hope donned his serious face and said, 'you see, this is exactly the kind of thing that

Peter thought I could assist you with. The answer is that it appears to be instinctive. It's not always immediate, but if you're in the presence of other Ascendants you will normally cotton on to it quickly enough.'

'It's not foolproof though?'

Hope made a weighing up gesture with his hands and replied, 'we all have instincts. I'd say it would be foolhardy to rely on any of them totally.'

Harman accepted the advice, told Hope again to stay out of trouble, and entered the building. He went to the front desk, introduced himself to the stern-faced receptionist, and asked if he could see Dr Grosschild.

Being the diligent gatekeeper, she wanted to know if he had an appointment. He asked if she might call Dr Grosschild because he was sure he would be willing to meet him. He posed the question in such a way that her resistance evaporated. She made the call and with evident surprise informed him that Dr Grosschild had said he should go straight up. Harman skipped up the stairs with the lightness of Fred Astaire in his prime and was soon knocking lightly on the academic's door. Grosschild was not built for speed and so it took a few moments for his lumbering bulk to reach the door and invite Harman inside.

Grosschild's smile spread as broadly across his face as his stomach did over his trousers.

'What a surprise and pleasure to see you again, Sergeant Harman,' he said, as he ushered him in and towards a chair.

The office was exactly as Harman remembered it. There were the heavily stacked bookshelves. With pride of place were copies of Grosschild's best-selling *World War III* series: *World War III: Cyber Attack - World War III: Ethno-bombs - World War III: bankrupt states - World War III - Biocide!*

Since their previous meeting, Harman had read them all.

On one wall were a set of framed certificates, including Grosschild's doctorate in Philosophy. Next to the window was a straight-backed chair in front of a table that could not have been more than three feet across. On it was an old-style electric typewriter. To the chagrin of his colleagues and publishers, Grosschild was wedded to it and refused to prepare his work on anything else.

Grosschild slumped down on his heavily padded and thinning wing-backed leather armchair. Its legs creaked under the weight. Harman sat across from him on its matching and less battered partner.

Harman said, 'I'm grateful that you could see me at such short notice.'

Grosschild said, without sounding prickly, 'or to be precise, no notice at all.'

'Either way, I'm glad you hadn't forgotten me because it would be hugely helpful to pick your brains again.'

'How could I possibly forget you? It's not every day that I get a visit from a Detective Sergeant no less from the Ministry of Defence Police Force. I had ascribed the incursion into my office as a prank of some kind until you appeared on my doorstep. After all, who climbs into a building in the dead of night to leave a business card taped to my books? Which reminds me, did you ever catch the culprit? Peter Salt, wasn't it?'

Harman adopted a pained expression and said, 'I'm not sure that it was ever worth pursuing through the courts, but in any event, Mr Salt died recently so whether to prosecute has become a moot point.'

'Was it natural causes?'

'I am afraid not. He was killed in a shooting incident in the US.'

Grosschild's nose wrinkled in distaste. He said, 'yes, rather too much of that goes on over in the Old Colonies. Well, there is nothing more I can tell you about him, so to what do I owe the pleasure of your company today?'

Harman did not want to waste time talking about Salt and so took the chance to move the conversation forward. He said, 'he is not why I'm here. I'm on another case and, having met you and subsequently enjoyed all your books, it struck me that you might be able to help with an angle I'm pursuing.'

Grosschild immediately sat straighter in his chair. He said, 'did you really enjoy them? It's a constant struggle to pitch them at the right level. My publisher is forever rapping me across the knuckles for not dumbing them down enough. The final draft always and predictably becomes something of a battle between us. I wield my academic integrity. They wield a cheque book. To my shame, the pen might be mightier than the sword, but it tends to bow to pound signs, so I do crave honest feedback as reassurance that I have not totally sacrificed my soul on the altar of filthy lucre.'

Harman resisted the urge to offer up praise without thinking. Grosschild had been courteous and generous with his time and thoughts. A little gratitude would not go amiss. After a few moments of genuine contemplation, he said, 'they were easy to read and genuinely thought-provoking. I can see why they have become best sellers. And I gave them all five-star reviews on Amazon.'

Grosschild said, 'you are very kind. It's a shame that you are not a celebrity because that would make a great endorsement for my publisher to use. Can you believe that for the last paperback edition they put a quote from some TV chef that I'd never heard of on the back, but when I went to his restaurant in London, they still charged me full price? The world can be full of petty disappointments, can't it?'

For a man whose specialism was predicting the routes to apocalypse, it was strange that he was ever worried by petty disappointments, and Harman said, 'I suppose you're right, but I try not to sweat the small stuff. None of it seems that much of a deal after reading your books. Which brings me back to the purpose of my visit. If I could jump right in, hypothetically, if you had some toxic agent, what would be the most effective way of deploying it? I mean if you were a serious scientist and not someone with a chemistry set in a kitchen.'

The smile that had so far been ever present on Grosschild's face was shut down as quickly as Venetian Blinds could be flipped. He said, 'that is jumping in very deeply, Sergeant Harman. When you were here previously you were a Detective Sergeant with the MoD police investigating a burglary that was linked to an MoD official. That seemed like overkill at the time, but I was happy to overlook that and co-operate. This line of enquiry seems to be many steps removed from that.'

Harman remained relaxed. Grosschild was nobody's fool and he had done enough consultancy work for the British Government to know how things worked. No matter how many times on the flight over Harman had considered how to pitch his question to Grosschild, every possible outcome had included the potential for

Grosschild to smell a big fat decaying rat.

Harman raised his hands in mock surrender and said, 'I could spin you a yarn about it being research for a novel I want to write, but we both know that would be a lie. All can say is that it does relate to a live case, albeit that I am no longer acting for the MoD police. I cannot tell you any more than that. All I'm asking for is your informed views. Nothing more than an avid reader might ask you at a book signing or a conference.'

Grosschild steepled his fingers and tapped his nose with them while he thought about it. His sleeves were pulled down as a result, revealing swollen wrists. They were even redder than his cheeks. Eventually he relented and said, 'I suppose it can do no harm. If you were a terrorist, which would be such a nasty shock, you would presumably have found out what you wanted from published research and whatever nonsense could be found on the internet. On the contrary, my instincts tell me there is something trustworthy about you.'

Harman smiled wryly, 'funny you should say that. An acquaintance of mine told me today that instincts can't always be trusted.'

Grosschild's smile returned. He said, 'then your acquaintance is either a wise man or somebody who eats too many fortune cookies.'

Harman returned the warmth and said, 'I don't know him well enough yet to say which of

CLIVE HAWKSWOOD

those it is, but I aim to find out. Coming back to my question, would you care to enlighten me?'

'Very well. My first comment is that your *hypothetical* question is like asking me to say from here how long a piece of string is in a darkened room in Moscow. There is simply insufficient detail to make my assessment anything other than futile. Is there anything you might be able to offer up that would colour the picture for me?'

'As I say, it would be something sophisticated and designed for maximum impact. Safe to assume it has been manufactured in sufficient volume to achieve that, but the volume itself is small or was made in such a concentrated form that it could be carried in your hand. It could be biological, chemical, or a combination of the two.'

'Would it, *hypothetically,* be targeted or non-discriminatory?'

Harman said, 'since neither of is, I trust, recording this conversation, maybe we can dispense with prefacing everything by saying hypothetical or hypothetically? It will certainly save us time and breath.'

Grosschild smile became a tight grin through which he said, 'I appreciate your attempt at levity and your call for brevity, but a feeling of trepidation is coming over me.'

Harman took the prompt to move on quickly and said, 'it would be targeted at a majority population. I recall that's a phrase you used in your latest book.'

'Would it be selective or non-discriminatory?'

'Selective, definitely.'

Grosschild's flabby neck rippled like he was having trouble swallowing. He said, 'that sounds worryingly like a weapon directed at a specific racial type. That scares me. It also makes me wonder again why you have sought me out when the government has own experts in this field. I might be brought in for consulting purposes. That is only ever to augment them. It is never in place of them. To be blunt, if this threat is real, why are they not dealing with it and, with no offence intended, why is a lowly police sergeant asking these questions of me?'

Harman thought briefly about whether to influence Grosschild to get the information he wanted. He discounted the idea. He didn't know Grosschild well, but he liked and respected him. To dabble with such a fine mind was more than distasteful. Who knew if influencing Normals had any lasting effect on them? He had assumed until then that it was harmless, but he had nothing to base that on. He determined to persuade Grosschild by usual means and, if that meant failure, then he would accept it and leave. He said, 'I can't say much about my changed circumstances. Let's just say that I'm on secondment to another arm of government.

You probably won't have heard of it, but they do things slightly differently there.'

'I am familiar with the many arms and agencies of government that take an interest in my endeavours. I like to think I am trusted by them and not solely because I have signed the Official Secrets Act. Consequently, if you want my help, and silence afterwards, you will need to be a little more specific.'

'With absolutely no disrespect, 'Harman said, 'it doesn't help much. Hundreds of thousands of government employees have signed it as well, but we don't trust any of them with anything above and beyond their respective security clearances.'

'Your use of the word *we*, suggests that you are currently attached to the security services in some way or another.'

Harman said, 'you must draw your own conclusions about that. So, will you help me or not?'

Grosschild stared past Harman at an invisible spot on the wall while he reviewed his position. When that process was finished, he said, 'to be of any use to you, I will need more. Why don't we pretend that you are writing a film script rather than a novel, and that a fictional supervillain has a hypothetical weapon that they wish to use. What would that weapon be like?'

Harman nodded conspiratorially and said, 'I can't be certain because I haven't written that part of the script yet, but it would be a weapon that targets the DNA of a majority population while leaving untouched a specific minority population. One that is a very small minority.'

Grosschild did his staring into the middle distance again, then he said, 'I can't stop my mind journeying across the map trying to think where this attack might take place. Can you help me with that? It might narrow the field somewhat.'

'I genuinely cannot. I suppose the film might be shot anywhere.'

'In that case, would the attackers favour speed over effect?'

Harman paused to corral everything he knew or thought he knew and said, 'I am guessing they want both, but if I was in their shoes then speed would come out on top. It reduces the chance of them being found, provides a demonstration of power to their enemies, and an act of confirmation to their supporters.'

Grosschild frowned and said, 'that probably rules out putting it into the food chain. How wide is the geographical coverage they want to seek?'

'As broad as they can without reducing its effectiveness. They would want that one big hit.'

Grosschild made an umming sound in the back of his throat that rose and fell as if he was seeking some precise note. When that stopped, he said, 'air or water transmission then. Both methods have their strengths and weaknesses. Currents in the air and in the seas make dispersal and effect difficult to predict. Also, viruses and bacteria act and react differently to their surroundings. If your DNA-based weapon is attached to one of those that would add a serious complication. If it is some stand- alone toxin it is anybody's guess. I mean that quite literally.'

'How would they decide which to use then?'

'You intimated that they were scientists?'

'Their leader certainly is.'

Grosschild said, 'therein lies your answer. Scientists rely on experimentation. Trial and error. Any decision would be based on that.'

The thought filled Harman with dread, but he gave no indication of that as he said, 'would they need to conduct lots of tests?'

'No, not many. Enough to populate modelling software in order to create accurate computer simulations. That's all.'

'How long would that take?'

Grosschild said, 'that's the piece of string question again. It could be weeks or months. Without knowing the scientists involved, the resources available to them, or the results they are seeking it would be foolhardy to suggest an estimate.'

Harman was determined to extract every iota of help from Grosschild and so said, 'alright close your eyes, imagine you're in that fictional room in Moscow, and take a guess. Whatever your estimate is it will be better than anything I could come up with.'

Grosschild said, 'I can see that you are not to be deterred. I will give you an informed guess, not an estimate. Take it with not a pinch of salt but with a whole bag. I can tell you that the experiments and their analysis would take more than days. Even the best brains and computers in the world would need more than that. Which means that your piece of string will be weeks, maybe even a month or two but no more than that if they have the right knowledge and assets.'

Harman was sure that Virginia Bright had both. Within a small part of him there had been the slimmest of hopes that a visit to the guru of future wars would short circuit his hunt. That somehow it would narrow down the field to a single rutted corner that he could go straight to. If nothing else his conversation with Grosschild had clarified his own thinking and confirmed there was no alternative to dragging himself up the chain of Brightwell's subordinates to find her.

He said, 'you'll never know how much I appreciate your advice, Dr Grosschild.'

Grosschild levered himself up from the protesting chair. As he showed Harman out of the room, he said, 'I like films to have happy endings. I truly hope that yours does.'

Even the old rank and file Sergeant

Harman would have easily recognised the meaning behind Grosschild's words. To Alan Harman, still getting to grips with being an Ascendant, they were as subtle as being hit over the head with a cricket bat.

*

Sebastian Kent stretched out in the bed of his private room at The Denver Health Medical Centre. The bullet wound in his thigh was packed and bandaged. The medical staff told him it was healing well. There was no infection. Four days after being shot he had recovered enough strength to walk around his bed with the aid of a nurse and a walking stick. The small trip had exhausted him. And so, he was left lying there alone again. He was sick of being immobile, he was sick of the blue walls and wooden floor, and he was sick of being told that full recovery would take many months. And he could not bear being out of the hunt for Virginia Brightwell.

He was head of the British Emerging Threats Department One in London, or for short ET1. Every inch of him demanded that he should be back there, co-ordinating its efforts. He got regular reports from his team. It only served to make him feel more sidelined.

Kent bent his knee and lowered his leg. He was no longer getting morphine for the pain, and his eyes watered as shafts of heat shot out from the hole in his leg. It didn't deter him. He would not allow his leg muscles to atrophy. He flexed the leg and did it again. He winced. Then he did the exercise again. He could cope with the discomfort. The half of his face that was still scarred and disfigured as a result of an explosion in Afghanistan was testimony to that.

What he could not cope with was being trapped in that room while the world outside went on without him. They were at war with the Ascendants as surely as he had once been at war with the Taliban. His place was on the battlefield, not cocooned in a hospital.

His thoughts kept drifting back to the time when he had been shot in the mine complex on the 191 Ranch in Colorado. What he had seen before being put on his back was enough to terrify anyone. The vision of first seeing the room where Brightwell had left the men, and parts of men, she had experimented on was burnt into his memory as surely as if a branding iron had been used on him. They had been so close to catching her. He could not understand how she had gone without a trace after that. It was the second time she had slipped away from him. The first was when he had become aware of her at the Marston Creek research facility back in the UK. Everything pointed to her finalising whatever barbaric weapon she was developing. And what was he doing? Lying flat on his back with the four walls for company.

Then there was the truly troubling rogue element that was Alan Harman. Pragmatism had led to Kent taking Detective Sergeant Alan Harman and Detective Inspector Carol King on secondment to ET1. They were so far into the investigation of Peter Salt that it would have been foolhardy to take them off it when ET1 had taken over the case. They had proved their worth. Now both were gone. She had been killed, sacrificing herself to save her friend and colleague. He had discarded ET1 and gone off on some personal crusade against Brightwell and her followers. That wasn't the worst of it. Something had happened to him in those caves. During Kent's first bout of lucidity after the shooting, Harman had come to him, sat on the chair next to the bed, and recounted his transformation into being one of the Ascendants. Something dormant had been triggered in him. Harman had not asked for it, but he intended to make the best of it.

Kent looked at that same chair and imagined Harman sitting there. He had re-run the conversation so many times. Had reported on it as best he could back to London, to his team and to his masters. His mental reflex had been to assume that Harman was having a breakdown of some kind. He had lost his wife and best friend in quick succession and had then endured the trauma of coming face to face with Virginia Brightwell. Who could blame him for coming off the rails, doing a somersault, and bursting into flames? Kent wasn't sure when he had changed his mind. Somewhere in the exchange of words a switch had been flipped. Kent came to believe what he was being told. The subordinate that he had come to trust and, in his own guarded manner like, became in that instant a threat and potential enemy.

When Harman had said that he would be going after Brightwell alone and that it would be better for ET1 to stay out his way, Kent was offended, and he had not tried to hide it. The Ascendants hid in plain sight, and they were very good at it. That was why they had evaded detection for so long. Everyone in ET1 said so. They were the hidden enemy, so certain of their superiority that it was hard to predict what drove them or what they might do. Peter Salt had tried to help. He had alerted them to the existence of Ascendants in their midst and had led them by the nose to Brightwell, but when he had been given the chance to shoot her, he had let her go. Kent could not trust him after that. Use him, yes, put faith in him, no. Kent had now filed Harman in the same category. It was the only rational decision. Except Harman had gone rogue and that made using him very much harder.

None of which would change while Kent was having to concentrate on avoiding bedsores and being able to stand on his one good leg. He punched a pillow to vent some of his frustration and then chided himself for wasting his energy. He gritted his teeth and began the painful leg exercises again.

When the door to his room opened, Kent automatically looked sourly towards it. The lack of privacy was a perpetual irritant, and the nurses, doctors and physiotherapists came without warning and, seemingly, whenever they felt like it. They were without exception polite and professional, but it felt like their pleasantries were turned on and off automatically and he couldn't shake the feeling that to them he was no more than the next slab of meat for them to work on.

His mood brightened when he saw that his visitor was FBI Special Agent Qianfan Reilly. If not a friend, then he had proven himself to be a trustworthy comrade and ally. In Kent's line of work that was no small thing. Kent had found it hard, as did everyone else, to read Reilly's thoughts through the dead-pan expression that was fixed on Reilly's face like some emotional army of occupation. The fact that on this occasion Kent could so readily see that the agent was troubled was a worrying sign.

Neither of them was comfortable in overtly social situations, but Kent broke the silence by saying, 'I figured you would at least have brought me some grapes.'

Reilly pretended not to hear him. Without

waiting, he pulled back the visitor's chair and sat down on it. He faced Kent squarely and upright as if about to give evidence in court.

Without a 'hello' or 'how are you coming along', Reilly said, 'We've got a problem. A big one.'

'There's never a shortage of those. Are you telling me you have another to add to the list?'

'A dead body has been found in Palo Alto. He's been identified as Thibault Blanc. He worked at Stanford. We're building a picture of him. He was involved in some genetics project. No trace of family or friends.'

'Is that meant to mean something to me?'

'You've never heard of him?'

'Not that I can recall, but I've got an alibi if he was killed in the last few days.'

Reilly cocked his head slightly as if trying to understand something that had been said to him in a foreign language. He said, 'were you trying to make a joke?'

Kent did not have to be told that Reilly would be every comedian's idea of a nightmare. Somebody they would happily pay not to attend their shows.

'Forget it, Qianfan, I'm on drugs, I don't know what I'm saying. Maybe you could get to the point?'

'Blanc was murdered. Slow and nasty. Whoever did it tied him to a chair, emptied the contents of the bookcase around him and set fire to the books. If you've ever seen one of those old movies where a witch is burnt at the stake, you'll get the picture.'

'Torture? You think whoever did it was trying to get information from him?'

'Not likely, his tongue had been cut out. The killer was plain crazy or had some personal gripe to settle in the most extreme fashion. Or maybe a bit of both. The neighbours raised the alarm when they saw smoke.'

'I can see that's a problem, but how is it ours?'

In response, Reilly pulled an envelope from inside his jacket. He extracted from it a handful of photographs. As he handed them to Kent, he said, 'it's a modern apartment building. It has good CCTV at the entrance, the garage, and on every floor. At some point the whole system crashed. We have specialists investigating that. Before everything went haywire though the footage is of a good standard, and we didn't need to clear up the resolution too much. They show a man sneaking into the garage and later entering and leaving Blanc's apartment. Look familiar to you?'

Kent recognised Harman clearly from the first photograph. He didn't need to inspect the rest.

He said, 'I don't believe it.'

Reilly said, 'that was my first reaction too, but the evidence doesn't lie. Establishing a precise time of death for a badly burned body is difficult but given everything we know Blanc was killed very close to the time stamps on the CCTV film of Harman being there. I thought I owed you a heads up on this.'

Kent rubbed his forehead. None of it felt right. Then again, as he'd told himself so often, how could any of them really know what was going on in the head of an Ascendant, especially a new-born like Harman. Whatever his thoughts might be, this was indeed a problem and one that would have to be dealt with.

He said, 'you think this Blanc character was an Ascendant, don't you?'

'What matters is what I know and not what I think. And what I know is that your man, Alan Harman, has gone off the reservation. I don't mind bending the rules, but they're important. Is it too hard to imagine that Alan has decided they're no longer for him?'

'We won't know that until we catch him, will we?'

Reilly said, 'they all get caught in the end. If he's still here in the US, we will do that. You can see that Homeland Security will be excited by that prospect.'

'And if he's gone?'

'Then he will be your mess to clear up. That will come down through official channels in the clearest way. You're going to find that any co-operation from our side will dry up until you do.'

Kent stared out of the window for a few moments. He found he was still holding the photograph of Harman. He let it fall to the bed and said, 'I appreciate you bringing this to me.'

'I'm sorry it's played out like this. I'd like to think I've given you a small head start. Use it wisely.'

'Not easy when I'm stuck here.'

'We've seen guys crawl off battlefields with worse wounds than yours. What have they told you about recovery time?'

'At first, they said it could be ten days before I was on my feet again. Sod that. I can already get around the room. Then maybe two months for the wound to heal properly. If it all mends well the limp might go in six months. The pain could last longer.'

Reilly was pleased that Kent made every recovery milestone sound like a personal affront. He got up and left, returning only seconds later. In his hand he held a dark ebony wood cane. Its handle was made of carved bone. He propped it beside Kent's bed and said simply, 'you might need this.'

'Looks like I will. Keep your head down, Qianfan, it's getting harder to know what direction the bullets are coming from.'

'That's why old Rangers like me used to take two helmets on choppers. One for your head and one to sit on, so your ass don't get shot off.'

He gave Kent a curt nod and went from the room. He had said all he needed to.

Kent painstakingly swung his legs from the bed and reached for the walking stick. He weighed it in his hands. It was substantial, unyielding and supportive, just like the man who had given it to him. He concentrated on what had to be done. Reilly had been right. It was what you knew rather than what you thought that was most important. Alan Harman had killed in the heat of the moment when under attack back at the mine. That proved it was something he was capable of, but Kent could not bring himself to see Harman as a cold-blooded killer and certainly not one who would deal out the kind of sadistic death that Thibault Blanc appeared to have suffered. Unfortunately for them Kent could not afford to be wrong. Faced with the evidence and the forthcoming deluge of angst from Homeland Security and the FBI, there was only one course of action open to him.

He grabbed his phone from the side cabinet. After establishing a secure line, he called Dr Amy Bishop back at ET1 in London. He told her about Reilly's visit, warned her that bad things would be coming down from on high, and instructed her to turn every asset at their disposal to locating and apprehending Alan Harman. Finally, he directed her to get him a seat on the next flight to London.

CHAPTER THREE

The Ryanair flight from Scotland to Gran Canaria took nearly five hours. Neither Harman nor Hope slept during the journey. It was one of the Ascendants' traits that they required less sleep than the Normals around them. Harman wanted nothing more than to spend the time on is hands by firing questions at Hope. It was a desire he could not fulfil. With so many ears in the cramped aircraft they could not risk discussing anything of importance. Hope, as was his way, tried to indulge in harmless small talk as if he found any silence between himself and Harman impossible to bear. It soon dried up in the face of Harman's unwillingness to engage with him.

After disembarking at Las Palmas de Gran Canaria Airport they hired a car, or at least the young Spaniard who served them was led to believe by Hope that they had paid for the hire of a car. In reality, he had been influenced to register the loan of a car to two elderly women and had paid for it with his own credit card. Then he had handed them the keys and led them to a white SUV.

As they drove off, Harman said, 'how much do you think a kid like that gets paid for working there?'

Hope shrugged and said, 'what does it matter?'

'It doesn't feel right making him pay for the car.'

Hope said, 'you are serious, aren't you? I can see it will take a long time for me to understand you. You are on a mission, dare I say a quest, to stop Virginia Brightwell from putting thousands, maybe millions, to the sword and you're bothered about whether someone you've never set eyes on before might go a little overdrawn at the bank. I'm not criticising, just observing.'

'Yeah, well thanks for the observation,' Harman said. He didn't need to explain himself to Hope, and he regretted saying anything about the kid at the dealership being out of pocket. Instead, he reconciled to leave the duped employee a big tip when they returned the car. He figured the cost of the rental plus ten per cent should do it.

Harman brought the car to a halt as they reached the junction with the Autopista Del Sur. It was the highway that joined the capital city of Las Palmas in the north with the east and south coasts. Long lines of cars, trucks, and coaches flowed in both directions. He had already put their destination into the GPS and chosen 'English' from the language options. It came below Spanish and German, but above French. A woman's electronic voice told him to turn left, and he did as he was told.

As they drove down the highway their views were dominated on one side by the sun-glistened Atlantic Ocean and the white-walled hotels and apartment blocks that catered for the hundreds of thousands of sun-seekers from across Europe who descended on the island annually. On the other side the sun-baked land sloped gradually away to the mountains in the centre of the island. That was their destination, but there was no direct road from east to west and so for about half an hour they had to keep going south, deep into the tourist heartland. Just where the road began to follow the curve of the coast northward again, they turned off on to the GC-60. About ten miles later they arrived in the picturesque town of Fataga. It wasn't somewhere that tourists normally stayed, but they did visit to get a taste of a more authentic Gran Canarian lifestyle. Up there on top of a hill surrounded by mountains and much more natural greenery than was to be found down on the coast, the town had grown organically, but the white buildings with their terracotta roofing gave it a cohesion that any town planner would have been proud to achieve.

Emerging from the far side of the town, Harman reduced the car's speed. He said, 'According to Thibault Blanc, Chen is hiding away about two miles north of here. Keep your eyes peeled for any signs to the Finca Klausen.'

'You got it, boss,' Hope said cheerily.

Harman scowled and said, 'don't call me boss.'

'Sorry, I guess I'm a bit over-excited.'

Harman had a question that he wanted to get off his chest without making Hope wary of him. It has been intruding on his thoughts for too long and so he asked, 'have you ever tried to influence another Ascendant?'

Hope snorted and said, 'down that path would lie madness.'

'You mean you've never tried, not even out of curiosity?'

'It can't be done, not as far as I'm aware. Why do you want to know about that?'

'That an easy one. It's because I need to learn everything that the likes of you have taken for granted all their lives.'

'That's exactly why Peter sent me to you,' Hope said, sounding even more excited. 'Why has it taken you so long to start firing questions at me?'

Harman said, 'I'm prudent by nature and patient by training. And don't make me ask whether you are still looking for that sign.'

Hope raised a querying eyebrow. The lightness had disappeared from his voice when he said, 'ah, how silly of me. You weren't asking because you don't trust me and therefore you could not trust whatever answers I might give you.'

'I barely know you,' Harman said. It was a statement without any animosity attached to it.

'And yet here I am. Why bring me along, if not to help?'

'You'll get a chance to earn your spurs. Until then I'm happier having you where I can keep an eye on you.'

Hope stared wistfully down the road. After a few moments of contemplation, he said, 'how did Peter Salt win your trust?'

Harman quickly turned hard eyes on the man next to him and said, 'by dying for me.'

That killed their conversation as surely as a wooden stake through the heart of a vampire. They drove on in silence for the next five minutes until Hope shot out an arm and pointed to a wooden sign a hundred feet away, saying, 'there, up there.'

Elegantly carved in Gothic script on an oval board of darkened laurel were the words *Finca Klausen.* A private road led from it and meandered off deeper into the mountains.

The uneven surface was pitted with rocks and Harman steered carefully along it. The last thing he wanted was to bust the car's suspension and end up having to hike the rest of the way. His caution paid off when the car reached an S bend that was hemmed in on both sides by stony outcrops that were over thirty feet high. A heavy link chain was stretched across the road where it emerged from the shelter of the small false canyon. Even at less than 20mph, Harman had to stamp on the brakes to stop the SUV ploughing into the barrier. He and Hope lurched forward. Their seat belts brought them up short of the steering wheel and windshield.

Harman got out to move the chain aside.

A heavily accented voice called out from behind him, 'leave that alone.'

Harman turned slowly. Something told him it was the smart move. He found himself facing a man dressed from head to toe in black, like a nightclub bouncer. However, this man offered the extra security of a hunting rifle. He wasn't pointing it at Harman, but he could quickly do so if the mood took him.

'I'm here to see Daiyu Chen. A mutual friend told me she was staying here. She will want to see me,' Harman said with total certainty.

His assured manner seemed to confuse the man with the gun. It told Harman that the sentry was used to swatting away unwanted visitors with ease as soon as they saw the rifle, although it was hard to believe they had many visitors of any kind way up there.

The conundrum was too much for the man to solve on his own. He told Harman to wait and then used his phone to make a call. He said a few words in Spanish, listened, and grunted an acknowledgement.

He said again, 'wait.'

Hope decided that it was now safe to move from the wing of the car, but as soon as he did, he raised his hands above shoulder height.

Harman shook his head in disbelief and said quietly, 'you can put your hands down, Charles, it's not a hostage situation. He's not even raised the rifle.'

'Are you certain?' Hope said, his voice wavering.

'I'm sure.'

Hope reluctantly lowered his arms as if some unseen buoyancy aid kept trying to pull them skyward.

Harman said, 'take a breath and relax. But if I start running, you're on your own.'

Hope's eyes flared in horror. Before panic could take a grip of him, Harman said, 'joking, I was joking.'

Hope jutted his jaw toward Harman and said, 'that's not funny. You've had days to make jokes and you choose now to start?'

While Harman was still deciding whether to apologise or not, another man appeared from around the bend in the road up ahead. He was dressed like the first man and carried a rifle, barrel down, with an easy familiarity. A couple of yards behind him came a woman in sandals. She was wearing a yellow bikini top, and a patterned sarong was wrapped around her waist. Long, silky black hair draped over her shoulder. Harman was struck by the flawless beauty of the

Chinese woman.

'Is that her?' Hope asked quite unnecessarily. There was nobody else it could have been.

When she was close enough to be heard without raising her voice, she said, 'Alverado tells me that you are here to see me?'

Harman, doing his best to appear non-threatening, replied, 'that's right. My name is Alan Harman, and this is Charles Hope. We were acquaintances of Peter Salt. He told us that you had been helpful to him in the past and we're hoping that you might help us as well.'

'Peter could not have known I was here,' she said, making the underlying challenge apparent.

'No, that's true,' Harman said, 'it was Thibault Blanc who told me where to find you.'

She raised a delicate and well-manicured finger and plucked at her lips. It was provocative rather than childish. Then she pointed the finger at Harman and said, 'Alverado and Hugo are ex-Spanish Special Forces. They were both in the *Boinas Verdes.* They are totally devoted to me. They would, literally, kill for me. I say this so that you will choose your next answer with great care.'

Harman whispered so that the three Ascendants could hear what he was saying, but the two Spanish guards could not, 'if you were going to influence some Normals to protect you, it makes sense that you'd make sure they were well-trained.'

Only a twinkle in her eyes told him that she had heard.

She said, 'my advice to you stands.'

'Your advice sounds a little like a threat,' Harman said, using his normal voice again.

'Is there really any difference between friendly advice and a friendly threat?' She spoke as if posing the question to herself. 'It is an interesting point, but it would be wrong to digress at this juncture. Tell me, how did you come to know of Thibault Blanc?'

'That's easy enough. His name was on a list that Peter gave to me. A list that you provided him with.'

'If I ever provided such a list, I am sure I would not have included contact details for whoever was on it.'

It was Harman's turn to smile. He said, 'if you're asking me how I found him, then all I can say is that it wasn't hard. It is public knowledge that he's employed at Stanford University. After that, it didn't take Hercules Poirot to find him at his apartment in Palo Alto.'

His explanation seemed to satisfy her because she turned sideways on to them and, waving them up the road, she said, 'please join me for a cold drink or glass of wine. It seems there is much for us to discuss.'

Harman led Hope around the chain, and

they followed her at a respectful distance as she headed back to the finca. Alverado and Hugo tracked them. It did not go unnoticed that Alverado's rifle traced Harman's movements and Hugo's traced Hope's. Daiyu Chen's attack dogs were ready to pounce at the slightest command from her.

When they reached the finca, Harman applauded her choice of retreat. In traditional Canarian style the converted farmhouse was half built into the mountain behind it and much of the outdoor living area was overhung by pine trees. The one way to it was via the road they had walked up. The panoramic views across more mountains, rolling farmland, and the distant sea were magnificent. A telescope and chair were perched on the cliff edge. From there they could see everything in the valley immediately below them.

A small, yet modern kidney-shaped swimming pool flickered invitingly in the sunlight. It appeared to be one of many improvements made, Harman assumed, by Herr Klausen, whoever he might be.

On a small terrace above the pool was a circular table. A large umbrella shrouded it in a calming shade. There were four chairs around the table, each with blue and white striped cushions. On a tray were glasses, and jugs of Sangria and iced water. Chen ushered them over and invited them to sit.

Harman and Hope waited for her to take her seat first. She aimed her dazzling smile at them and said, 'what good manners you have. Politeness is truly the currency of kings.'

As Harman settled himself down, he said, 'won't your Spanish friends be joining us?'

She looked around, having seemingly forgotten of their existence, and said, 'don't give the boys a second thought. Alverado will be heading back to the road, just in case you have brought any friends with you, and Hugo will be where he can see you, but you can't see him. Close enough to shoot you if you make any move to threaten me, but too far away for you to sense him.'

'Who exactly are they protecting you from? Virginia Brightwell or somebody else?'

At the mention of Brightwell, Chen's face and shoulders tightened. The reaction passed almost immediately. Harman had still seen it.

When she spoke again there was no hint of concern, 'these are dangerous times. One cannot be too careful. Virginia has stirred up the proverbial hornet's nest and I do not intend to be stung by anyone. Hence my temporary exile here.'

'Is your play to sit on the sidelines and then to swoop in and pick up the pieces?' Harman said. 'It would be a clever move for an ambitious woman.'

Chen lowered her head slightly to look at

him doe-eyed and said in a husky voice that was designed to melt men's hearts, 'you over-estimate me, Alan. I am alone and vulnerable. I have merely sought sanctuary until the craziness in the outside world evaporates.'

'You're not exactly alone, with Alverado and Hugo for company.'

'You wouldn't deny me one or two simple pleasures, would you? With one on guard there is always room in my bed for the other. They really are delightful specimens of manhood, aren't they?'

Hope, who had poured himself some water and was taking his first sip, spluttered. He put the glass down and mopped at the drops that had landed on his shirt.

Chen immediately switched her attention to him and said, 'do I shock you, Charles?'

He cleared his throat and, not sure what the right answer should be, said uncertainly, 'no?'

'I love your sunglasses, Charles, they are very chic,' she said, pursing her lips as if about to lean over and kiss him.

'They're not sunglasses. They're prescription reactive tinted spectacles. My eyes are light sensitive.'

'Really? Such a weakness is rare amongst us. I don't believe I've ever come across it before.'

With more petulance than he had intended, Hope said, 'we are evolved, not perfect.

We are not all the same.'

Her smile cooled by a few degrees as she inspected him more closely and then said, 'it appears that you are very much the evidence that proves your claim.'

Harman was anxious to keep her in a co-operative mood. If Blanc had been honest with him then Chen should be more than willing to provide him with his next destination point on his journey to Brightwell. He deliberately re-directed her attention away from Hope before their exchange could develop into a damaging spat.

He said, 'It can't have been easy to slip away from the Institute of Genetics. I'd have thought that the Chinese Government keeps a very close eye on the comings and goings at its Academy of Sciences.'

The frown that was forming on her forehead took flight and her complexion remained smooth and flawless. Harman would normally have put her age at about thirty or even younger, but she was an Ascendant and so it was anyone's guess what her real age was. It was easy to be distracted by her beauty and he reminded himself to be wary of her. He recalled a conversation with Peter Salt when he had told him about the list of names that Chen had passed to him. Harman had asked if she could be trusted. Salt's exact words came to mind as if the dead man was speaking into his ear. He had said, 'trust her? not for a second, but I do believe her.'

'It was not easy. I think the question you really wanted to ask was whether they are also hunting for me. To which the answer would be, I have established a grace period of a few months so do not expect the tanks of the People's Army to come thundering across the hills any time soon.'

'That's good to know, Daiyu, I genuinely wouldn't want any harm to befall you.'

'Ahh, how gallant of you. Are you a chivalrous knight come to protect me, Alan? Wouldn't that be nice.'

Harman bowed his head in mock appreciation of how nice that might be and said, 'you strike me as well able to protect yourself from most things. Except perhaps from Virginia Bright? After all, isn't she why you are here?'

'As Thibault will have told you, Virginia directed her inner circle to go to ground while she completes her work. Thibault should have paid heed to her. I for one was more than content to take her advice.'

'Wasn't it more of an order? Wasn't she afraid that not all her supporters could be trusted? Things haven't gone smoothly for her lately. Perhaps she suspects there is a traitor in her ranks.'

Chen laughed with the exuberance of a small girl and placed her hand lightly and fleetingly on Harman's. She said, 'Virginia was a great woman and a great leader. Her star is fading, but she is not stupid or paranoid. The appearance of Peter Salt after so many years may have distracted her. That is true. It may have clouded her judgement. It did not deprive her of it totally. It had to be one of us who set the dogs on her in Colorado. She may assume it was me, but she has other priorities right now than to seek out the viper in her nest. Instead, she has taken all the suspect pieces off the board. I cannot deny the wisdom of her strategy.'

'You need her gone before she can turn her full attention toward you. I can do that for you.'

'Even if you were capable of such an endeavour, you most certainly would not be doing it for me.'

Harman raised his arms in a you've-got-me gesture and replied, 'whatever my motives, you would benefit from the outcome.'

'You are a very intriguing man, Alan. What benefit would you derive from her death? Something must drive you to confront such a formidable opponent.'

'She is planning to kill countless innocent people. Isn't that enough?'

'Their day is done,' she said, matter-of-factly, 'the tide of destiny cannot be turned back. Whether you like it or not, evolution and replacement is the natural order. If you were to go over to that telescope and point it down the valley you would see a large cave and a path sloping down from it. That is where the Guanches made their last stand against the Spanish invaders. There is a myth that they were a lost tribe of blond-haired giants. More likely they were early settlers who had sailed over from the African mainland. Whatever the reality, they were the native population of these islands. When the conquistadores arrived, they wanted to rule, exactly as they did in the Americas. Conflict was inevitable, as was the outcome. The Guanches may have fought hard, but they were farmers with sticks and stones. What chance did they have against men with horses, armour, and muskets? None at all. The sole issue was how long their conquest would take. The Guanches were eradicated and hundreds of years later they are no more than a historical curiosity. The islands are unquestionably Spanish. History is littered with similar examples. There is one no more than a stone's throw away from here.

I say this so you will know that killing Virginia will not save those countless lives that you are so concerned with. It will do no more than delay their demise.'

'You paint a depressing picture, Daiyu. Maybe you're right and maybe you're wrong, but maybe those Guanches would have fared better with the help of some men who also had muskets?'

Chen wrinkled her nose in amusement and said, 'how quaint, Alan, you have a saviour complex.'

'Peter Salt told me that evolution will happen in its own time and that there was no need to hurry it along by committing genocide. That's not having a saviour complex, it's having a moral compass. Let's not get distracted by that, shall we? All that matters right here today is that our immediate aims are aligned. We both want rid of her. It does not have to be more complicated than that.'

Chen brushed her long satin-black hair back over a shoulder and said, 'the complication is that you might have it in mind to kill me once you have killed Virginia. Our world view is diametrically opposed. It might be in my long-term interest to have Hugo put bullets into you and your friend before you can leave.'

The threat was real. Harman was sure of that. So too was Hope, who began to stand as he scoured the surroundings for any sign of Hugo and his rifle.

Harman reached out a steadying hand and said, 'enjoy your water, Charles, we're safe enough.'

'I genuinely admire your certitude, Alan,' Chen said, enjoying herself. 'I wonder what you are basing it on.'

'I'm basing it on you, Daiyu,' Harman said as if it was glaringly obvious, 'you couldn't bear to rot on this island and that is exactly what will happen while Virginia Brightwell leads your faction. And that's if you're lucky. There is a scenario where she gets everything she wants and then has the time and power to be vindictive. What would your future look like then?'

Chen stared slowly around her like a camera taking a panning shot for the start of a film. When she had finished, she filled a glass with Sangria and took a couple of long sips from it. Finally, she said, 'what's that saying you English have? It's a nice place to visit, but I wouldn't want to live here?'

Harman knew he had her, but gloating would be counterproductive. He said, 'you helped Peter by giving him that list. I'm not asking for anything more than that. Blanc told me that Brightwell had moved you onto a chain system for communication. All I want is the next link in the chain.'

Chen drank some more of the Sangria before soundlessly putting the glass back on the table. She said, 'I have had my fun with you. It is time to conclude our business. You knew that I had helped the esteemed Peter Salt, and we both knew from the moment you arrived that I would assist you in the same fashion. I warn you that from here your task will become much harder. Above me are her die-hards. You must be prepared for that. Oh, and do feel free to kill them as well.'

'Sorry to disappoint you and your bloodlust, Daiyu, but all I want is Virginia Brightwell.'

'At least promise me that you will do a better job than Peter did,' she said, her voice almost purring, 'and kill them all.'

For a second or two it felt to Harman like his brain was vibrating in his skull. When it passed, he said, innocently, 'Daiyu, were you trying to influence me? I was under the impression, as was Charles, that Ascendants couldn't do that to one another.'

She shone her most disarming smile at him and said, 'you can't blame a girl for trying. Who knows what we are capable of if we don't try? I've heard stories about strong Ascendants being able to get into the minds of weaker ones. I haven't experienced it myself, but nothing ventured etc etc.'

'Why not give in gracefully and tell me where Hans Osterfeld is?'

Her mood changed abruptly and her sexily angelic features transformed into a sneer of distaste.

'Where do Jews go when they need to feel safe? He's in Israel, of course. You will find him with his nose in a book, probably the Torah or The Tanakh. He owns a small house in Komemiyut. It's not far from Jerusalem. Wait here while I get the address for you.'

She eased smoothly from her chair and, like a model on a catwalk, sauntered into the cave house.

Behind his heavily tinted glasses, Hope

was still eyeing the hillside nervously. He said, 'I don't like her. She's the same as Brightwell, but with a better figure.'

Harman squinted at him and said, 'I thought you'd never met Brightwell.'

Hope said, 'I haven't. I'm only saying that nobody can be better looking than that monster in a bikini.'

'Don't tell me you have a crush on her, Charles?'

'Mock me if you like, Alan, but the Devil comes in many guises and I'm damn sure that's one of them.'

He choked on whatever else he was preparing to say as Chen returned to them. She handed a slip of paper to Harman. He glanced at it before folding it in half and putting it in his shirt pocket. He said, 'how did you get hold of this?'

'Don't worry, he's there alright. I have good friends, deep pockets and a knowledge of Israel that brings into doubt his flawed belief in its sanctity. A word to the wise, Alan. Hans is a mouse of a man, but he is an absolute believer in manifest destiny. Virginia has persuaded him that after the Ascent he will be transformed into a lion. He will do anything to see that come to fruition. She has promised him the future that he has always dreamt of, where he will be a lord amongst lesser men. He has blind loyalty to her.'

Harman said, 'yet these deep pockets and

good friends of yours could not lead you to Yukio Hagihara or Virginia Brightwell?'

'Don't sound so suspicious, Alan. They are birds of a different colour. Even I respect Yukio and there is nobody closer to Virginia than him. The Old Man is old even by our standards. He is clever, maybe as clever as me, but he lacks ambition. He is like one of those legendary Japanese swordsmiths – he could make the best katana or tachi blade in the world, but he would never be a samurai that bears it. If Virginia ever really listens to anyone it's that old goat, he loves playing the guru.'

Harman took out his phone and scrolled through the picture gallery. He found the photograph he was searching for. He raised the screen for Chen to see and said, 'I downloaded this from The Genomic Sciences Centre, Yokohama website. Can you confirm that's him?'

She nodded and said, 'he looks like a gnome.'

Harman repeated the process and showed her a picture he had taken from the website of the Max Planck Institute for Molecular Genetics, Berlin.

'Is that Osterfeld?'

Chen confirmed that it was.

Harman said, 'any idea why neither of them tried to expunge the information and images of themselves from the internet?'

She looked as if the answer was obvious

and said, 'that is surely self-evident. They are powerful Ascendants under the wing of Virginia Brightwell. Who could possibly scare them enough to go to all that trouble?'

Harman rose and went around the table. He stroked Chen's luscious hair as an elderly man might to a loved and still innocent granddaughter and simply said, 'me.'

*

It was late afternoon when Sebastian Kent hobbled out of the lift at the ET1 base in South London. Dr Amy Bishop, with her neatly bobbed hair, WWJD bracelet, and weighted down with enough earnestness to sink the Titanic, was waiting for him in the corridor.

Through the relentless pain in his leg, he managed to give her a grin and say, 'I wasn't expecting a welcoming committee.'

She returned his grin. It was driven by an emotional cocktail of warmth and apprehension. She said, 'it is good to have you back but I'm not the welcoming committee. Sir Anthony is waiting in your office.'

'No doubt he's here to remind me that shit rolls downhill and I'm at the bottom.'

'That's not how I would have put it, Sebastian. What I do know is that it takes a lot for him to shift from the heart of government and drag himself out to our drab corner of town.

I thought you might want to take a few minutes to get your thoughts in order before bearding the beast in your own den.'

'How did he seem? You're the psychiatrist, analyse him for me.'

'He seems how he always seems. Polite and unreadable. Like he could spend all day wired up to a lie detector and not be caught out once.'

Kent squared his shoulders and said, 'thanks for the heads up, Amy. We'll speak properly after he's gone.'

He marched past her as best he could with one weakened leg and the walking cane clipping along, took the next corner and entered his office with all the presence of a superstar going on stage. A lesser man would have been sitting in Kent's chair, but Wildman did not need to play such low-level power games.

Kent said, 'it's good to see you, Sir Anthony. Do you mind if I sit down before I fall down?'

Wildman gave him a regal wave of assent. Kent exaggerated the extent of his immobility and slumped into his chair. He placed the walking cane that Agent Reilly had given him against the wall.

Without moving more than his eyes, Wildman assessed Kent as he might if he was an expensive car that had been returned from the garage repair shop after a crash. He had to decide if it was still safe to drive or whether it would be better to send it to the wrecking yard and invest in a new model.

Wildman adjusted the knot of his royal blue tie and tugged at the creases of his pin striped suit before saying, 'what I have to say won't take long. Putting to one side your failure to deal with this woman Brightwell in Colorado, this business with your man Harman is very embarrassing. You personally assured me of his value to ET1. You also persuaded me that he ought to be part of your jaunt to the US. You will have heard the saying that when the US sneezes the UK catches a cold. This is more like Washington getting a bad dose of the trots and us, particularly you, getting covered in fecal matter. It is a smell that never comes off completely. Do you understand me?'

A few salty options sprang to Kent's mind, but he restricted himself to saying, 'completely.'

The corners of Wildman's lips flickered upward in approval. He had not come there for excuses and whining apologies. He said, 'good. Harman is your man, your mess. Deal with him, deal with him expeditiously, or I will replace you with someone who can. Are we on the same page, Kent?'

'Yes, sir, down to the same letter, of the same word of the same sentence on that page.'

'Then our business is concluded. I told

you it would not take long,' Wildman said.

'Thank you for the clarity you have brought to my position, Sir Anthony.'

Wildman looked like a fox who had spotted a stout hen escaping from its coop. He said, 'how remiss of me. I forgot to mention that as of 10.00am this morning I have upgraded the threat level to Status Red. Until Brightwell is brought to book, it would be negligent of us not to recognise that an extinction event may well be imminent. You might reflect on that when assessing the scale of your failure in Colorado.'

Without any words of farewell to soften the blow he had landed on Kent, he left.

Under his breath, Kent said, 'and you have a nice day too. By the way, thanks for asking how I am – I only took a bullet for you.'

Before he had any time to take comfort from the familiar surroundings of his office, Kent was disturbed by a knock at the door. He knew it couldn't be Wildman coming back. The man would have flung the door open as if he owned the place, which in a sense he did.

Amy Bishop came in and said, 'I thought I'd stay clear until Sir Anthony was back in his car. Can I sit down?'

'Feel free. If I don't get on top of this Harman mess soon you could find this office becomes yours.'

'I wouldn't know what to do with it, although you could make it a bit more homely. Maybe some plants to assist with your wellbeing?'

'Everyone wants to be a comedian these days,' he gave her his tight grin again. He knew she wasn't after his job and that she was doing her best to lighten the mood after his roasting from Wildman. Her efforts probably deserved a full on laugh or big cheesy smile, but he wasn't renowned for those and that grin was the best he could manage.

Bishop sat where Wildman had been moments before and said, 'whatever the Americans or Sir Anthony say, I don't believe that Alan Harman is capable of torturing and murdering anyone. That is both my professional and my personal opinion.'

'Noted. Unfortunately, it counts for nothing. Whether he is innocent or not is secondary to us catching him. Did you put out all the alerts as I asked you to do?' 'You know I did. Your question is merely an attempt at conversational diversion.'

Much as he respected her work, it was times like this that he regretted having a psychiatrist on the team. He said, 'alright, what do you think I am diverting away from?'

'The obvious. Why are we directing all our efforts towards Alan and not continuing with the hunt for Virginia Brightwell?'

'Wake up, Amy, smell the roses or, as Sir Anthony said, the fecal matter. This is politics and that trumps everything else. We've had two goes at Brightwell and failed both times. The best we've done is slow her down. That's not good enough for the men and woman who sit high atop the decision-making mountain. To use a mixed sporting analogy, that ball has been passed to somebody else and we've been benched. Alan Harman is an unpleasant sideshow. Our one chance of redemption is to stop him before he can become a centre stage attraction.'

'And does that mean stop him by any means?'

'Mad dogs have to be put down.'

'And what about wrongly accused dogs?'

'That's not our call any longer. We don't know what Alan has been through or what transitioning to become an Ascendant has done to him. We can't take any chances and Sir Anthony Wildman will be watching to ensure that we don't. Whether he killed that man in Palo Alto or not, what we do know is that he has gone rogue. That is unacceptable. I repeat, our sole focus now is on him.'

'Dead or alive, as the cowboys used to say? That's beyond callous for one of our own, isn't it?'

Kent understood her feelings on the matter but didn't have the inclination to smooth them. He said, 'call it what you want. If you'd wanted an easy life, you should have gone into a different line of work. How about we get on with the job we are paid to do?'

She gave him a curt, 'yes, sir, I will get right on it' answer and left with the same level of friendliness towards him that Wildman had demonstrated.

Kent adjusted his leg while he fished in a desk drawer for a bottle of painkillers. It occurred to him that he had spoken to Amy Bishop in the same way that Wildman had spoken to him. It did nothing to ease the level of his overall discomfort.

*

Virginia Brightwell stared out at the barely rippling waters of Lake Geneva. At over 133 square miles in size, it was impossible to see across it to France on the far side. The boatyard that she had hired was not far from Lausanne, the small city built on hills between the Alps and the Jura Mountains. Until then it had been a calm, picturesque spot. That was before the arrival of the lengthy flatbed truck, the whirring of pneumatic brakes, and the clanking of the lurid orange crane that was being used to hoist the payload from the transporter to the concrete quayside.

The contractors knew what they were doing, and she did not have to oversee their work. Nevertheless, she had felt obliged to come and watch. With great care the workmen attached straps and chains to the cradle that held the bulbous piece of machinery. The object was nearly eight metres long and four metres wide. In total the package weighed nearly 18000kg. That was what the sales material had said, and she had no reason to doubt it, although it was a hire rather than a purchase.

As it was raised and swung across it appeared to her to swing about alarmingly. However, the men from the truck, the crane operators, and the shipping agent, all seemed relaxed despite the amount of shouting they were doing to one another.

The steel cradle screeched as it landed on the concrete and the thump that accompanied it could be felt through her feet. She stood aside as the crane was detached. The chains were reeled in. The straps untied and collected. Papers were signed and the truck departed. The crane was due to be collected the following day. Its operator and his mate got out, waved their farewells, got into a car and left.

She had a brief conversation with the agent. He confirmed that the team of three mechanics would be there in two days' time. It wasn't ideal, but they were specialists and were returning from a job in the South Atlantic. The support ship that she had leased, the *Duttweiller,* would arrive on schedule within three days. Brightwell displayed no impatience. She had known the timetable and had accepted it. She expressed her thanks and appreciation for his efforts. It was not the first occasion on which he had acted for a scientific team that was anxious to explore the mysteries of the great lake. It was good business. He assured her that he had everything in hand, but that she should contact him if he could help further. Satisfied that his client was happy with the service he was providing, he bade her *adieu,* returned to his waiting Mercedes and drove off.

The only ones remaining were Brightwell and the security guard. He closed the gates behind the departing Mercedes and went back to his tiny room inside the main workshop. He had shown no interest in the delivery nor in Brightwell. To her, that made him perfect.

Left alone with her special new toy she ran a hand over its smooth exterior. The Mir submersible was white all over except for the top, which was bright red, and the front which had a wide viewport. It carried a crew of three and could go to a depth of six thousand metres. Brightwell did not need to put it to the test. The deepest part of the lake was about a twentieth of that. It reminded her of a squat helicopter with the long overhead propellers being placed by a small, enclosed propeller at the rear.

She stood on tiptoes and stared through the viewport into the interior. When the lights and control panel were illuminated it might be fractionally more inviting, but it looked like a claustrophobe's worst nightmare. Being cooped up in there, elbow to elbow with two other people, thousands of feet under water would be somebody's idea of Hell. Brightwell was amused by the thought. This bulbous device would help her bring Heaven to Earth for the Ascendants. She was eager to get inside and be trained in its use. The mechanics would help her with that while they made it operational again. She could wait for them. In the meantime, there was still much for her to do. The time until their arrival would not be wasted.

Unlike the men she had hired, Brightwell had not driven there. She had walked along the coast from Lausanne, and she would walk back again. Next to the sliding gate that barred the road into the yard was a single mesh door. She stepped across the ramp that ran from the workshop and down into the water, used her key to unlock the padlock on the door and let herself out. She was aware that the guard was watching her through the grimy window of his room. For his benefit she made great play of securing the padlock so that the door was locked again. She knew it would please him.

Brightwell smiled sadly to herself. In some regard the Normals were like children, easily distracted and easily satisfied. If only that was all there was to them then the peaceful co-existence dreamt of by her brother, Peter Salt, might have become more than a dream. When had he become so deluded and dangerous? She often wondered if she could have acted sooner to keep him on the right path, but the blind cannot see and the deaf cannot hear. She knew deep down that there was nothing she could have said or shown him that would have changed his mind. Worse than that, she could never comprehend why she should have to when the evidence of the threat from the Normals was all around them and always had been. When placid, the Normals could be like happy toddlers, but they never remained like that. Their ignorance and latent savagery contaminated them like some awful disease. All their history showed they would resort to violence when threatened and there could be no greater threat to them than eventual replacement by the Ascendants. The Normals propensity for genocide would find its target sooner or later when they became fully aware of the rise of the Ascendants. That might not be for a year, ten years, or a hundred years, but Brightwell had pledged her life to preventing it from happening.

As she walked her mood brightened. Life did not have to be complicated. When the equation was reduced it came down to a straight choice between them and us. Unpleasant as the actions themselves might be, she had to be strong because there was only one solution, and it was incontrovertible to those with the clarity and will to see clearly. There would be before and there would be after. For her own peace of mind, she had to focus resolutely on the after.

*

About seven hours after Harman and Hope had departed to find a hotel for the night for themselves, Ernst Mannson cycled up the road from Fataga to the Finca Klausen. The sky was clear and absent of any light pollution from the seaside resorts. The velvety blackness above him was dotted with more stars than he had ever seen. The night air was pleasantly warm without being oppressive. It was joyful. He reflected contentedly on God's majesty and gifts.

The bicycle had lamps attached at the front and rear. He had not switched them on. There was no need. He could see perfectly well without them. Despite the meandering climb he was breathing easily. Earlier he had watched Alan Harman turn the car on to the road for the finca. It meant that he knew where he would find Daiyu Chen.

Before reaching the turn off, Ernst Mannson got off the stolen bike and laid it down behind a bush. It could not be seen from the road, but he would find it easily enough when he came back.

Without haste he took a detour around the road and came up the rocks behind one of the guards. It happened to be Hugo. Not that it mattered to Mannson. The former Spanish Green Beret was sitting with his back against a tree. The glow from the tip of his cigarette stood out like a beacon. The hunting rifle was within his reach propped against a boulder. It wasn't close enough. Mannson crept up silently behind him. He put one hand around Hugo's face. In the other he held a sharp camping knife. He stabbed it repeatedly into the former soldier's throat. Mannson held his victim like that until he bled out. He had strived to make it as quick and painless as he could. He took no more pleasure from the killing than a slaughterhouse worker did when butchering cattle. Hugo was no more than an obstacle that had to be removed. Mannson hoped, as he always did on such occasions, that God would be able to forgive him.

From there, he walked up the road to the finca. There were no lights on outside. He went to the cave entrance. He tried the door and found it unlocked. Easing it open, he wondered at Chen's carelessness and peered into the darkness. He had no idea what the layout was inside the finca, but how complex could a dug-out cave be? Taking each step with the slow certainty of a natural predator he moved along the short corridor. The odours coming from his right spoke of recently cooked food. The hint of washing-up liquid told him it was a kitchen area.

Pushing deeper into the cave, he heard

heavy breathing coming from an opening on his left. There was no door, just a doorway carved from the pale rock of the mountainside. The minimal light coming from outside and along the corridor was enough for Mannson's perfect Ascendant vision to make out the sleeping form of a naked man on an outsized bed. It was easily big enough for three. While that thought flittered through his mind, it was his perfect Ascendant hearing that saved his life. He jerked backwards as the blade of a kitchen knife swished past in what should have been a deadly arc. The thrust left Chen unbalanced. He grabbed the back of her elbow and shoulder. He twisted. She let out a scream and dropped the knife. Awoken by the scuffle, Alverado sat up groggily in the bed. Mannson hurled Chen back into the concealed corner where she had been hiding. He ignored her grunt of anguish as her naked torso slapped into the wall.

Mannson took two quick steps forward and rammed his own knife into Alverado's chest. The ex-soldier did not see it coming in what to him was total and immersive darkness. The big man let out a cry. His struggle ended soon after the blade pierced his heart. He slumped back. Mannson's knife was lodged between two of the man's ribs. Mannson should have released the knife, but he didn't. He found himself dragged on to the bed. He dropped beside the dead man, bouncing slightly as the bed springs resisted his weight.

No sooner had he scrambled up than Chen sprang at him, landing with all her athletic force on his back. He tripped forward under the unexpected burden. Her fingernails were clawing for his eyes. Her legs wrapped themselves around his chest. Her knees clenched tightly as she tried to squeeze the air from him. Even as he tottered about, he was able to grip her hands and prise them loose. Her screaming in his ears was deafening. As they wrestled, he laughed. She was not bawling at him she was yelling for Hugo to come and help. She couldn't have known that she was asking for a dead man to walk.

After steadying his feet, Mannson drove backwards, using her weight on his back to add impetus to the movement. When they hammered into the uneven, rough-cut wall her scream changed to one of wordless agony. He heard something that might have been the fracturing of bones, but the dull thud of hard skull against something even harder was unmistakeable. Her body went limp like a puppet whose strings had been cut. He moved away and let her unconscious body slide to the ground.

Mannson checked himself for damage. His face was unscathed, and any scratches and bruising would be hidden beneath his clothes. He found the light switch and turned it on. He checked his watch and rubbed his hands in glee. He still had plenty of time.

Looking at the bed he turned his nose up in disgust. Who in their right mind would choose golden satin bedsheets? He had misjudged Chen. He had assumed that her sense of style permeated all aspects of her life. It was disappointing to see that in the bedroom her tastes ran to the gaudy. The amount of Alverado's blood that was pouring over the sheets wouldn't do them any good either. The ghostly pallor of his victim told Mannson that he was now as much use to Chen as Hugo was.

Returning to Chen, he moved her chin softly. Although she was unconscious, a low groan escaped from her lips. As she lay there, his eyes swept over her body. She really was a magnificent specimen, but he felt no lust for her. She was an abomination and therefore utterly repulsive to him.

He grabbed her by her ankles and dragged her from the bedroom to the kitchen. Her long black hair splayed out on the floor behind her like waves of ebony. He turned on the light and hauled her up on to an old wooden chair. When he was sure she was not going to fall off, he rummaged through the draws of the tall traditional Canarian wood cabinet that stood next to the sink. He had hoped to find masking tape. All he could find was a ball of string. He shrugged. It would have to do.

He took a steak knife from the cutlery drawer and cut long lengths from the ball. After doubling up some of the lengths of string he tied Chen's arms and legs to the chair. He tested the fastenings to make sure they would hold and then lightly tapped Chen's cheeks. She did not respond. He raised one of her eyelids. She was still out cold. He tut-tutted and filled a bowl with water. He threw it into her face. While droplets trickled down her nose, off her chin, and through her hair, he watched with pleasure as her eyes blinked open. He waited until he detected a semblance of understanding in those pretty almond orbs.

'There she is,' he said as cheerily as if she had just come back after running some errand for him. 'How's my girl?'

It took a while for her to focus on him properly. She croaked, 'who are you?'

'That really isn't important. I'm not important. Tell me, Daiyu, how well do you know the scriptures?'

'I...I...don't understand.'

'Well, if you had the time, which you do not, I would refer you to Mark 3:15. It is one of my favourites. It says that the light of the devil shines from their eyes and I have the authority to drive out demons.'

'What are you talking about?' she said, as the fog slowly lifted from her mind.

'I will give you a clue,' Mannson said

playfully. 'The devil's light shines brightly from your eyes. I would go so far as to say that it shines intensely.'

'Are you mad?'

Mannson acted as if he had not heard her answer. He said to himself as much to her, 'sometimes I can be so forgetful. What am I like? Wait here for me, will you?'

He left the room and was back in under a minute. He found Chen tugging at her bounds. He said, 'you really shouldn't waste your energy doing that. I've always been very good at tying knots. I learnt that on the farm. So, where was I? Oh yes, the second part of Mark 3:15. I have the authority to drive out demons.'

Mannson raised the gore-drenched knife that he had just pulled out of Alverado's heart. He rested it on Chen's nose and said, 'let's begin here, shall we?'

CHAPTER FOUR

Alan Harman settled into his window seat and looked out at Las Palmas airport. The flight to Gatwick was scheduled to leave at 12.35. They were already running ten minutes late, but he wasn't concerned by that. Pilots always seemed to be able to make up periods of up to an hour through some kind of airline magic. The connecting flight to Tel Aviv was due to depart at 19.10 and he was sure he would still have time for an insipid drink and shrink-wrapped snack at the London airport before boarding time.

For both flights he had obtained seats for himself near the front of the plane and for Charles Hope at the rear. He didn't yet trust his new companion enough for them to take separate flights. fly separately, but equally if Brightwell or anyone else was on the looking for him it made no sense for the two men to be so visibly travelling as a pair.

Over the past few days, the bricks had been gradually falling away from the wall he had put up between him and Hope, but he was far from seeing the American as a reliable ally, let alone a friend. It did not help that Hope lived on a spectrum with nervous anxiety at one end and boyish excitement at the other, with precious little in between. He was like a mistreated puppy who had never learned to play and who perpetually flinched for fear of receiving another beating. For all of that, for the lengthy periods when they had been travelling rather than confronting Thibault Blanc and Daiyu Chen, Hope was a ready and willing source of information about Ascendants and their abilities. The pleasure he derived from being of any assistance at all appeared to be genuine. There were so many gaps in Harman's knowledge about the Ascendants that fresh queries came to him as frequently as hungry birds to a grain store. Whenever they were fired at Hope, he answered patiently and as fully as he could. Occasionally, he would admit that he wasn't sure and would have to think about it some more before giving a response that was worthy of the name. Without fail, often hours later, he would supply an answer that was as thoughtful and thorough as he could construct.

Harman's decision to bring him along seemed vindicated. Whether he could afford to babysit him when he really had to put the pedal to the floor was a different matter. The list of people who were close to him that had died recently was already too long. Not that Hope was close to him like they were, but each in their way was an innocent and Hope was a fish that fell into that same net.

In the seat behind Harman a little girl

squawked and began to cry. He craned around to see what was wrong. Next to her was a boy, at maybe nine or ten he was several years older than her. He had snatched some handheld game device from her and was teasing her by repeatedly pretending to throw it away. A woman, who Harman presumed to be their mother, was ignoring the sibling spat by resolutely reading emails on her phone. The faintest twang of music could be detected from the buds that were plugged into her ears. There was no way of knowing whether she had been listening for a while or whether she had resorted to the tracks from her chosen album to drown out the bickering of her offspring.

'Hey,' Harman said in his most child-friendly tone to the boy, 'why not give it back to her?'

He would have been happy with a 'sorry, mister' response and would maybe have been amused if the kid had cheekily stuck his tongue out. Neither of those things happened. Instead, the boy went red, bared his teeth, gave Harman the middle finger, and said, 'you can do one, or my dad will cut you a new arsehole.' Which made Harman neither happy, nor amused.

Harman winked at the little girl and said to her, 'would you care to see a magic trick?'

Distracted from her obnoxious brother and wary of being spoken to by a stranger, even if there was a row of seats between them, she stopped wailing and turned her red-rimmed eyes on him. With a little hesitation, she nodded.

'Good girl. How about if we put a spell on your brother? We could make him do whatever you want for the rest of the flight.'

'You're funny,' she said in a tinny, little voice.

Harman's gut feeling about influencing people hadn't changed, but he could forgive himself this once. He said to the boy in a low monotone that verged on the hypnotic, 'you will behave nicely for the rest of this trip, and you will do whatever your sister tells you to do.'

He turned back to the girl and invited her to say the magic word.

Still unsure, she said, 'abrcabragra.'

He laughed and said, 'close enough. Try asking for your gadget.'

She glowered at her tormentor and said, 'gimme my game.'

The boy handed it over without question.

She looked with delight at Harman and was soon happily pressing buttons with the speed of a striking snake.

As Harman turned around to face forward, he noticed the appreciative glances of the adult passengers all around him. All except the children's mother who pretended not to have noticed anything. With relative peace assured he took a laptop from his flight bag. Prior to boarding he had downloaded from the internet as much information as he could about Komemiyut. It wasn't the same as a proper reconnaissance, but it was better than going in completely blind. He began to read.

*

A couple of hours later, shortly before Harman's plane approached mainland Europe and left the coast of Africa behind, Amy Bishop dashed into Sebastian Kent's office. He barely had time to note that she had failed to knock prior to entering.

Her cheeks flushed as she hurriedly said, 'we have a match.'

'Facial recognition or documentation?'

'Facial. 85% match. The angles aren't perfect, and the tech isn't as good as ours, but we can't ignore it.'

'Is that after AI enhancement?'

'It is. That's as good as we will get it.'

Kent stifled the urge to remind her that he knew more about the technology than she did. Pettiness was not one of his failings. He limited himself to asking, 'is the facility ready?'

'It's as functional as we could make it. I would have preferred longer.'

'Me too, but we go with what we've got. If we learned anything from our acquaintance with Peter Salt, it was that whatever we had before was not good enough. Even if it's a work in progress, the new place is our best option. You take charge of that, and I will make the other arrangements. Maybe for once, we've struck lucky.'

'You know that I don't believe in luck,' Bishop said, sounding vaguely offended.

Kent did know that he simply didn't care that much about her minor sensitivities when they had an undeclared war to fight. He said, 'would it be better if I cited divine intervention?'

'That's a conversation for another day. Perhaps when you are fully recovered from your injury. By then, you will have one less excuse for your rudeness towards me.'

Bishop was off to carry on her work before he could respond to that. She left the door ajar in an act of defiance that was guaranteed to be recognised as such by each of them. He scratched his jaw. The roughness there reminded him that he needed a shave. With no small effort and leaning wearily on his stick, he walked to the door to close it. He had been away for a matter of weeks, rather than months, yet during that short period Amy Bishop had grown some claws. He liked the change in her.

*

When the flight landed at Gatwick, Harman was deliberately slow in unbuckling himself. He was even slower in putting his laptop away. And he made no effort to join the cramped queue that was gathering in the aisle to escape from the plane as soon as the fresher air announced the opening of its passenger doors. He wanted to get as good a look as he could at the other passengers as they disembarked. Somehow, he was sure he would know if anyone was taking the wrong sort of interest in him.

As they shuffled off, only one of them paid him any heed. It was the little girl. She gave him a small wave with her bunched fingers. He waved awkwardly back at her. It wouldn't be long before she discovered that her brat of a brother was returning to his old self. The spell that had been put on him would expire when he set foot on the tarmac. The magic would end abruptly. She would have to adapt and grow, just as Harman was learning to do. He felt sorry for her, because he felt sorry for himself. Neither of them had asked to be placed in the situations they were in, but both were there, nonetheless. There were two paths open to them. Thrive and survive or wither and die. As he caught his final glimpse of her something told him she would be just fine.

Charles Hope went past as the line snaked forward. It was hard to tell where he was looking with his eyes hidden by those darkly tinted spectacles, but his head pointed resolutely forward. There was no hint of recognition. If anyone was watching, they would not see any obvious connection between the two men.

After Harman had joined the end of the passenger line, he thanked the cabin crew at the exit and headed casually towards the maze of corridors that funnelled disembarking passengers to where they need to be next. Most took the route to the baggage pick up and passport control areas. He followed the signs to the connecting flight lounges. As expected, the plane had landed close to its scheduled time. He saw from the screens that he had no need to rush to catch the flight to Tel Aviv.

He stepped on to a travelator and let it carry him down the lengthy corridor. One wall was made up of windows overlooking parked aircraft. The other with a procession of glossy adverts for duty free goods, and union jack bedecked souvenirs of London.

Maybe two hundred feet ahead, were a clutch of passengers congregating at the exit from the corridor. He couldn't see what was causing the bottle neck, but it was a common enough sight at airports. It was inevitable when people were being herded around like cattle, that sometimes they would adopt a herd mentality and grouped together.

When he stepped off the travelator, he walked the remaining short distance and peered around the corner and over the heads of those ahead of him. A woman in a blue border control uniform sat at a table. Another woman and man, similarly clad, stood beside her. Seemingly at random they were requesting that passengers go into a side room to have their bags checked. All three staff on view had adopted looks of bored indifference which did not change one iota in the face of grumbling passengers, some of whom were waving their passports around as if they were golden tickets to Willy Wonka's Chocolate Factory.

Harman was pleased to see Hope being ushered through. He watched as his new ally walked ahead for a bit and then knelt to tie a shoelace. To Harman it was obviously a pretence so that he could hover close by to see whether his partner in crime would catch up with him soon. Nobody else took any notice of Hope.

The line nudged forward. Harman turned sharp eyes on the three uniformed personnel. If they were anything other than bored bureaucrats, conducting a boring bureaucratic process, then they were better actors than he had seen on stage or film.

As he reached the table, the woman, turned her head up toward him and said, 'good afternoon, sir, what's your onward destination today?'

'Tel Aviv, next plane out,' he said pleasantly.

'For security reasons, we are conducting additional checks on visitors to Israel. Please accompany my colleague into one of the adjoining rooms where your hand luggage will be searched, and you may be asked some further questions.'

The waiting uniformed woman took a pace forward. She managed a tired smile and said with an Afro-Caribbean lilt, 'would you come this way please, sir?'

'Lead on,' he said, trying to sound jaunty but fearing that it had come across as sarcastic. He had nothing to hide, and a delay of a couple of minutes wouldn't do any harm. If it turned into something that might prevent him catching the Tel Aviv flight, he would reluctantly influence them to pass him through, although it hardly seemed likely that would be necessary.

He followed the woman into a room where a stoic official was working his way through the contents of a rucksack while its owner berated him for persecuting the already oppressed. There was another door beyond that. She led him through it into what was little more than a windowless cubicle.

She directed him to a metal chair and said, 'please wait here, one of my colleagues will be with you momentarily.'

It sounded like she was reading from a script. Harman put that down to repetitive training and actions rather than her actually being an aspiring actress. The door clicked shut behind her. He sat on the chair and placed the bag on his lap. He unzipped its cover and pockets in preparation for the quick search that would reveal nothing more threatening than an unsharpened pencil.

If he had not been an Ascendant, he would not have heard the second click as something slid into place around the doorway. And he would not have heard the faintest of hisses as an odourless gas was released from the air vents that were set into the foot of the walls.

His eyes closed. The world disappeared from him. His muscles relaxed. His bag dropped to the floor. He slid from the chair like limp jelly off a warm plate.

*

As Hope straightened, he pretended to accidentally drop loose change from his pocket. He had seen Harman being led away and was desperate to buy time until he reappeared. When he had clumsily picked up each coin, and dropped one or two again, he accepted that he could not loiter there for too long without attracting some unwanted attention. While he deliberately brushed some non-existent dirt from the knees of his trousers, he saw the man who had been pulled out of line behind Harman reappear and come towards him. He tracked the man down the corridor. When Hope was out of sight of the border patrol guards, he waited. He grabbed a landing card from one of the dispensers and made great show of reading it while the remaining passengers strolled by him.

When they had all gone and Hope found himself standing there alone, he had to accept that Harman was not coming. He rubbed at his stomach. It suddenly felt empty apart from acid. He looked back the way he had come, and forward to the departure lounge. He couldn't stand in that empty passageway indefinitely. He was sure of that much, but not much else.

Hope went to the lounge area. He needed a way out. Something was seriously wrong. His every instinct told him so. In any normal situation, Harman would have been able to talk his way out of it or, with reluctance, used his significant influencing powers to extract himself. After spending a lot of time with Harman, Hope had observed him closely. The Brit from ET1 was a novice. His perpetual questions about what it meant to be an Ascendant were evidence enough of that. Hope had been guarded as he drip fed the information he chose to share. He had become even more wary as Harman bloomed before him like a flower in one of those nature documentaries where trick photography condensed months of growth into a few seconds. Harman seemed unaware of his own progress. After all, what did he have to compare it to? Harman's latent talents did not frighten Hope, but they were making him uneasy.

What was making him even more

unsettled in that moment was a single thought: with all the Ascendant advantages that Harman had, what could possibly have stopped him from reaching the departures loung?

Hope ran a hand over his bald pate as his gaze darted around for exits and threats. It was the wrong time to worry about how powerful an Ascendant Harman was becoming. All that mattered in that moment was that he had been taken or killed. Hope rationalised that he had so far been allowed to pass and he inferred that nobody had drawn a connection between him and Harman. The precautions that Harman had insisted upon had proved their worth, but for how long?

On the flight manifests, their seats were recorded as vacant. They were travelling without passports and so no records of matching names were there to betray them. But what they could not hide from, or influence, was security cameras. What if an investigator was even now going through the footage passengers going to and from Gran Canaria? When would someone spot that Hope was the only one to fly out of Edinburgh and back to Gatwick on the same planes as Harman? By backtracking further, pictures would inevitably emerge on some hard drive of them arriving together at the airport in Scotland. It was all a question of time and Hope concluded that it was not on his side.

Getting on the flight to Tel Aviv would be

to trap himself like a mouse in a cage knowing that vermin hunters might be waiting for him at the other end.

He watched a maintenance worker heading for a door behind an unoccupied boarding gate. That was his way out. Wherever it led to had to be safer than where he was.

*

When Harman woke his chin was on his chest. He raised his head. His neck felt like it had been set in concrete. His mouth was dry, his eyes were gritty. His head was telling him that a heavy-handed carpenter was hammering nails into it. He wiped his face with a clammy hand and slowly got his bearings. He was lying on a cot. An unused pillow was above him. Whoever had dropped him there hadn't bothered to make sure that he was comfortable. He rolled over and sat up. A second carpenter joined the first and they both beat away at his brain as hard as they could. He screwed his eyes up at the pain and waited for it to subside.

When it became bearable, he inspected his surroundings. He was in a cell of some kind, but it wasn't the kind found in police stations or prisons. Harman had been in plenty of those. He knew the differences well enough. To begin with this place had no windows and no discernible door. Logic said there must be one. He would find it later. The walls and ceiling were painted a relaxing sky-blue colour. Some psychologist or other would no doubt have recommended it to help keep any inmates stay calm. A toilet and sink were in one corner. As there was no shower or bath, he decided that this wasn't a place for long term incarceration. Apart from the cot, the only other furniture consisted of a table and chair.

He eased himself to the bare floor and looked under the cot. There was a cardboard box. He pulled it out. It contained plastic bottles of water and stacks of energy bars. Harman grabbed one of the bottles, tore off the top, and gulped down half of its contents. While there he ran an eye over the bedframe. It was made from a single mould. There were no screws or nuts. Next, he checked the table and chair. They were of the same design.

The lights were in recesses in the ceiling. Thin steel bars protected them from being touched, although by his estimates he could not have reached them even if he had put the table on top of the bed, and the chair on top of the table. He was not surprised that there was no light switch in the room.

The high ceiling gave the room a sense of space, but as he toured the room, he found it measured no more than ten of his paces from end to end. He grimaced at the sight of the air vents sited at ankle height. They were identical to the ones in the cubicle that he had been lured to.

Harman checked his pockets. They were all empty. He touched the spot on his wrist where his watch had been. There were no clocks on the walls. Textbook disorientation tactics. With no windows either it was impossible to guess what time of day or night it was. Which meant that the lights would remain on perpetually or would sporadically be turned on and off to throw his body clock out of kilter. It was unoriginal, but no less effective for that.

A sudden wave of fatigue engulfed him, and he stumbled back to the cot. He glugged down more of the water. He used a sleeve to wipe a trace of sweat from his forehead. The room wasn't hot, so he put it down to an after effect of whatever toxin they had put in his system. As his head cleared again, he went to the sink and doused his head and shoulders in cold tap water.

A disembodied voice said, 'good to see you are awake at last, Alan. I'm afraid we had to guess a bit at the dosage. Don't worry, you will be back to your new self quickly enough.'

Using the tiny towel that his hosts had supplied, Harman dabbed at his face. In his own time, he said, 'is that you, Sebastian?'

'Large as life and twice as ugly. I really hadn't expected to see you so soon again. Arrogance and over-confidence seem to be a bit of a curse to Ascendants like you. I suppose it comes with the territory.'

'I get that you're not happy that I went off on my own, but this is a bit of over kill, isn't it?'

'You're a dangerous man, Alan. We can't be too careful.'

'Dangerous? What are you talking about? And where are you? Why can't I see you?'

'You are not a policeman any longer, Alan. It's not your job to be posing questions in these circumstances. Things will go better for you if you accept that reality.'

Harman breathed deeply through his nose and exhaled slowly. Having calmed his thoughts, he said, 'I haven't done anything wrong. You can't hold me here.'

Kent's mocking laughter echoed around the cell. He said, 'come on, Alan, that must have sounded as lame to you as it did to us.'

'Us? Who else is with you?'

'Dr Bishop is here with me. And before you ask, in this instance by here, I mean my office at Faulkner House. She designed the facility you are being kept in. She's more than a little curious to see if it comes up to expectations. It's something she's been working on ever since we discovered that Peter Salt, God rest him, had the ability to seemingly walk through walls and that no cell could hold him. It was later that we became aware of the Ascendants' propensity to control most people they came across. You do remember that don't you?'

Harman's memory roved back to the time that he and Carol King had gone to Charing Cross Police Station to investigate Salt's disappearance from police custody. It seemed an age ago, but it wasn't.

After less than a minute, Kent continued, 'I can see that you do. Anyhow, you know as well as I do, that Amy is very good at her job. We are nowhere near your location and there is nobody there for you to influence. You are, in every sense of the word, alone and isolated.'

'This is vindictive, even for you, Sebastian. Why go to all this trouble to bring me back in?' Harman said, the tiredness in his body reflected in his voice. 'Is ET1 like the mafia? Once you're in you can never leave, is that it? Are you making an example of me to keep the others in line? I'd say it's a lot of trouble to go to just to show who's boss. I didn't know I had dented your ego so badly.'

'My ego is intact, Alan, which is more than can be said for Thibault Blanc. You do know him, don't you?'

As the question was as heavily weighted as a dead body in the river with anvil attached to it, Harman did not rush to reply. As a reputable interrogator himself, he knew how to set bear traps for suspects. He knew better than to fall straight into one. His position was weak, but he wasn't powerless. If they wanted information from him then he would want information from them in return. It might be no more than scraps. Whatever it was would be more than he currently had to draw on.

Harman said, doing his best not to sound defensive, 'I know him, what I don't understand is how you do?'

'Was he a friend of yours?'

Harman couldn't miss Kent's use of the past tense when talking about the French-Canadian. The conclusion was obvious. It was information, but it wasn't welcome.

'He's an acquaintance,' Hamran countered. 'I've only met him once.'

'How did you come to know him?'

Harman saw no point in lying when Kent probably knew the truth already. He said, 'he was on the list of Ascendants that Peter Salt gave to me. The one I told you about while you were in hospital.'

'Would you care to confirm what other names are on that list?'

Harman allowed himself a wan smile and said, '*confirm* implies that you already know who they are. I don't think you do and so I will keep them to myself if you don't mind.'

'The list won't do you any good in there, Alan. You need to accept that you won't be going anywhere soon and, when you do, it will probably be a lot worse that where you are now.'

'If and when I reach the same conclusion, maybe I will tell you then.'

'What a shame,' Kent groaned theatrically, 'and there I was thinking we were on the same side. Has the awakening of your dormant Ascendancy led you to reassess your loyalties?'

'Then again, if we were on the same side, you wouldn't have me locked up in here.'

'You make a valid point, Alan. Let us return then to Mr Blanc. How was he when you last saw him in Palo Alto?'

Harman admired the way that Kent had slipped in a reference to Palo Alto. It was a signal that he wasn't bluffing and a clear message that Harman should not pretend ignorance. He said, 'I would say he was...unsettled.'

'Being tortured and set alight would do that, wouldn't it? Hard to imagine anything more unsettling. Why did you do it, Alan?'

The iron hard edge in Kent's words meant that he was not playing around any longer. Harman felt them like a jab to the chin. Then he felt a follow up punch to the guts as full realisation hit him that Blanc was dead, and Kent thought he was responsible. It totally changed the rules of engagement. This was not an exercise in ET1 bringing him to heel. His head was being put on the chopping block of a guillotine and the executioner was waiting for the command to drop the blade on his neck.

Harman scanned the room intently, more anxious than ever to find the hidden door.

As if reading his thoughts, Amy Bishop joined the conversation and said, 'please don't waste your time, Alan. I'm sure you are clever enough to find the door eventually. If you do, we will simply release more gas and you will be back where you started, except with the addition of physical restraints when you re-awaken.'

'Amy, you know me, you can't believe I would have killed Blanc.'

'You shot and killed someone at the mine on the 191 Ranch. I also believe you intend to kill Virginia Brightwell if you find her. That was true before your latent Ascendancy was activated. You had a capacity for death when I knew you, and for all we know that capacity has grown after the changes you have gone through.'

All Harman heard was the complete professional speaking. There was no inkling of the friend he had hoped she was becoming. Those few sentences from her were harder to take than anything Kent might say.

He had to try one more time to get through to her. He said, 'but torture, Amy? Surely you can't believe I would be capable of that?'

There was a pause, during which his expectations rose, but they soon crashed down again when he heard her say, 'my previous answer stands.'

Kent came on again and said, 'the first fact is that this fellow Blanc is dead, and he died badly. The second, is that you are on camera breaking into his apartment building, entering his home, and leaving it. The timing is incontrovertible. You were there long enough to torture him, get whatever information you wanted so that you could continue your pursuit, kill him and leave. What is it you policemen say? Means, motive and opportunity. You had all three.'

'I had no need to hurt him,' Harman said, 'all he wanted was a quiet life. He could return to that as soon as he told me where to go next. So, he told me, and I left. He was happily enjoying some expensive cognac when I last saw him.'

'If someone else had told me that story, I would advise them to get the best defence attorney they could afford. In your case, that would be bad advice and a waste of money even if you could follow it. You see, I really do not expect you will ever see the inside of a court. We might have caught you my little trapped bird, but you are the property of Homeland Security and in due course you will be handed into their caring arms. They are even less happy with you than we are. Naturally, I would prefer to hang on to you myself so that we can drain you of every ounce of knowledge about your Ascendant abilities, but they have pulled rank and so it must be.'

Harman wasn't fooled. Despite what he was saying, Kent was not totally convinced of his guilt, and his resentment at playing second fiddle to his US counterparts irked every inch of him. Harman might not be able to see Kent and Bishop, but his heightened insight as an Ascendant told him more from their voices than they could know.

'Well, they do say that travel broadens the mind.'

Kent scoffed and said 'humour in the face of adversity. Admirable yet worthless. I think I've had enough of your company for now and it is past my bedtime. Let's resume this in the morning.'

Harman picked up the faintest click as the interaction was terminated. While he could not hear them anymore, he had no doubt that he was still being watched and listened to. He was also sure that Kent was probably off for breakfast or lunch rather than it being close to his *bedtime*. They would have to try much harder than that to make him lose sense of time. He decided that outside it was probably still morning. What he could not tell was whether it was the day after his planned flight to Tel Aviv or if they had kept him sedated for longer than that.

He lay back on the cot. He bunched the pillow up under his head and began to re-run everything that had been said. There was useful information in there and he intended to mine it for every spec of value. He had not killed Blanc and if he could put enough doubt in their minds about that then he might yet talk his way back into their good graces. What other hope did he have to latch on to?

When Kent engaged with him again, Harman guessed it was four to six hours later. And the slim hope that he had nurtured during that period was immediately snatched away from him.

*

Virginia Brightwell looked out from her room on the top floor of the Lausanne Palace Hotel. A low haze hung over the Swiss city like a dirty veil. It hid Lake Geneva from her view. Below her the buildings were a mix of young and old. It was clean and orderly without being regimented. On her frequent walks she had been surprised to see graffiti on some of the walls. In the urban sprawl of cities across Europe and the USA it had been part of the scenery, so commonplace as to be totally unremarkable. Here in this wealthy lakeside city which esteemed bodies, including the International Olympic Committee, had chosen to call home, it seemed odd and out of place.

Her eye was caught by a procession of young schoolchildren walking in pairs while eagle-eyed teachers watched over them. They turned a corner awkwardly like a rheumatic snake and began the descent down the hill towards the waterfront. There always seemed to be lots of school parties visiting the Olympic Museum and she wondered if that was their destination. She could just about hear their chattering and giggling. It reminded her of a flock of small birds fighting for scraps in a garden. Their innocent joy was lighting up the faces of everyone they passed.

What a blessing true innocence was, she thought, and what a tragedy its passing. How many years would it take for those same children to become a hate-filled mob? When would their ignorance and unconstrained fear lead them to hunt her people down? Hyena cubs were cute. They had big eyes and almost round ears that were too big for their heads. They stumbled about in a goofy way. Their fur was as soft as velvet. Anyone who saw one would be tempted to pick it up and give it a big hug. But in less than three years, that same cub would be part of a pack that was one of the most predatory in the world. It would hunt and slaughter its prey without mercy. It would kill not just to sate its hunger, but because that was part of its very nature. Brightwell could not blame the hyena for that, any more than she would an ant for having six legs or a giraffe for having a long neck. It was in their DNA. It was who they were, and it was unavoidable. Those cheery children below her were no different. That was why when, not more than a child herself, she had decided that the only way to ensure the safety and longevity of her people, the Ascendants like her, was to eradicate the Normals.

Such an aggressive response was not part of the DNA of an Ascendant. Brightwell had always known her actions were not pre-determined by her evolved genes. She did not delude herself by pretending that what she planned was driven by some irrational instinct. She was no hyena. She had considered the existential threat to the growing number of Ascendants. She had looked back at the history of mankind. She had tried and failed to identify evidence of any real change. Over several years she had assessed the challenge logically and without emotion. And she had reached an unassailable and irrevocable conclusion.

Within a few days she would finally be able to act on that conclusion.

Brightwell laced her fingers behind her back and stretched. There was always more work to be done. Trying not to hunch, she sat again in front of her computer screen.

She scrolled through the projections and calculations. It was something she had done countless times. She checked, double checked, and triple checked the statistics for the Rhône River water that flowed through Lake Geneva on its path to its eventual destination, the Mediterranean Sea. About 1.5 million people lived around the lake and it provided the drinking water for over half of them. They would be first to feel the effects, but her aspirations were much, much, higher than that.

*

'What are you playing at, Sebastian?' Harman shouted at the spot where he imagined Kent's voice was emanating from. 'First you tell me Thibault Blanc is dead and now you're telling me that Daiyu Chen has been murdered. These mind games won't work because I have nothing else to tell you. We should both be out there tracking Brightwell down rather than messing about like this.'

Kent's tone was like a sharp icicle as he said, 'Chen wasn't murdered, she was tortured to death. The two men with her were butchered. Becoming an Ascendant had turned you into a maniac, Harman. I notice you didn't try to deny meeting her while you were in Gran Canaria. She was the second name on your list, wasn't she? Were you planning to kill them all, one at a time?'

Harman felt like his cheek had been slapped. Kent was serious. It wasn't something from the interrogators' textbook designed to put him on the back foot. Once again, he was desperate for information. He said, 'there is no reason for me to deny it. I went there to see her, to ask for her help in finding Brightwell. There was no reason to hurt her. If she is dead, what makes you think I'm responsible for it?'

'I am glad you aren't denying that you went to see her. It would add insult to injury. Since you ask, we know you went there because the car you hired at the airport had a GPS tracker on it. They all have them so that they can trace any cars that are stolen or unreturned. The Spanish police enquiries are at an early stage, but they were able to tell us that much. The apparently confused young man who rented the car to you couldn't explain why the fee had been debited from his card, but he explicitly remembered the tip you gave him when you brought the car back. He said there was another man with you. Would you care to say who that was?'

Harman digested what he had heard and did not hurry to reply. He would not give them Charles Hope's name. It would do neither of them any good. He needed to steer what barely passed as a conversation back in a direction where he would glean something from it. He said, 'I've already admitted that I visited her. I have nothing to hide on that score. When the local police complete their forensics checks they might find proof that I was there. What they won't find is a stroke of evidence that I laid a hand on Chen or her guards. There is not a court in Spain or anywhere else that would be able to prosecute me.'

Harman could picture the sneer on Kent's

disfigured face as the head of ET1 said, 'let's add naivety to your list of crimes. You are never going to see the inside of any court. You are already in your coffin and your ungodly acts in Gran Canaria will provide the nails to hammer into the lid. Before too long you will be transported from the facility to a waiting plane. When you wake again you will be in an American equivalent. What they do with you until Kingdom come will be their business. It will be a relief to get you off my hands.'

Harman said in disbelief, 'you will really let them disappear me? Based on circumstantial evidence? I know we haven't always seen eye to eye, but that doesn't sound like you.'

'It's out of my hands,' Kent snapped. 'You were the one who chose to go off on a one-man crusade. You decided that we weren't good enough for you. You said we would get in your way. Did you think there wouldn't be a price to pay for that? Then in no time flat you leave a trail of corpses in your wake. The first of those was in the US, so they get first crack at you. Nobody is going to rush to defend you. It's bad enough that you being an Ascendant makes you a threat, but everything points to you being a deranged mass killer as well. If you're looking for pity, you are looking in the wrong place.'

It occurred to Harman that it was Kent's turn to protest too much. All that mattered was that he had said *it's out of my hands.* The rest was him trying to justify the unjustifiable. Kent had been given his orders and, like the good soldier he was, he would follow them. Such mindless obedience left a bitter taste in Harman's mouth. He took a swig from the water bottle to get rid of it. He knew he was doing Kent a disservice. He might be obedient. He was never mindless. Harman decided that it would be a waste of breath to protest his innocence any further. The deal to repatriate him to America had apparently been struck and it was not within Kent's power to change that even if he wanted to.

There was nothing further to be said. Harman settled back on to the cot again. He didn't know when the cell would be flooded with debilitating gas. Or when or where he would wake up again. He concentrated instead on what he knew and what he might be able to do about it.

Blocking out Kent's increasingly irritated calls for him to respond, Harman fleetingly thought of Charles Hope. His timid short-term companion was alone and probably feeling rudderless. For his own sake, he didn't want Hope to summon untapped reserves of courage and proceed without him to Israel and even beyond. The man wasn't equipped for the task and his life expectancy would quickly diminish. He felt guilty for dragging him into the mess he had created, but there was nothing Harman could do for him while trapped in that box.

His thoughts moved on to Thibault

Blanc and Daiyu Chen. They had not just been murdered they had been tortured. The implication to Kent and Bishop was obvious: he had done it to them because they had refused to give him the information he demanded. Any claims that he made about them being willing collaborators would sound hollow. In Kent's shoes he would not have believed them either. Harman had reluctantly been persuaded that Kent was telling the facts, as he perceived them. As he hadn't killed the two Ascendants and the two Spanish sentinels, somebody else must be responsible, but who? Whoever it was had been clever enough to avoid detection, and cunning enough to leave the fingers of accusation pointing at him. That could only happen if he was being followed or someone had the same list as him. He supposed that it would have been possible, but not easy for the killer to dog his tracks. It seemed more likely that this was Virginia Brightwell cleaning house by removing those who might betray her. Then again, if that was the case, why would she employ torture? What information could they possibly have that was not already in her possession? It made no sense. That gave him pause for more thought. Maybe, she had given her assassin carte blanche. Maybe, there was information that she thought they had. Maybe, he would never know.

It was all academic while his future life was to be lived out in cells like this one. His existence would serve solely as the subject of experimentation. He was the caged rat that would be tested to better understand and combat the disease that was Ascendancy.

Kent gave up trying to persuade him to resume their remote communication. Harman caught the now recognisable click of disconnection as the audio link was severed.

In the silence, Harman's eyes roved over every inch of the cell. Amy Bishop, whose intelligence was matched by her commitment to the cause, had designed his temporary prison with the utmost care. If it had any flaws, they would be hard to find.

Fully aware that he was being monitored, he made great show of eating an energy bar before casually walking around the table several times. He waved his arms around and rubbed his legs as if fending off cramp. All the while he was doing that, he stared at the walls, as his Ascendant hyper-sight probed for indication of any crack or line that might indicate where a door might be. There was nothing.

He scolded himself. Amy wouldn't make it that easy. He knelt, as if to adjust his socks and shoes. Doors didn't have to be in walls. There could be one in the floor. His optimism was short-lived. As hard as he tried, he couldn't detect anything.

Harman's face remained impassive. He refused to give anyone the satisfaction of seeing the blanket of defeat that was being pulled inexorably over his head. After the failure of his covert search, he had nothing to lose from conducting an overt one. With his knuckles he wrapped on different parts of the wall closest to him. Each tap was met by an unyielding thud. There was nothing thin or hollow about that wall.

He moved on to the next one.

A voice came from the ceiling, 'please stop doing that, Alan. If you persist, you will be immobilised.'

Harman cocked his head and said, 'is that you, Amy? Will you really gas me again?'

'The consequences of your actions have already been made clear to you. My request will not be repeated.'

Harman lifted his hands to signify submission and he sat in the chair by the table. He said, 'is this what you really want, Amy?'

'You've betrayed us all, and I do not want to dwell on the crimes you have committed. I did not set the price you are now having to pay for that.'

As much as she tried to hide it, he heard the regret that permeated those two sentences.

He sighed and said, 'I'm sorry, Amy, I know there's nothing you can do.'

The microphone went dead, and he was alone again. Was this really the end? If it wasn't for Virginia Brightwell, he wasn't sure that he would have cared that much. He had no surviving family or friends. He had nobody to love or protect. There was nobody to miss him.

Harman ran an angry hand through his hair and pulled hard at the strands. He would not let himself give in. His eyes watered as a tuft came loose. It was as if some part of his brain screamed at him. Had Amy Bishop witnessed his moment of weakness and despair? She would at some point because, as sure as his middle name was Patrick, cameras were recording every instant of his imprisonment.

What she could not know was that his warring emotions of impotence and rage were not the result of self-pity and the prospect of endless days filled with pain and bereft of hope.

He could bear that. What he could not live with was the prospect of Virginia Brightwell escaping his vengeance.

CHAPTER FIVE

Harman was startled by the sound of a hydraulic motor buzzing quietly by his head. He bounded off the cot and watched as a panel opened in the wall behind where he had been laying. As it smoothly grew into a man-sized portal, he applauded Amy Bishop's cunning in hiding the doorway there and realised why she had been so quick to stop him tapping away at every inch of all four walls.

He braced himself. It hadn't occurred to him that he would have the chance to fight for his freedom, but if the opportunity arose, he would not go quietly. He flexed his knuckles and bunched his hands into fists.

Something was already bothering him. They had used the gas to get him there and had said they would use the gas to transport him out again. So why weren't they using it now?

Before he could get his head around that, two-uniformed policemen appeared. They looked uncertainly around the room and with some disbelief at the single bed that stood between them and the man they had come for.

Then a shrill siren began to wail repetitively. The overhead lights switched from unremitting whiteness to a flashing red. The cell was transformed into a hellish disco but with alarm bells playing instead of music.

Over it all one of the policemen called, 'Mr Harman? Please come with us.'

Which struck Harman as more than odd, mainly because the officer sounded no more concerned than he would have been if returning a lost dog to its fretting owner. On the basis that he couldn't be any worse off than he already was, he dropped his fists and went with them. The second policeman even gave him a helping hand to clamber over the cot.

The earache inducing wow-wow-wow of the alarms followed them along a metal gantry and down a set of steel stairs. The policemen were not moved to rush by the racket. They walked at the one pace with no more care than if they were on patrol in a shopping mall. They didn't speak to him again, nor did they give any indication of coercing him. They reached a landing, traversed it, and went down a second flight of steps. The clanging of their feet went some way to drowning out the alarm as they left its source further behind.

As they neared the bottom, Harman saw another figure waiting for them. He was sure it was a man, but he couldn't make out any features because of the motorcycle helmet with full visor he was wearing. The hidden man was fidgeting about. He certainly wasn't sharing the stoic indifference of the men in uniform.

When they reached him, Harman saw a door ajar. It was dark outside. Freedom was apparently no more than ten feet away. The man span on his heel and with urgency waved them to follow him. As soon as they were out of the building, the man said, 'thank you officers. Your help is greatly appreciated. Please go back to your normal business.'

The policeman nearest to him touched the peak of his cap and said, 'glad to have been of service, sir.'

Nearby was a standard police patrol car. The two uniformed officers got in it a drove away.

Although his voice was muffled by the helmet, there was no mistaking that it was Charles Hope. Before Harman could ask any questions, Hope took another helmet from the back of a waiting Kawasaki Ninja high-performance motorcycle and thrust it into Harman's hands. He swung a leg over to mount the bike. There was no time to argue. Harman got on behind him. He had barely grabbed hold, before the engine growled into life. The back wheel skidded, gained traction, and they tore off into the night.

Risking a backward glance, Harman saw the outline of the cube-shaped building that had been his personal prison. It was surrounded by a field. The only other sign of civilisation was the access road that he was hurtling down with his unlikely rescuer.

His head was full of whats and hows. That was where they would have to stay for the time being. All he could do until they stopped was trust that Hope knew what he was doing and that they could get far away before a small army of ET1 stormtroopers descended on the facility. Amy Bishop had been right not to have anyone on site. The risk of them being influenced was too high. But she seemed not to have prepared adequately for the possibility that somebody else might find the location of the facility and help whoever was incarcerated there to escape.

Harman did not want her to have any black marks on her record because of him. She and Kent had seen the evidence and decided he was not the man they thought they knew. In their eyes he had become a freak with a penchant for sadistic murder. He couldn't really blame them for that, although he was disappointed not to have earned a more of their trust during the albeit short time they had worked together.

When push came to shove it was Charles Hope who had stood by him. He was proving himself as an ally, while Amy and Sebastian had become enemies. It was painful to think of them like that, but what could he do other than judge them on their actions?

The world rushed by in a blur of traffic lights. It was accompanied by a cacophony of engines and squealing tyres. Harman blocked it all out and re-focussed. Kent, Bishop and ET1 were literally behind him. What mattered much more was what lay ahead.

*

Virginia Brightwell, like Alan Harman, like most Ascendants required little sleep. She averaged three hours a night. It was her custom to be up by 4.00am and the change in time zones did not affect that. Apart from streetlamps, and the odd neon shop sign, it was unremittingly dark across Lausanne. She pulled back the hotel curtains to see a cloud filled sky and a rolling mist drifting down from the mountains. She found it eerily beautiful. Unfortunately, she had a busy day ahead that left no room to dwell on the wordless poetry of nature. She let the curtains fall back into place and went for a shower.

After that she towelled herself down and used the hotel-provided dryer on her blonde hair. It would be dawn at about 5.30am and by then she planned to be well on the way to the boatyard. She dressed herself in locally bought garb. The black ski jacket, grey pants, and tan hiking boots were functional. They were also completely unremarkable in Lausanne and that was a bonus. If anyone noticed her at all, they would categorise her as a harmless woman of late middle-age who was merely there to enjoy the simple pleasures of lakeside life.

She wrapped a scarf around her laptop

and then placed it securely in a backpack. Alongside it she placed a bottle of the hotel's complimentary spring water. From a tray on the desk, she took the two packets of equally complimentary biscuits. She shoved them into a pocket and zipped it up. They were not for her. When she reached the lake, she planned to break them up and feed them to the ducks. She saw nothing wrong in permitting herself that small distraction.

Her key and small wallet went into her hip pocket. Her fully charged cell phone was about to join them there when it rang. Her lips pursed tightly in response to the interruption to her plans. She soon relented. It was more secure to have the conversation in a hotel room than while striding through the streets of a waking city.

The display on her phone said *285679*. It wasn't the number of her incoming caller it was one of the codes she attached to her contacts rather than putting their names into the phone's memory.

She accepted the call and said, 'hello, Old Man.'

It was a term of affection rather than one of disdain. It was also factually accurate. The son of Nippon had achieved his hundredth birthday earlier in the year.

Yukio Hagihara said, 'we are blessed to see the sun at the start of another day.'

It was an unusual greeting, but one

that Brightwell had become accustomed to. From anyone else it would have seemed embarrassingly pretentious. From him, it was instead a reflection of the man himself and it was not to be mocked or belittled. There were few people in her lifetime whose wisdom she acknowledged and whose opinions she respected. He was one of them. He was the one that she had placed at the top of the chain. He was the one direct link to her from amongst the committee that had given birth to their great solution. There was no greater way for her to demonstrate her esteem for him.

'Indeed, we are, Yukio. To what do I owe your call?'

'Daiyu Chen did not check in as scheduled.'

Brightwell had always viewed Chen as a necessary evil. She reviled her and her ways as much as she revered Hagihara.

She said, 'she has never been reliable. She was probably too busy rutting with her latest pets to remember her responsibilities.'

Hagihara said wistfully, 'it is true that even the most beautiful diamond can have flaws beneath its surface. However, it may be that our concern cuts deeper than that. Mere days ago, Thibault Blanc was murdered. That is already a matter of public record. Taking that together with Chen's silence have led me to surmise that a wolf is perhaps loose amongst our flock.'

'I don't see how that could be, but the coincidence is too great to ignore. Thibault's weakness and Chen's ambition could have lured either of them to betray us to those who hunt us. That possibility is why I distanced them from me. If one of them has turned on us, I cannot understand why their new allies would reward them with death.'

'All we know is that Thibault is dead. Of Daiyu, all we can be certain of is that she is incommunicado.'

Brightwell latched on to that and said, 'so you believe she has turned traitor and is somewhere safe plotting against us? Could she have killed Thibault?'

Hagihara mulled it over for a while before saying, 'I do not believe that. Your assessment of Chen is correct. Her ambition shines out from her like a flaming beacon. You are incorrect if you believe that makes her foolhardy. Do not let your personal views about her blind you to her qualities. They are why you recruited her, aren't they?'

'You know they were, Old Man. So, what are you saying?'

'I am humbly suggesting that Chen is intent on challenging you. Of that there is no doubt. I am also suggesting that she is too clever to attempt that while failure remains the most likely outcome. She would not have retreated to the Canary Islands if she was about to strike against you. Which surely implies she deemed the time not to be ripe for revolt. Her strategy is transparent to me. Her intention was to wait there until we had achieved success or endured the cold dead hand of failure. If it is the former, she will ride on your coat tails and claim as much of the credit as she can. She will seek to strengthen her status further and bide her time until another window for progress opens. If we fail, then she will swoop in to pick up the pieces. As for Thibault, she would have wanted to win him over. There is no benefit to her in his death.'

Brightwell's lips curled upwards. She could not fault the old man's logic. And he was right, again, that she should not view Chen solely through a prism of antipathy.

She said, 'what then is your conclusion?'

'That is simple, Virginia. We must beware the wolf and keep him at bay until our work is concluded.'

'What then?'

Hagihara cackled. It sounded like dried leaves being crushed underfoot. He said, 'our lives will have served their purpose. Nothing matters after that.'

Brightwell supposed he was right. She said, 'very well, Old Man, let's complete our work then. If there is a wolf, I want you here with me when it arrives. How long will it take for you to finish up there?'

'Two or three days at the most.'

'Make it less,' she said, for the first time sounding like a commanding officer rather than a supine pupil.

'I will see you soon, Virginia. You can bank on that.'

Given the task he was undertaking for her, she wondered if he was attempting to make a joke. She thought better of it. Humour was largely missing from his impressively broad range of skillsets. She told him to let her know if Chen reappeared and then ended the call.

She sat down at the dressing table and took a few minutes to digest what Hagihara had told her. If there was a wolf, was it a lone wolf or the leader of a pack? A shiver ran up her spine and spread across her shoulders as she thought of the man who she had confronted at the 191 Ranch in Colorado. Apart from her brother, Peter Salt, whose death she had ordered and whose passing she had not lamented for one fraction of one second, she had not encountered another Ascendant who had scared her like that.

It was an unfamiliar and unwelcome sensation. The Normals were not to be underestimated, but she had an unshakeable faith in her ability to quash any threat they might mount. Blanc was weak, but he was no fool. Chen may be a preening prima donna, but she would be a formidable opponent for anyone. If the wolf had eaten them so readily then it could only be because he or she was one of them, an Ascendant. Nothing else made sense. And her mind was inexorably drawn back to the Englishman in the caves. There was a dryness in her throat and a dead weight in the pit of her stomach that she had not experienced before.

She shook her head like a boxer who had taken a hard punch to the chin. Hagihara's sagacity gave her a rock to cling to. If she completed her work...no, she corrected herself, when she completed her work, her purpose would have been served. If the wolf devoured her after that, it wouldn't do them any good. The Ascendancy would have begun, and she would have achieved everything she ever dreamed of.

With a grim determination that had not been there when she had awoken, she slid the backpack over her shoulder and left the hotel. If the wolf was coming, she would make sure that he was too late.

There would be no feeding of the ducks that morning after all. Even those few moments of peaceful enjoyment had become time that she could no longer afford to spare.

*

The first flicker of daylight was scratching the horizon on the English Channel as Hope and Harman arrived on the coast of Sussex. Roughly south of them on the other side of the sea was the French town of Dieppe.

Hope had brought them to a grassy hill. He tapped his helmet and removed it to indicate that his passenger should do the same. They were flanked by a row of bushes. As soon as they had dismounted, Hope pushed the heavy motorcycle into the undergrowth and let it fall there. He stepped back to see if it was sufficiently well-hidden. Satisfied with his efforts he re-joined Harman.

Hope took Harman's helmet from him and said, 'we won't be needing these again. I know you have lots of questions, but there will be time to ask them while we walk down to the shore.'

Harman watched as Hope, buzzing with nervous excitement, took their helmets and threw them deep into the bushes. When he had finished, he pointed at a path and said, 'come on, down there.'

'Time for questions now?' Harman said, amused by the way that Hope's new-found decisiveness sat so uncomfortably on his shoulders. It was like watching a sparrow struggling to lift a brick so that it could get to some seed underneath,

Hope nodded anxiously.

'Grateful as I am for the rescue, can you tell me where we're going?'

Hope cocked his head, again reminding Harman of a startled sparrow, and said, 'Tel Aviv, of course.'

'That's good to hear, but more specifically, what's your plan for getting us there?'

Without breaking his scurrying stride, Hope said, 'we're going to get one of the local fishermen down there to sail us to France. Flying from Paris would be too obvious, so we steal another motorbike when we get to France and drive to Lisbon. By tomorrow we should be on a plane to Israel. After that, we are back on course. We will be, won't we?'

Harman had become accustomed to Hope gabbling when he was stressed. He only slowed down when Harman posed the question about them getting back on course. That was when Hope's deep-rooted lack of confidence reasserted itself. With those few words he was handing control back to Harman and they both knew it.

'Sounds like a great plan, I didn't know you had it in you.'

'To tell the truth, I've surprised myself,' Hope said managing a fragile smile of self-congratulation.

'And how does that feel?'

'Like I never want to do it again. I've been shaking so much that it's been a struggle to keep my glasses from falling off my nose.'

Harman laughed good-naturedly at Hope's weak attempt at a joke. He said, 'much as I love your plan, we're putting ourselves at risk by going to any airports. Who knows how wide the net has been cast for us?'

'I thought of that,' Hope said, seemingly in search of more approval. 'Unfortunately, I could see no alternative. No other mode of travel would get us to Israel quickly enough. I did consider influencing some pilot of a light aircraft to fly us, but their planes don't have the range. Even if we could refuel somewhere along the line, they'd soon be detected on radar if they had not lodged a prior flight plan and adhered to it. Which means we must travel on scheduled international flights and mitigate the risks associated with that. I did some reading up and there are ways to confuse facial recognition. I also believe that we can use our skills to board the flight without going through high-risk areas such as passport control and the security scanners where bags and passengers are x-rayed. And, as I've said, not traveling from the more obvious points of departure will help.'

As they scrambled down to the shingle beach, Harman said, 'take a breath, Charles. I don't want you getting a heart attack.'

Hope said sheepishly, 'I've been living on my nerves since they took you. I've had nobody to turn to. Sorry for blurting. It's been hard to hold it all in.'

'You've got nothing to apologise for, Charles. Quite the opposite. If it wasn't for you, I'd be spending my life in whatever the Ascendant equivalent is of Guantanamo Bay. Homeland Security would have buried me so deep, that I'd never walk free again.'

'That could still happen to both of us. It's not something I could cope with. I would go mad,' Hope's voice wavered as he spoke as if that dreadful thought had never been far from his mind.

'Don't let it bother you. We've outsmarted them once and we can do it again,' Harman said. He wasn't sure he believed it, but he felt honour bound to reassure Hope. The best solution was to get him off the subject, so Harman continued, 'to be more accurate, we didn't outsmart them, you did. All on your own. Tell me how you did it?'

'From the beginning?'

'If you can fit it all in before we commandeer a boat?'

Hope did not recognise Harman's gentle teasing for what it was and said, 'I will try.'

'Maybe just the edited highlights then?'

Hope also did not recognise the sporting reference, but he said, 'when you didn't come out from that inspection at Gatwick, I knew something was badly wrong. My first instinct was to get away from there in case they came for me next. With the help of some unknowing maintenance staff, I was able to get out of the danger zone. It was later that it occurred to me that in other circumstances, those behind-the-scenes workers could also help us into an airport and on to a plane. But I mustn't digress. Once outside I thought of running. I don't know how or where to. I was simply filled with a desire to be away from there. I'm sorry...'

Harman said cheerily, 'I've already told you not to apologise. Besides, whatever you were thinking, you still came back for me. Do you know how brave that was? To confront your fears and overcome them is no small thing.'

'I wish I could say that I have overcome them. I haven't. At best, I am managing them.'

'That is good enough for me and it should be good enough for you too. How about the rest of your story?'

'As we weren't named on any flight list, I assumed that they were searching for you, and maybe me, by description or facial recognition software or both. Before reading up on it yesterday, I barely knew of its existence. In any event, I needed to hide my face and what better way than behind a visor and helmet? And where to get those other than from someone with a motorcycle? And I know a whole lot more about bikes than I do facial recognition. I persuaded a man who, because of his ownership of that beautiful Kawasaki Ninja, was probably going through some midlife crisis to hand it over to me. He was on his way to Los Angeles and is no doubt there by now. As far as he is aware, his beloved bike is in long term parking awaiting his return.'

They reached the beach. Small stones clanked beneath their feet as they walked parallel to the waves of the outgoing tide. Harman was no sailor, but the sea seemed calm enough. If they could get a boat with a competent crew, the crossing should be straight forward. That was their priority, so he gently asked Hope to edit the highlights even more than he was already doing.

Hope was thrown off his verbal stride, however, he was quick to regroup and said, 'yes, yes, stick to the key events. It was self-evident that whoever had detained you would want you out of there and in the most discrete of ways. I waited with the Kawasaki where I could keep watch on the rear of the terminus. The only non-airport vehicle that departed from the airside exit was a private ambulance. Had it been alone I might still have let it pass. As it was, a substantial black car which smacked of anonymous security trailed right behind it. I followed. It took you to that nightmarish block. It was about forty-five minutes away. Mainly it was on major roads, and it was easy enough to hide in the traffic without being noteworthy. They went through a gate. I drove on. I came back on foot and saw a stretcher being carried inside. I kept well-hidden while the car and ambulance departed. I kept watch for the next few hours. Nobody else came or went and no vehicles of any description were parked there. Whatever that place was, it was no hospital. Emboldened to think that it must have been you on that stretcher, I sought assistance in my efforts to recover you.

It seemed a prudent course of action when I could not be sure what I would find inside there.'

Harman was quietly impressed by Hope's resourcefulness. It was unexpected. He said, 'let me guess the rest. As a solid citizen you thought to yourself, who do you go to for help when you need it?'

Hope stood taller as he replied, 'exactly, when you need help, ask a policeman. After nightfall, I drove up to the freeway...'

'Motorway,' Harman couldn't help himself saying, 'over here we call them motorways.'

'...whatever, on the big road thing I came across the two nice men in their patrol car. They were parked on a verge watching out for speeding motorists. That hardly seemed fair, but I was willing to forgive them. Once I had influenced them to believe that my good friend, Mr Harman, was trapped in a building and in fear for his life, they were most glad to break in for me and rescue you. There is a lot more I could say, but as highlights go that tells you all you missed. In return I would love to hear what happened to you while you were in there.'

'Edited highlights again?' Harman said rhetorically, 'I talked to some old friends, and it turns out they're not friends anymore. Oh, yeah, and it seems somebody is killing off everyone that I meet.'

Hope swallowed hard and for a while the silence was only interrupted by the gently rolling waves, some skittish seagulls, and the scrunching of pebbles as they trod on them. When he had summoned the courage to speak again, Hope glanced over both shoulders before saying, 'but...but...I've met you more than anyone recently.'

Harman slapped him on the arm and said, 'I did warn you when we first met over a cup of coffee that this could be very dangerous.'

Hope's eyebrows pushed up towards each other. 'I'm not sure you did, Alan.'

Harman shrugged and said, 'well, if I didn't. I should have done.'

Hope adjusted his tinted glasses and stroked a reassuring hand across his bald head. 'What did they tell you about who's stalking us?'

'Nothing except that Blanc and Chen are both dead and not by accident' Harman said, opting to not make Hope feel any worse by referring to the unpleasant manner in which the brace of Ascendants had been despatched. He pointed up ahead to where two men in orange waterproofs were loading nets and baskets onto a low-sided fishing boat. 'More highlights later once we're safely on that thing.'

*

Sebastian Kent was a precise man, and precisely thirty-four minutes after being alerted to Harman's escape he stormed into Faulkner House. On being awoken by the calamitous news at 3.32am, the first thought that broke through the fug of drowsiness told him to go to the detention facility. His second thought was to chastise himself for the first. Going to that black box in that isolated field in Surrey would be as useful as closing a barn door after not only the horse had bolted but also every animal on the whole farm. There would be nothing there to help him recapture Harman. What he needed to see was the film from the array of cameras at the facility. That was stored on hard drives and servers at ET1's headquarters. Which was why he had gone there with the body language of a bull scraping at the dust before charging at a matador.

The staff at ET1 tended to work in silos. It was good for security, but bad for office morale because they rarely mixed and water cooler moments were few and far between. Even when the full roster of staff was on site, the place tended to have an atmosphere like the abandoned *Marie Celeste.* In the early morning hours, it was worse. As Kent unlocked his office door it seemed like he might be the sole occupier of the building, but he knew better. He was tempted to put on some coffee. He decided against it. His blood pressure was high enough already. Instead, he booted up his desk top computer and switched on the large wall screen. Then he called Amy Bishop's extension. She picked up on the first ring. He told her to get Bill Trantor, the duty officer, and come to his office.

Both had been waiting for the summons and were there in no time flat.

Bishop knocked and they entered. By way of welcome Kent looked from one to the other and very slowly shook his head. It summed up how they were all feeling. He nodded towards the small meeting table, and they sat down. He came around his desk to join them.

Kent said, 'right, the shit has hit the fan. Let's see where we are before it blows back and blinds us. Bill, you start.'

Trantor had spent a while in the Parachute Regiment, and a long while in the SAS. It took a lot more than a major screw up and an irate senior to throw him off his stride. He was in his forties but still lean and compact. He placed strong hands together on the desk and said, with the detached calm of someone reading names out from a telephone directory, 'the alarm at the facility was triggered automatically when someone gained unauthorised access. Two teams were immediately sent to the site as per standard operating procedure. I then notified those on the red list, including yourself and Dr Bishop. Descriptions of Mr Harman have been circulated to the police, airports, and shipping ports.

From the internal cameras we were able to see the force identification numbers of the two policemen who committed the ingress. They were traffic cops. Both are currently logged as off duty. We have men on the way to their homes as I speak.

As for the third man, he was in civvies, and his face was hidden by a helmet. It could have been anyone. He led Harman to a bright green Kawasaki Ninja motorcycle, and they departed the scene separately from the police car. A description of the bike has also been circulated.'

Kent expected nothing less than informed efficiency from Trantor, and so he did not praise him for his diligence. All he said was, 'get every detail written up into a full report.'

'Already done, sir. Preliminary filing is in your in-box.'

'Alright, Bill, get back to your post and keep me informed the moment anything comes in.'

When Trantor had gone and the door was securely closed behind him, Kent said, 'well at least one of us has done their job properly.'

Unsure whether it was a general airing of frustration or an implicit criticism of her in particular, Bishop deemed it best not respond. She did so on the basis that when you are in a minefield it is usually sensible not to move from the spot you are standing on.

Kent said, 'alright let's begin the self-flagellation. Get the recordings up on the screen so I can see exactly what happened.'

Turning to the screen Bishop used an app on her tablet to get the camera feeds up. They watched in silence as Harman's escape was depicted from multiple camera angles.

When they were finished, Kent said, almost to himself, 'can you tell me how this is possible when we constructed that place specifically to hold Ascendants?' 'We will learn lessons from this,' Bishop said.

'Is that all you've got to say, Amy? That place was built to your specifications. It took a good chunk of our budget. How do we explain that its first inmate walked out while the paint was barely dry on it?'

'It was constructed to keep Ascendants in, not to keep them out. In hindsight, greater attention should have been paid to external security, but then again, we had not anticipated that anyone would know where it was in order that they could launch a rescue attempt.'

Kent's aggressive energy was fast dissipating. He said, with a weary resignation that threatened to overwhelm him, 'it didn't take you long to prepare your excuses.'

'I have provided an explanation. That is not the same as an excuse,' Amy said. There was an unwavering stillness about her to the extent that even the tips of her bobbed hair did not sway in the slightest.

'I've said it before, you're a clever woman, Amy.'

'Unless that ever becomes a crime, my conscience will remain clear.'

Kent had never told her how much he admired that sharp psychiatrist brain of hers. It was the wrong time to rectify that. Anything that sounded like a compliment could too easily be misconstrued as a lure for her to drop her guard.

He plumped for saying, 'what we need are solutions rather than recriminations. Every second while Alan's out of our hands will make it harder to recapture him.'

'I was surprised that we managed to catch him so easily and so quickly the first time around,' she said more openly now that they were moving on to practical matters.

Kent made a pish sound and said, 'Alan's an Ascendant. Ascendants are arrogant. That makes them complacent. It's their Achilles Heel. And before you say it, yes, I'm well aware that's what I always say.'

'Or alternatively, he was telling us the truth. He knew nothing of the murders and had no cause to believe that a major search was underway for him. That being the case, he would have no need to take extreme steps to avoid identification. Is it not plausible to consider that innocence rather than complacency was his downfall?'

Kent's eyes met hers. There was sympathy in that look of his. He said, 'you've had a soft spot for Alan since the day he walked in here. And before you protest, I know you haven't let that colour your professional judgements. All I'm saying is that even the best of us sometimes sees what they want to see.'

'You might hold that mirror up to yourself, Sebastian. If all you look for is the worst in people, then that is all you will find.'

Her emerging spikiness no longer gave him pause for thought. All that mattered to him in that moment was harnessing her intellect and directing it towards an outcome that would avoid them both joining the ranks of the unemployed.

It cost him nothing to concede the point and he said, 'you might be right. We won't know either way until we find Alan again and get to the bottom of this.'

She raised an eyebrow and said, 'we are past that, aren't we? Are you forgetting that we were only supposed to be holding him prior to his transfer to US Homeland Security and whatever other agencies they care to involve that have three letter initials? Irrespective of whether he is guilty of the alleged crimes, he will never stand trial and we will have no say in what happens to him. If we can trace Alan quickly, it will partially redeem our reputation, but we will never be trusted again to hold or question him.'

Kent said, 'we have twice missed out on Virginia Brightwell and now we've lost Alan. I won't lose sight of the existential threat that she represents, but we will be out of the game completely if we don't get him back. Everything else is secondary to that.'

He was interrupted by the ringing of the phone on his desk. He picked it up, listened, and acknowledged that he understood. He slowly put the receiver down. After staring longingly around his office, he said, 'that was Sir Anthony. I'm suspended indefinitely pending a full enquiry. You're to take charge until a new head of ET1 can be appointed.'

'I'm sorry, Sebastian,' Amy Bishop said, knowing that it was a wholly inadequate response. It was a potential penalty that each of them had been aware of, but which neither had cared to voice. Even so, she did not have to be a psychiatrist to recognise that the heart had been torn from Kent's broad chest. ET1 was his baby. There was precious else in his life. If there had been any women after his divorce, she had not heard about them. It had been a childless marriage that was doomed from the moment his wife had been unable to suppress her revulsion when seeing what the bomb in Afghanistan had done to his face. It would be no surprise if he had chosen chastity over any further painful rejections. Faced with a choice of platitudes and empty words, Bishop decided that silence was the kindest option.

Kent rubbed his face. His palm came to rest on his scarred cheek. His remaining time at ET1 could be measured in minutes. He refused to waste those precious moments by drowning in pity and regret.

Unbidden a memory came to him from his first patrol in Afghanistan. It was nighttime. They had been ambushed. He'd led his men into the sparse cover of a dry riverbed. He had hugged the bank like a child might cling to its mother when hearing a firework cracker for the first time. One of his men took a round in the side. He screamed as a medic worked on him. The high-pitched anguish cut through the cracks of rifle fire. A mortar shell exploded behind them. He knew the Taliban would range in on them. The darkness was speckled with flashes of gunfire and sliced through with tracer bullets. The madness of it all was stunning. Desperate for anything of substance to cling to he had thrust a hand into the sandy soil and ground the grains between his fingers. To retreat would be to run into the mortar barrage. To climb forward out of the ditch would surely to be cut down by the bullets that screeched all around them. He tried to muster a semblance of rational thought. It kept being driven away by the screams of the injured soldier.

The platoon sergeant, who Kent considered to be an old veteran but who was still in his twenties, scrambled round to settle beside him. Kent had swallowed his pride and through tightly clamped teeth asked what they should do. The sergeant leaned in closer so that their helmets were touching and said, 'we can't hide here forever. And we can't surrender. You know what they'll do to us.'

'So, what then?' Kent said, his voice trembling as the shock wave from another detonating mortar pushed against them.

The sergeant shrugged and said, 'we fight, sir, we fight. Sometimes, that's all you can do.'

It was a lesson well learned.

The memory acted as a jolt to his system. He said to Amy, 'Sir Anthony told me not long ago about the importance of redemption. For me and for ET1. I need another chance to do that. Can you see me as a salesman in the arms industry or a security adviser in some emirate where the ruler has more oil wells than brain cells? And you, Amy, what about you? You know you've been tainted by all of this. Not long ago you would have been a shoo-in to replace me. Instead, you'll be asked to hold the hand of some know-nothing interim chief until he knows enough to get rid of you. After all you've seen and done here, will you be satisfied treating some sad pop star with mummy issues, or anorexic starlets? Because that's the best you would have to look forward to.'

Bishop inspected her fingernails. She knew there was truth in what he was saying, but she would not be rushed. When she was ready, she said, 'what are you proposing?'

'Working alone, I can find Alan. I can bring him back.'

'You condemned Alan for going renegade and yet you are saying you should do the same. Without the resources of ET1 behind you, how could you possibly succeed?'

'I couldn't. Alan at least had a chance when going it alone because he has the advantage of being an Ascendant. My task would be hopeless without the resources of ET1 to assist me...'

The light of understanding came on in Bishop's eyes. She said, 'you can't seriously be asking me to help you? You're suspended. I shouldn't even be talking to you about this.'

'I am asking you to help us both. It may only be for a day or two, but you'll be in the big seat. Mistress of all you survey. You could help me, and nobody would know.'

Bishop ran her fingers over the WWJD bracelet that she had worn every single day since becoming a born-again Christian. When all else failed, it gave her a reliable springboard to jump from. So, what would Jesus do? The question was applicable to every choice she made in her life, but divining the correct answer was frequently difficult.

She said, 'if Alan is innocent, and if he may be our best shot at finding Virginia Brightwell, then what's best for him and us is for you to get to him first. On that basis I might be willing to help you. My offer comes with an important proviso...'

'Which is?' Kent said, suddenly unsure if he was playing her or if she was about to play him.

'You don't hurt him, and you don't turn him over to anyone else unless you're sure, one hundred percent sure, that he is the murderer we've been told he is.'

'There's that soft spot I told you about.'

'Do you agree, or not? It won't be long before you're escorted from the premises. You should make your mind up quickly.'

'As you have me trousers down and bent over a barrel, what else can I do but agree?'

'I knew you would, but I wanted to hear you say it. Tell me what you want, and I will tell you if I can get it.'

'As before, we need eyes and ears internationally to spot Harman when he's travelling. We can't be sure why he's moving around so much. All we know is that he is and that it isn't aimless. I need to be informed if you get any scent of him, but I won't be holding my breath. He fell for that once. I'd be surprised if he does again.'

'Why ask for it then?'

'Belt and braces, Amy. Alan is smart, he's not infallible. Put that to one side. What I really need is to identify whoever is helping him. The man in the motorcycle helmet. He is an Ascendant. That's how he got those dopey transport cops to do the heavy lifting for him. Whoever he is, there is no reason that he would randomly appear and help Alan get out of the facility. We also know that there was a second man with Alan when they picked up the hire car in Gran Canaria. It's reasonable to assume these two men are one and the same. Which means he and Alan have been together before and are probably still together now. We know that Alan flew to Gran Canaria from Edinburgh and then back to Gatwick. There can't be many people apart from Alan and his mysterious companion who were on both of those flights. What I want you to get for me is all the tapes you can find from those airports and any adjacent CCTV. If I can identify that man, then it will lead me to Alan.'

'That's all?'

'Don't sound so suspicious, Amy, it doesn't suit you. Will you do it?'

She didn't get to answer before the door was opened. Trantor and another man, who could have been a younger version of himself, entered. Without any trace of embarrassment or discomfort, Trantor said, 'I'm sorry, sir, but as you've been suspended you are required to leave Faulkner House.'

'After all this time I think I can find my own way out.'

Trantor said, 'rules are rules, sir. We will see you safely out.'

'Not even time to gather up my personal possessions?'

'They will be collected and delivered to you, sir.'

'My car?'

'ET1's car, sir. It will remain in the garage,' Trantor put his hand out, palm up, and said, 'the key's, sir?'

Kent rummaged in his pocket, removed his front door key from the key ring, and handed the rest over. He said, 'before you ask, the keys to the door, filing cabinets, desk and so on are all on there as well as the car keys.'

Trantor went through the keys one by one before saying, 'so they are, sir, thank you. We have a car waiting to take you home, unless there is somewhere else you would prefer to be taken?'

'Home's as good as anywhere,' Kent said, pretending to be sullen and downcast for the benefit of his two escorts.

Less formally than the Changing of the Guard, yet with the same effect, Trantor handed the keys to Amy and said, 'you'll be needing these now Dr Bishop.'

As he was led away from what had been his own office, Kent cast the slightest of glances towards Amy Bishop.

The nod of her head would have been imperceptible to anyone who wasn't looking for it.

CHAPTER SIX

Harman had acquired fresh clothes in Lisbon. By the time he disembarked from the five and half hour flight to Ben Gurion International Airport in Israel, they felt anything but new. His khaki shirt was creased, and his beige trousers had a small coffee stain on them, courtesy of mid-flight air turbulence over the Mediterranean when he was taking a sip from the plastic cup. It reinforced his emerging dislike for long plane journeys.

As he made his way through the terminal, he followed the signs towards the taxi rank. Hope was keeping his distance and Harman trusted that he would follow the instructions he had been given. As Harman came out of the air-conditioned Arrivals Hall, the heat closed in on him. The air bore the taint of oil and hot plastic. Armed men and women were readily apparent. Some wore olive uniforms. Others looked dressed for a day at the office or college. He was struck by the sight of two young bare-headed women. To him they seemed barely old enough to qualify for a driver's licence. That did not stop them from casually toting automatic weapons over the shoulders of their drab Israeli Defence Force outfits. It reminded him that there was more to be wary of in that country than the Ascendant threat.

When he reached the front of the queue, he slid on to the tired rear seat of a waiting taxi and passed a slip of paper to the driver. On it was the address of Hans Osterfeld's hidey hole in Komemiyut. The swarthy middle-aged man behind the wheel half-turned towards him. He read the handwritten details on the paper and said, 'are you American?'

Harman had to concentrate to understand what was being said to him because the man's words were so heavily accented. He answered with a tight grin, that he assumed to be a common sign of reassurance around the world, 'English.'

The driver threw a glance at the airport buildings and said, 'no luggage?'

'The airline seems to have lost it. Hopefully it will turn up and they will send it on behind me. What are you going to do?' Harman said trying to get the right balance between indignation and resignation.

'And you want to go to Komemiyut? Are you sure? Not Tel Aviv or Jerusalem?'

'I'm sure. I'm staying with a friend who lives there.'

The driver scowled. Whatever suspicions were brewing in him were interrupted by the tooting of a horn from the taxi behind him. He shrugged and made a vague gesture with his hand out of the car window. He put the cab in gear and the car pulled away.

It had barely gone two hundred yards when Harman saw Hope waiting in isolation at the roadside. He tapped the back of the driver's seat to get the man's attention and asked if they could pull over. The man mumbled something unintelligible but did as he had been requested. While Hope got in, Harman promised the driver that he would get a big tip for being so accommodating. While that was true, Harman said nothing about also influencing the taxi man to forget having ever met him. He didn't want to do it, but he couldn't have a suspicious and disgruntled Israeli voicing any concerns to the authorities.

It took them less than an hour to reach Komemiyut. Harman had the driver drop them off a couple of streets away from their true destination. He retrieved the slip of paper, left the promised tip, and made the driver forget having ever met the two strangers he had picked up at the airport.

As the taxi headed off in a small cloud of dust and exhaust fumes, Harman looked about him at the square sand-coloured buildings that made up the small township that was home to less than six hundred souls.

Hope said, 'why did we stop here?'

'How do you think Osterfeld might have reacted to a taxi pulling up on his doorstep? If

Daiyu Chen is really dead, then he will probably know about it by now. I don't want to spook him more than we have to.'

'Can we be sure she is dead, though?' Hope said. 'just because your old friends at ET1 said so, doesn't make it true.'

'Don't fool yourself, Charles. They couldn't lie to me even if they wanted to. I would have heard it in their voices. She's dead alright and they think I did it.'

'But you didn't.'

'Us knowing that won't carry much weight in the face of the evidence.'

Hope kicked at the paved surface beneath his feet and said, 'what worries me more is that some killer is following us around and we have no idea who it is.'

'Maybe there will be time to worry about that once we've found Virginia Brightwell. Until then we can't afford to lose our focus.'

'Doesn't it scare you? If someone can get rid of Chen and her ex-special forces boyfriends, then what chance would I have?'

'There's nothing wrong with being scared if it keeps you sharp. Use it for that, don't let it paralyse you.'

'I will do my best,' Hope said in a way that didn't convince either of them.

An aged man dressed head to foot in black stepped out of a doorway up the road. He glanced nervously towards them, his grey ringlets swaying into his grey beard.

In an attempt to put the local resident's mind at rest, Harman gave him a little wave. In a community of Hasidic Jews, he knew that he and Hope stood out like Martin Luther King at a Ku Klux Klan convention.

'Time to go,' he said to Hope and led them unhurriedly to the other end of the street.

There were a couple of parked cars, but no other signs of life. Harman had memorised a map of the town and led them unerringly around the next bend and the one after that before slowing at the final corner. The road ahead was made of pale stones cemented together. There were no more than three connected houses on each side. Purple flowers draped from a balcony. Potted plants were dotted along terraces. A bush that was crying out for more water wilted on a tiny patch of grass.

The house they were looking for was at the end. At road level a narrow door and two windows were heavily barred. They were all painted over. Beyond them, steps with a metal rail went up to a higher level. It was populated by more plants, some iron chairs and a wooden table. It was clean and orderly. The door and windows up there were white and, although also heavily barred, had clean blue drapes hanging behind them.

Hope said, 'are we going to knock on the front door?'

Harman said, 'yes and no. And don't sound so dubious.'

'I am dubious. And don't mock me for it,' Hope said with more humour than irritation. 'Anyway, what do you mean by yes and no?'

'I mean you will knock on the front door while I go around and climb into the walled garden at the rear. While he and whoever he has with him come to the front I will find a way in. We can take it from there.'

Hope harrumphed and said, 'I was right to be dubious, wasn't I? You've seen the house on Google Maps and will simply let yourself in from the garden. That's your plan, is it?'

Harman couldn't stop himself from laughing at the look of dread on Hope's face. He said, 'hey, we're Ascendants aren't we, what more do we need?'

Hope grimaced and then said, 'in for a penny, in for a pound, I suppose. What do I say if someone opens the door?'

'Just tell them that you've come to visit your Uncle Shmuel.'

'And who might he be?'

'In a town this size there must be a couple of Shmuel's at least. Besides, Osterfeld is only a visitor himself. He won't know if there's anyone called Shmuel living around here.'

'And when he denies any knowledge of my fictional uncle, what do I do then?'

'Improvise for a bit. I won't need long.'

'I don't think I will be any good at improvising.'

'You'll do fine,' Hope said, patting him on the shoulder, 'just give me five minutes to get in position.'

'What? You want me to stand here for five minutes on my own.'

'Should anyone come along, be friendly and tell them you're waiting for your Uncle Shmuel, and he should be there any moment.'

'And what if I'm accosted by someone called Shmuel?'

'That's easy. Say what a lovely coincidence it is and...improvise.'

Hope said sheepishly, 'that's not who I am.'

Harman said, 'you'll be fine. It's five minutes, no more.'

Without waiting for Hope to throw up more skimpy barriers to progress, Harman jogged back the way they had come so that he could skirt the block of buildings and get to the garden.

*

Hope swallowed hard and tapped on the door. There was no response. He checked again that there was no bell, buzzer, or knocker to use. As he couldn't see one, he knocked again, longer and harder. He was about to try for a third time when he heard slow steps coming down the hallway inside. He took a pace back from the door. If it was going to be opened, he did not want to seem confrontational.

The drape over the frosted glass in the door twitched. Hope pretended not to have seen it. He took off his heavily tinted glasses and made a show of cleaning them with a handkerchief. While he was doing that he blinked and squinted at his surroundings. He was doing his best to appear non-threatening.

A muffled voice from behind the door called out, 'what do you want here?'

Hope adopted a playful smile and said, 'is that you, Uncle Shmuel? Stop kidding around and open the door.'

After a pause, the disembodied voice said, 'there is no Shmuel here. Please leave.'

Hope adopted a look of mild confusion and, stroking his goatee beard, said, 'it's me, your nephew, Aaron. Is there something wrong, Uncle?'

'I've told you, there is no Shmuel here. You are mistaken. Leave now or I will call the police.'

Hope had given Harman the full five minutes he had asked for and then some extra time on top of that. He knew he couldn't keep talking to the door indefinitely and was running out of things to say. He resolved to try a bit longer and if that failed to give up and go in search of Harman. The thought of that chafed at Hope. He had saved Harman once already. He didn't want it to become a habit. He was more than happy to trail around behind Harman while Peter Salt's protégé pursued his quest, but there was a point at which risk would outweigh reward.

With concern replacing confusion on his face, Hope chose to bluff it out. He said, 'have you stopped taking your medication, Uncle? I'm worried about you. If you don't open the door right now, I will call the police myself. I tell you I am not leaving this spot until I have seen with my own two eyes that you are safe and well.'

In the uncomfortable silence that followed Hope wondered if he had pushed his luck too far. He swiped at a fly that was circling his head. A bolt grated behind the door. Hope forgot about the fly and watched as the door opened a few inches. A chain stopped it going any further.

A face appeared in the gap. Sharp eyes were framed by close cropped grey hair and a grey beard. They latched on to Hope. When the man spoke a flap of skin under his chin quivered.

'As you can see, I am not your uncle, and nobody of his name resides at this address. Listen carefully to me. You will leave here, you will forget us having spoken, and you will never return.'

When Hope did not comply, the man's face flickered through emotions ranging from surprise to fear as it dawned on him that the unwelcome caller could not be influenced. Until then his hands had been hidden. Now one of them appeared. It was holding a gun.

Hope's eyes widened and he took half a pace back. He had no idea what type of gun it was. All he knew was that it was black, big, and pointing straight at him.

Before he could retreat or protest his innocence, there was a rush of movement inside the house. There was a thud, a gasp, and the grey man slipped from sight.

Hope heard shuffling before the chain was removed and the door was pulled open just wide enough for him to get in. He got a glimpse of Harman waving to him. Hope darted through the doorway and pushed the door closed behind him. Without being told to, he slid the bolt and chain back into place. In the dark hallway he watched as Harman dragged the unconscious body away.

He scampered after Harman and said, 'is that Osterfeld?'

Without looking up, Harman grunted, 'that or he's got a twin brother.'

'Is he badly hurt?'

Harman paused in his labours to say, 'if I had a degree in hitting people over the head, maybe I could tell you, but I'm a beginner so let's hope for the best, shall we?'

'I was only asking.'

Harman resumed dragging the limp

figure deeper into the house and said, 'I came through the kitchen. It's down those stairs over there. Go and see if there's something we can tie him up with.'

Hope did as he was told. He found the kitchen easily enough. It was full of modern appliances but had an old feel to it. He hurriedly searched through drawers and cupboards. When he found some nylon washing line and a pair of sharp scissors he ran back to Harman. Waving his haul triumphantly, he said, 'these will do the trick.'

Harman rolled Osterfeld on to his front and pulled the man's arms behind him. He said, 'tie his hands and feet and make sure you do a good job. I'm going to check out the house.'

They were already on the top floor, so after picking up the fallen handgun, Harman checked the rooms there first. There were two bedrooms. One had been slept in. There was a living room. The walls were white. The furniture was beige. The large black HD television dominated everything else. The last door led into a study. It was windowless. He found the wall switch and turned on the overhead light. Book-lined shelves pressed in on him from all sides. A high-end laptop computer stood on a wooden table. Harman booted it up, but as expected it was password protected and he could not access its contents. Something told him that this was where Osterfeld spent most of his time.

Coming out again, he nodded with approval at the progress Hope was making with his knot making skills, and then skipped down the stairs. He went past the kitchen door that he had forced to get into the building. As for the kitchen itself, it had been very tidy before Hope had messed with it. There was nothing that Harman had not seen when entering. A heavy door to his right led him into a dining room. It was musty and brightened solely by a slim vein of sunlight from the garden. Next to it was a smaller room. It contained a single bed. The pillows had no covers, and the mattress was bare. Satisfied that it was no more than some barely used guest room, he backed out. A hallway from the kitchen led to the street level door. It was immediately obvious that it had not been used for years. The bars across it were still sturdy, but the paint on them was flaking and cobwebs were splayed across the gaps.

Harman's search was nearly complete. There was only the basement to go. That was reached by a set of stone stairs at the far end of the kitchen. Strip lighting illuminated the path downwards. A rolled iron banister gave him something to hold on to as he descended. This seemed to be the most recently decorated part of the house. Three doors led from a small landing at the foot of the staircase. One opened into a utility room that was stocked with white goods. One opened into a storage room. Its wooden shelves were full of towels, bedclothes and linens.

The third and final one took Harman into the biggest bathroom he had ever seen. In spite of himself, he took a few moments to dwell on it. One wall was covered in seashells. One was dominated by a painting of a mermaid. One had a mosaic image of a beach on it. The fourth wall was completely taken up with a wooden sauna. The toilet facilities and the twin sinks were the most mundane aspects of the place and were made even more so by comparison to the huge sunken bath that filled the centre of the room. Marble steps led down into it. If it had been any bigger, Harman would have considered swimming widths of it.

Mentally shaking himself free of the unexpectedly opulent bathroom, he allowed himself to relax. He had got what he wanted from his tour of the house. He had satisfied himself that Osterfeld had no minders on site, and he had found the perfect place to hold his prisoner while he questioned him.

Without any further delay, he ran back to Hope. He checked that the bindings on Osterfeld were secure and then with Hope's help hauled the stricken figure back down the two flights of stairs to the bathroom.

After cutting another strand from the washing line, Harman tied Osterfeld to one of the sinks. While Hope did an orbit of the sunken bath and repeatedly muttered, 'wow, just wow' to himself, Harman took one of the plush towels from where they were hanging and doused it in cold water. As gently as he could, he lowered Osterfeld's head to inspect his handiwork. He breathed a sigh of relief on finding that he had barely broken the skin and that the fast-swelling lump was not a sign of lasting damage. After carefully parting the short hair around the wound, he placed the cold towel against it. It brought a groan from Osterfeld, although their prisoner was not yet awake.

Harman said, 'Charles, when you've finished admiring this underground paradise could you see if there is any ice in the kitchen freezer? And while you're there, have a look for a medical kit, aspirins, anything like that.'

Tearing his gaze from the mermaid, Hope said, 'uh, ok, sure thing.'

Harman stretched Osterfeld's legs out straight and formed the towel into a pillow before leaning the man's head back against it. He pulled down another couple of towels and shaped them around Osterfeld's neck. It was the best he could do to make him comfortable.

When Hope came back, he carried a glass of water in one hand and a bundled tea towel in the other. He put the glass on the floor and handed the dripping bundle to Harman. He pulled a small brown bottle from a pocket.

He said, 'I crushed some ice up into that. I

found some painkillers and the water is to help him wash them down.'

Sensing Hope's need for further approval, Harman said, 'you've done a good job. And nice improvising while you were keeping him occupied upstairs.'

'What took you so long? I was running out of small talk.'

'I couldn't move up on him until he'd opened the door and was solely concentrating on you. Were you getting worried?'

Hope raised an eyebrow and said, 'what have I told you about mocking me. It's not nice.'

'No offence intended, Charles. We're a team, aren't we? We should be able to enjoy some banter.'

'A team, eh? I like that. I've never been part of a team before.'

Harman winked at him and said, 'I think this team should get on with it.'

He took Osterfeld's chin in his hand and tapped his cheek with the other. At the first indication of Osterfeld coming around, Harman slid the wet towel away and replaced it with the ersatz ice pack that Hope had made. It was a jolt to Osterfeld's system and the German Ascendant's eyelids strobed for a second before he squeezed them shut. He tried to sit forward. The washing line stopped him.

'Easy does it, Hans,' Harman purred, 'take a few moments to get your head straight.'

Osterfeld was struggling to focus. He clamped his eyes shut and tried again. It took a while before he could blearily ask, 'who are you?'

Harman whispered to Hope, 'stand back and don't say a word. Just stare at him.'

Hope opened his mouth to speak, thought better of it, and did as he was told. He repositioned himself by standing on the edge of the bath.

Osterfeld turned his head from side to side and let out a squawk as a shaft pain sprang out from the lump on his head. Almost in disbelief, he said, 'you hit me...'

'We're not here to hurt you unless we need to. Here take these...' Harman unscrewed the brown bottle, shook out three white pills, and held them to Osterfeld's lips. Then he raised the glass and poured some of the water into his prisoner's mouth. There was some spluttering. Trickles of the liquid ran down Osterfeld's chin and on to his shirt. With great effort he managed to swallow the painkillers.

Harman's act of kindness was not well rewarded. As soon as the pills had gone down Osterfeld's gullet, he took a lungful of air, and began screaming at the top of his voice, 'HELP, HELP, HELP, HELP.'

The screams resounded around the palatial bathroom. Harman did nothing to stop the racket. When a panting Osterfeld finally stopped, Harman said, 'I'm glad you've got that out of your system. It's best you understand that nobody can hear you down here. Did you know that this place wasn't originally built as the glorious sauna and bathroom you see here today? This, Herr Osterfeld, was constructed as a bomb shelter beneath the house. I can't say which threat to Israel it was constructed in response to. That doesn't matter. What I can say is that it has reinforced walls and ceiling. Those, coupled with the fact that we are already some way below ground level, means that nobody out in the street will ever be able to hear you. It would help no end if you could accept that and the reality of your situation.'

Osterfeld shut his eyes again. Harman left him to his thoughts. The sooner that Osterfeld came to his own conclusions, the easier it would be to get information from him.

When Osterfeld was ready he looked at Harman and said, 'why would you do this to your own people?'

Harman saw past the accusation to the fear that hid behind it. It was telling that he hadn't asked, *why are you doing this to me?* It meant that Osterfeld knew they were Ascendants and, more than that, they were the people who had hurt others and not just him. If word had reached him of the deaths of Thibault Blanc and Daiyu Chen, then his fear was understandable. It was something that Harman could use to his advantage.

'You were expecting us then, Herr Osterfeld?'

'I was aware of the possibility.'

'Given that you are such an intelligent man, you don't seem to have prepared very well for it. One gun and some rusting bars on your windows? I had expected better.'

'Armed guards did not help the good lady Chen, did they?'

'My, word does get around quickly in your circles, doesn't it? You will know then what you face, if you don't co-operate with us. I had no appetite for what was done to her or Blanc, but if you believe anything, then believe that nothing will stop me from reaching Virginia Brightwell.'

Osterfeld managed a defiant sneer and said, 'for someone with no such appetite, you went beyond what was necessary to extract information from them. You are a traitor and a monster.'

Harman drew back as if personally offended by the accusation. He said, 'what, you thought that was me? No, Herr Osterfeld, I have no stomach for such work. I could not even watch. Those acts and others that I care not to think about again were perpetrated by my ally here.'

Osterfeld stared over Harman's shoulder at the impassive Charles Hope. After inspecting him like a bug under a microscope, Osterfeld said, 'that weak fool could not cut the crust from a loaf of challah bread. He is the one who was jabbering foolishness at me from outside.'

'In this country of all places, I hesitate to mention the word Nazi, but try to imagine Heinrich Himmler without his black SS uniform and trappings of power. You would see a small man who was no threat to you. A man in cheap clothes with the ink-stained fingers of a petty clerk. My point is that appearances can be deceptive. And your hope should be that you are never left alone with the man you have been so rude to. I promise you he will not forget that. If you could see the eyes behind those dark glasses of his, you would be pissing yourself.'

Harman stopped himself there. He was already at risk of either laughing or going so far over the top as to sound ridiculous. He knew his decision was the right one when Osterfeld's gaze dropped from Hope to the floor. He was like a man who had gone to stroke a puppy only for it to transform miraculously into a snarling, slathering Rottweiler.

Harman put what he intended to be a reassuring hand on Osterfeld's knee and said, 'put him out of your mind if you can. I've already told you that we are not here to hurt you and I meant that. If you give me the information I want, you can be out of here in a day or two completely unharmed. You are the next link in the chain that will lead me to Brightwell. That is all you are to me. I bear you no malice personally.

You are a clever man, Herr Osterfeld. A Senior Fellow at the Max Planck Institute for Molecular Genetics in Berlin, no less. So do the smart thing and tell me what I want.'

'No malice, you say,' Osterfeld barked, 'yet you bring that animal with you.'

Harman made great play of leaning closer to him and saying out of Hope's earshot, 'we are all playing for great stakes. Can you honestly say that you have not supported Brightwell in her use of extreme measures when they were needed? It's not a question of liking them, it's a question of their necessity, isn't it?'

Osterfeld's bottom lip shook as if his mouth wanted to argue the point, but his brain couldn't provide the requisite ammunition. All he could manage was, 'I don't know where Virginia is.'

'That's okay. It's disappointing, but not surprising. Maybe we should turn our attention to what you do know, rather than what you do not? I'm familiar with the chain that Virginia Brightwell set up. It's why I referred to you as a link. Let's start with who the link is above you and where he or she might be?'

'You won't stop her,' Osterfeld said.

'So other links in the chain have been saying to me. That, however, is an answer to a completely different question.'

'And one that I suspect Daiyu Chen would happily have given you. She would not have endured a single instant of torture to protect Virginia or me. She was a supporter of the cause, but I knew her well enough to be sure she would not suffer for it. My belief is that she told you what you wanted, and that you still let her be mutilated by your Golem over there. I conclude therefore that I am a dead man either way and so there is no incentive for me to help you.'

Harman could feel his leverage slipping away. Osterfeld was proving that even under threat his rationality was not deserting him. Harman could not afford to falter. He said, 'that is not exactly how it played out. You see, Chen thought she was better than us. Hell, she probably thought she was better than everyone. She did tell me about you. Unfortunately, that wasn't the end of it. By giving me that information she must have thought our guard would drop. Backed by her two men, she chose to fight. It did not go well for her. My friend's reaction may have been rather...extreme...but he would not be contained. It did not have to end that way for her, and it does not have to end that way for you.'

'You won't stop Virginia. You do know that?' Osterfeld said, his chin jutting resolutely forward.

Harman checked his wristwatch as if he had somewhere he needed to be. He said, 'so I keep hearing. Then again, if you're so confident of that, you might as well tell me how to find her.'

'I do not know where she is.'

'We've been down that cul-de-sac already. All I want is the name of somebody who does know where she is. I'm on something of a tight schedule so if you plan to tell me voluntarily, you'd be best to tell me now. In a while, I will be leaving here. It would be in your best interest to speak to me before that.'

'If you are late for another appointment, please don't be late on my account.'

'You misunderstand me, Herr Osterfeld. Maybe that bang on the head has left you dazed. I will leave temporarily because I have a weak stomach. I am not ashamed to admit it. When you begin to scream, I do not want to hear it. I will go and make myself a cup of tea, or coffee if you don't have that, and wait for him to come and tell me what he has extracted from you.'

As he spoke Harman jabbed a thumb in Hope's direction to leave no doubt about who would be bringing agony to Osterfeld's immediate future.

'I am not afraid.'

Harman shook his head sadly and said, 'your voice betrays your words.'

He went to Hope and led him by the arm to the door. When they were outside, he said, 'I will try to reason with him, but he's going to be a stubborn bastard. We will need a bit of theatre to tip him over. I want you to go back to the kitchen and come back with anything you can find there that a psychopath might enjoy using on someone.'

Hope pulled a face like a child taking medicine. He said, 'how am I supposed to know what that would be. I can just about manage standing still while you depict me as some madman, but that's about as scary as I can get. The minute I open my mouth, he will see through me and know it's an empty threat.'

'Use your imagination, you might surprise yourself.'

'I don't want to imagine the sort of things you're talking about. Some lunatic is out there actually doing those things and we might be next on his homicidal shopping list. The last thing I want to do is think about that any more than I have to.'

'Relax, Charles. Deep breaths. I don't get my kicks from scaring people but remember who we have in there. He's no angel. All I'm asking you to do is play along. Get whatever you can, come back, lay them out and start inspecting them, like you would if you were shopping for fresh vegetables in a market. Don't look at Osterfeld and don't speak to him. Maybe you don't want to imagine *those things,* but he won't be able to help himself. His head will be filling with gruesome possibilities. They will eat away at him.'

Hope was still muttering away to himself about deep breaths as he reluctantly trudged up the stairs to the kitchen.

Harman paused to get his tactics straight and then grim-faced he hurried back into the grand bathroom. He strode across to Osterfeld and crouched in front of the bound figure.

'We don't have long, Herr Osterfeld. Please tell me what I want. There is no need for you to become a martyr to Brightwell's cause.'

'Her cause is my cause.'

Harman stabbed a finger into Osterfeld's chest and said, 'how can you, a learned Jewish man, support genocide. That sticks in my throat.'

'Pah, what do you know? I've been watching you. I've seen the signs before. Tell me, how recently did your Ascendant DNA become dominant?'

Harman couldn't guess what Osterfeld was getting at, but there was no apparent reason for deception. He said, 'weeks ago rather than years.'

Osterfeld's eyes blazed with triumph. He said, 'I thought as much. You are like a child with a new toy. You don't know the price that comes with it or how to use it properly, but you will play with it, nevertheless. If you had been born different and aware of it from your earliest days, like me, like Virginia, you would be whistling a different tune. You would be whistling our tune.'

'No, you're wrong. Virginia Brightwell had two of my friends killed and she's prepared to kill millions more. Whether I was a Normal or an Ascendant from the day of my birth wouldn't change that. She is evil and I will stop her.'

'I understand better then,' Osterfeld said accusingly, 'you are not on some holy crusade. Your real motive for all of this is a lust for personal vengeance.'

'It's not my motives that are in question. It's yours. Why are you willing to be tortured to protect her? How can you countenance for a single second the deaths of so many innocents? Tell me, I'm desperate to understand.'

Osterfeld flexed his aching arms and rolled his neck. When he was ready, he said, his voice deep and angry, 'my days of giving lectures are over, but, yes, I will tell you. I grew up as a Jew and as an Ascendant. For most people on this over-populated world, I am the perfect target for their blind envy and hate. I determined not to be a victim. Meeting Virginia Brightwell was the best day of my life. She showed me and others how to fight back. She showed us that the real lesson of the Holocaust was not that genocide was wrong, but rather that if applied correctly it could make the world infinitely better. Cauterising a wound is unpleasant, but it can be the only way to staunch a critical loss of blood. You yourself mentioned the Nazis. What if in the 1930s we had the ability to kill them all? That drastic action would have prevented the Second World War. There would have been no death camps. Would anyone now blame the Jews for defending themselves like that if they had been able to? Maybe they would still be vilified and condemned. How can we know? But I can be certain that millions would have been saved and that a true evil would have been eradicated.'

'And what's your point exactly?' Harman said.

'I would have thought that was obvious. If we don't act the Ascendants will be the Jews of this century or the next, except if there are any survivors, we will not be able to create a country of our own to retreat to. There will be no ancestral land for us to return to and defend from our enemies. This is how we draw a line in the sand. The Jews might not have had the wherewithal to save themselves in the 1930s, but we Ascendants have it today and will use it to ensure we have a future.'

Harman leaned back on his heels as if his body feared contamination from being so close to Osterfeld. He rubbed his face hard and said, 'I don't know where to begin with logic as warped as that, but for starters how about the blindingly obvious fact that the people you plan to kill are not Nazis? They are men, women, and children of all races and religions who have done nothing to you.'

'Let's see if you feel the same way when they come for you, your children, or your children's children. History talks to us. Only fools do not listen to it. Hitler was an innocent artist creating daubs to scrape a living before WW1, but if you had a time machine to take you back to 1913, you'd still kill him, wouldn't you?'

Harman remembered his first meeting with Sidney Grosschild at the Institute for Defence and Security. The sagging bookcases behind the academic were full of tomes about the atrocities that man had committed against man across the centuries. Alongside them were crisp copies of Grosschild's own bestsellers in his World War Three series about how science was increasing the opportunities for targeted genocide. Harman bit his lip hard to stop his thoughts drifting. He could not let Osterfeld get inside his head. He had another chip to toss into the pot. The last name on the list that Peter Salt had given him.

He said, 'I'm not here for debate. Tell me who is next in the chain. Is it Yukio Hagihara?'

Osterfeld looked like a mugger had produced a knife and was waving it at him. The blood drained from his sallow cheeks.

Harman smiled coldly at him and said, 'that's nice. You answered without saying anything. All I need is for you to tell me where he is.'

Osterfeld took a breath. It sounded like a sob. He said, 'how dare you preach to me about genocide when your hands are already wrist deep in Ascendant blood.'

'Let's not get sidetracked by that again. You know, I was feeling guilty about what will happen to you. Now I don't. When Charles is ready, he will hurt you. Did I mention that his name is Charles? It's an inoffensive name for someone who enjoys doing what he does, isn't it?'

Osterfled pulled at the cords holding him to the sink. It served to make them tighter on his wrists. That didn't stop him trying even harder when the door opened, and Charles Hope entered.

Hope stayed side on to Osterfeld as he knelt by the bath. His profile gave nothing away. He was seemingly completely focussed on his haul from the kitchen. From under his arm, he took an electric toaster. He held it up as he searched for somewhere to plug it in. He dejectedly put it down and proceeded to take a meat tenderiser and a selection of knives and forks from his pocket. They clinked as he lay them on the top of the marble steps that led into the bath.

Turning back to the toaster, he slid his fingers into one of the two slots for bread and tested to make sure that the depressor would still work with them inside. Nodding contentedly to himself, he left the room.

Harman said, 'you really are running out of time to tell me where to find Hagihara.'

'You think your Gestapo methods will

work on me?'

'More importantly, do you think they will? As an Ascendant, you probably have a high pain threshold. That doesn't mean you will be able to hold out. All it will do is extend your suffering. I don't want that, and it makes no sense to me that you would either.'

'Would you really stand by and let him commit these atrocities?'

'No, as I've explained, I will leave rather than stand by. I don't want the memory of what he will do to pollute my mind. Some things can't be forgotten. For both our sakes tell me where to find Hagihara.'

Osterfeld's tongue flicked across his dry lips like a thirsty snake. The saggy flap of skin under his chin shivered. Clammy sweat seeped on to his forehead.

Hope reappeared. He did not once look at them. He was slowly unravelling an orange extension lead that ran from somewhere outside the bathroom. When he reached the bath, he plugged the toaster into it. He pressed a button, and a small red light came on. His hands clapped together with delight.

Harman stood up and said, 'Hans, this really is your last chance.'

Osterfeld's eyes were locked on the toaster like a laser-guided missile system.

Harman said, 'I hate to think whether he will begin with that or build up to it. I've never been partial to the smell of cooked meat. Time for me to get that cup of coffee.'

He had barely taken one step, when Osterfeld said, 'Gibraltar.'

He said it so quickly that Harman had to ask him to repeat himself.

'Yukio is in Gibraltar. You will find him there.'

'Where exactly?'

'He's staying at that floating hotel. I can't remember its name.'

Harman crouched down once more and said, 'stop looking at him and look at me. Slow down and answer me, ok?'

With an effort that there was there for all to see, Osterfeld managed to tear his gaze away from Charles Hope. He said, 'you won't let him hurt me?'

Harman saw the first swell of a tear in Osterfeld's eyes, 'I promise. If you tell me what I need. What's Hagihara doing in Gibraltar? It doesn't seem like an obvious destination for him.'

'He's at a conference about the regulation of cryptocurrencies.'

Which wasn't what Harman had expected to hear. He said, 'that hardly seems likely, when the rest of you all went to ground? You wouldn't be sending me on a goose chase, would you?'

'No, no, no, I'm not. You've got to believe me. Even by our standards, he's a genius. We have accounts in banks there. He holds the purse strings for Virginia. Wherever she is, he is arranging for everything to be paid for. The conference gives him an excuse to be there.'

'When are you due to speak to him again?'

'Tomorrow. It's a scheduled check.'

Harman stared unwaveringly at Osterfled as if he was peeling back the layers of the German's mind to find the absolute truth that was hidden at its core. Something about it brought Osterfeld to the brink of panic. He started to thrash around.

The violent reaction broke Harman's concentration. He took Osterfeld by the shoulders. His fingers dug into the other man's flesh. He said, 'that's enough, Hans.'

He held him until Osterfeld subsided.

Osterfeld managed to ask what would happen to him next.

Harman said, 'I keep my promises. No harm will come to you. Not from me, anyway. I can't have you warning Hagihara that I'm giving him a visit. Which means Charles will stay here with you until after your call tomorrow. Say the right things to Hagihara, and Charles will leave you untouched. If you do anything to alert Hagihara, then you will have to bear the consequences. Are we understood? Is that clear enough for you?'

Osterfeld's nodded rapidly.

Harman said, 'good. If you behave,

Charles will leave here straight after the call. As soon as I know he's on a plane out of this country, I will call the local police and have them come release you. You will be uncomfortable for a while, that's all. After that, you're on your own. My advice would be to make sure our paths don't cross again. Given what you've been involved with, I'd say you're getting off lightly.'

Before his anger could rise, Harman gestured to Hope and the two of them went to the kitchen. Good as his word, Harman made them some coffee. After he had poured, he handed a cup to Hope who took it. His shaking hand made some of the brown liquid slop over the rim.

'What are you so nervous about?' Harman asked.

'He could have told us anything to get us to leave. It feels too easy. How do you know he's not lying?'

'Instinct. And I've got the insurance of you babysitting him until I can be sure he's been straight with us. Make yourself comfortable tonight, make sure he behaves himself tomorrow, and then make tracks to Gibraltar. I will meet you there unless something goes wrong.'

'I don't like it when you talk about things going wrong.'

'Hey, the world's chaotic, shit happens sometimes. I'm not expecting anything, but it would be crazy not to allow for the possibility.'

'I'm not a philosophical man. All I want is for this to be over and for you to tell me everything will be alright.'

Harman sipped carefully at the hot drink. He said, 'this will be over soon, and everything will be alright. Is that any better?'

Hope adjusted his glasses and said, 'it would be better if you sounded like you believe it.'

Harman said, 'something else has its hooks in you. What is it?'

Hope tried his own coffee and winced as it burned his tongue. He blew on it several times and then said, 'I'm not happy about staying here on my own.'

'You will be fine. Keep an occasional eye on Osterfeld. Say nothing, look intimidating, like someone who will rip his heart out if he looks the wrong way at you.'

'There you go with the intimidation again. I won't be able to keep that up.'

'It will be easy. Say as little as possible and keep your face blank. All he will see is a psycho.'

Hope put his cup down with more force than he had intended. Half the contents splashed on to the table. He shrilled, 'and what if the real killer turns up? If someone is following us this is where they will come next. You'll understand why I don't want to be sitting here alone if he shows up.'

'It's alright to be scared. Just sit very tight. You've got Osterfeld's gun for protection and this place is built like a fort. Keep the blinds down and the doors locked. I will secure the garden door before I go so that nobody can get in the way that I did.'

'And after that? Do you really have no idea who killed Blanc and Chen? How about your old employers? Or could it be Homeland Security and their friends? Black Ops they call it, don't they?'

Harman couldn't pretend that he hadn't been thinking about that himself. It was hard enough pressing on forward after Brightwell without having to worry about who was coming up behind them. He said, 'who knows? Maybe it's Virginia Brightwell pulling the ladder up after herself. She knows somebody betrayed her by telling Peter Salt where she was in Colorado. Maybe she's got someone removing the likely candidates so they can't let her down again. Maybe you're right and it's some arm of the US government upping their war on terror. Then there's always....'

Hope put his hands on the table to steady himself and said, 'always what? What is it you don't want to say? You're really scaring me now.'

Harman had very deliberately kept the final possibility to himself. Thinking about it did him no good and it was sure to unsettle Hope even more. Somehow though, it did not seem fair or right to hide it any longer. He said, 'Homeland Security had a tame Ascendant or so they thought. He went off reservation and disappeared. From what I hear he was certifiable. They kept him in a straitjacket half the time. He thought he was on a holy mission to destroy every Ascendant.'

'Even though he was one?'

'Apparently God had told him they were abominations and demons. From what I heard he planned to kill them all and then kill himself.'

'You're joking!' Hope said, his voice going up through the scales.

'I only wish I was.'

'What was his name? how do we spot him?'

'Charles, I'm not saying it is him. Try to calm down. It is another possibility. No more than that.'

Hope raised the cup. Ignoring how hot the remainder of the coffee was, he swallowed it all in one go. After a small cough, he said, 'please, please, tell me.'

Harman shrugged. He owed Hope some straight answers. He said, 'his name is Ernst Mannson and assuming he's not been put back in a straitjacket he won't be easy to spot.'

'But you'd recognise him, right?' Hope said, with a neediness that would have shamed a beggar.

'I'm not sure I would. I barely saw him

in passing. I've never heard him speak. All I really remember is this crazy hair that he had sprouting off in all directions. Plus, he had this eye-rolling thing going on as well, but he was drugged up at the time and maybe it was no more than part of his act to get inside DHS. That aside, he was average height and average build.'

Hope's frown was so deep that it seemed to be pointing accusingly at Harman, 'that could be almost anyone.'

'Put him out of your thoughts. Do your job and leave the rest to me.'

'That's easy for you to say. You won't be sitting here like a tethered goat waiting for a hungry tiger to show up. I won't be opening the doors to anyone with a German accent.'

'What?'

'You said his name was Mannson, that's German right?'

'I hate to pull the rug out from under you, but he's American, just like you. He might be from German stock, but he isn't German.'

Hope jumped to his feet and said, 'where did you leave that gun of Osterfeld's?'

Harman went to get it for him. He had made a mistake by telling Hope about Mannson. His new partner looked as horrified as Osterfeld did down in the bathroom. He retrieved the Masada 9mm pistol, made sure it was loaded, and put it on the table. He said, 'do you know how to use one of these?'

'Of course, I don't.'

Harman wasn't familiar with the make or model, but modern automatic handguns had so much in common that it was easy for him to show Hope how it worked. Hope's initial unease at handling the firearm was overcome by his desire for additional protection.

When they were finished, Harman wanted to change the subject. As much as he had quizzed Hope about Ascendants, there was one other question that gnawed at him. He had been reluctant to pose it for two reasons. The first was that he did not know if he could trust Hope with something that had been tearing at his heart. The second was that he dreaded what the answer might be. If it was the wrong one, he did not know if he could cope with it. Whatever the outcome, it wasn't something he could hide from any longer. He had to know, and he couldn't be certain that he would ever get the chance to ask it again.

With Hope still uneasily handling the pistol, Harman took the cups and placed them on the draining board. He came back feeling as twitchy as Hope looked. He pulled his chair a bit closer to Hope and said, 'Charles, I need your help. There's something I've been wanting to ask you, but the time has never seemed right.'

'I've lost count of the questions you've asked me. By now you must know as much about Ascendants as I do. What's so special about this one? What's bothering you?'

'I appreciate your concern, I really do, Charles. You're a good man.'

'It must be bad for you to prevaricate like that. Whatever it is, it will do you good to get off your chest.'

Harman cleared his throat and said, 'how much is really known about the Ascendant ability to influence people?'

'You told me Peter Salt had explained that to you already,' Hope said, suspicion beginning to replace his encouragement of Harman.

'He did. It's not voodoo, it's not exactly mesmerism, it's more a triumph of will, it works on most Normals, but not all. I get all of that.'

'Chill man,' Hope said, 'there's no need to get impatient with me. I haven't seen you like this before, Alan. What's bugging you?'

Harman's lips clenched tightly together as if his subconscious was trying to gag him. He berated himself for his weakness. It was now or never. He didn't choose the words they just came out. He said, 'I think I might have killed my wife. Since the first time I influenced someone, I can't get the thought out of my mind. It's eating away at me.'

'Whoa,' Hope said, 'what are you talking about? I can't help if you don't tell me exactly what's bothering you.'

'Sorry, I know. Maybe this was a mistake.'

'Listen to me, Alan, you will need all

223

your wits about you to put an end to Virginia Brightwell. You should unburden yourself, if you can. Say it now, say it as simply as you can, and we'll see where that takes us.'

Harman concentrated on the fingers of his left hand. His wedding ring had rested there once. When he was ready, he said, 'I was married. It didn't work out, but I still loved her. Francesca, that is. I was working too hard, drinking too much. I don't know what came over me. I was alone, drunk, feeling sorry for myself. I got angry. For the one and only time in my entire life, I wished her dead. The day after that I found out that she had been knocked off her bicycle. She was in a coma for a long time before they switched the machines off.'

'I'm sorry, Alan, I really am, but tragic accidents happen sometimes. How could that have been your fault?'

'Isn't it bloody obvious? Harman's eyes flared with rage. 'I could never understand why I blamed myself quite so much. I do now. I do since my Ascendant genes were awakened. I influenced her to ride in front of that truck. For that millisecond I wanted her dead and I influenced her to destroy herself. How's that for sick?'

Hope reached out a hand to touch Harman. He thought better of it and rerouted his fingers so that they thrummed in distress on his forehead. He had no idea how to manifest empathy in such a situation. He had never had a friend to seek solace from him. He was a stranger in a strange emotional land with no map to guide him. He didn't know what the right thing to say was, but he was sure he should say something.

'Alan, it seems to me that you have already answered the question that you wanted to ask me. But what if your answer is the wrong one?'

'What do you mean?' Harman said, making it sound more of a challenge than a plea.

'I mean that in the court of your own mind you seem to have condemned yourself without hearing all the evidence. Tell me, were you there when the accident occurred?'

'No, I was at home cuddling up to a bottle of vodka. What's that got to do with it?'

'Then you have been punishing yourself unnecessarily. I have never heard of an Ascendant being able to influence anyone unless they are with them in person or via some other direct media. Whatever you may have been thinking and no matter how guilty that makes you feel, you did not cause that accident.'

'You're sure? You're really sure?'

'As sure as I can be. Look, you've been around me, Peter Salt, and Virginia Brightwell. You've seen how the influence is used. You've even used it yourself recently. Have you once witnessed it being used other than as I've described?'

Harman looked at his hand again. He tried

to remember every instance. Most of all he remembered Peter Salt dying in his arms back in the caves of the silver mine system in Colorado.

Harman's first act as an Ascendant had been to influence Cornel Culpepper, the man who had shot Salt, to turn the gun on himself. That power was dangerous and frightening. It had to be used carefully and sparingly. Above all it had to be controlled, and he had worked hard at doing that. He flipped from his limited experience of influencing Normals to the incidents where he had seen Salt and Brightwell use it. It came at a cost. It compelled him to picture Salt, the virtuous man, who was the anthesis of his sister. Salt influenced people to protect them or to shine a light where it desperately needed to be shone. Brightwell influenced people in the name of her cause, and she had no compunction about them killing others on her behalf. She had used Culpepper for that, and she had used Ministry of Defence guards at the muddy riverside at Marston Creek research facility to shoot his best and only friend dead. Every image from that and the other scenes which sprang to mind opened wounds that had barely had time to scar over. It was a relief when he could bring himself to stop.

Harman sighed with sorrow as much as with relief. He said, 'maybe you're right.'

'That doesn't happen very often,' Hope said, lamely trying to inject some levity into their exchange.

Harman closed his eyes and rubbed them.
Hope could not tell whether it was to wipe away the fatigue that was sweeping over him or, in the interests of his manly pride, to conceal a tear. Either way, when Harman rose, said he was going to check flight routes to Gibraltar, and left upstairs in the direction of the living room, Hope was sure it was best to leave him alone for a while.

*

As it transpired, flying to Gibraltar from Israel was far from easy without going via London and Harman had no intention of trying that again any time soon. Instead, he flew by way of Madrid to Malaga in southern Spain. From there he took the ninety- minute taxi drive to the small British dependency at the tip of Europe which looked out across the entrance to the Mediterranean Sea. As the breezy taxi driver had told him, and he assumed every passenger that made the long journey, the coast of North Africa was no more than fourteen miles away.

Harman had the misfortune to arrive at the Spain-Gibraltar border crossing at one of the busiest times in the morning when the small horde of foreign workers were streaming across for their jobs on the small peninsula which tenaciously clung to its British roots. He paid off the taxi driver and joined the queue of those crossing on foot. He influenced the border guards to believe that he was holding a British passport and strolled in. The Rock soared skywards ahead of him. The mountain dominated the territory. He would have enjoyed its grandeur more if the summit had not been hidden by clouds and if rain was not pouring down around him.

The modern airport was across the road to his left. He turned away from it and walked towards the harbour. He had never been anywhere before where the airport was walking distance from just about everywhere you might want to go to. The concept appealed to him at a time when he was fast getting sick of the sight of airports and the monotony of getting to and from them. Whatever awaited him after he had dealt with Brightwell, he was determined that it would not involve flying.

He went into at a gas station and bought an umbrella. There was no point in getting drenched while he went about his business. With the flimsy black brolly covering his head he resumed his walk.

Harman had to stop when barriers came down across the road. It was not for a train to pass, but rather for a plane to land on the runway that cut across the road. It was both curious and quaint, like seeing the policemen in uniforms that would not have been out of place in London. He liked it. After the plane had landed, the barriers had been raised, and the procession of vehicles had started up again, he turned off into a quieter road. There were some industrial buildings, warehouses, and a modern football ground that was hidden away behind graffiti covered walls. It seemed like the young and bored of Gibraltar enjoyed aerosol paint as much as their counterparts in Spain and the UK. The area soon gave way to more modern buildings and apartments. He went through the archway of a residential complex and found himself facing the marina and rows of modern boats and yachts. He turned left along the narrow promenade until he came to a café. Tables and chairs were available outside, but they were all dripping from the rain and so he went in. Even Ascendants needed to eat, and a Full English Breakfast was just what he wanted. Hagihara could wait that long. Or so Harman thought.

*

Sebastian Kent sat on a bench overlooking a field of wheat. Beside him was a rucksack. Inside it was a flask of tea and a laptop computer. Resting against his thigh was the walking stick that Agent Reilly had presented to him. He hid his amusement as he saw Amy Bishop trudging up the country path towards him. This was not her natural habitat.

As soon as she close enough to hail, he got

the flask out and called to ask if she would care to join him for a drink. The scowl on her face was answer enough. When she reached him, she said, 'did you have to pick somewhere that was so far off the beaten track?'

'I thought you would approve. It wouldn't do for the disgraced head of ET1 to be seen with his successor so soon after his fall from grace, would it?'

Without being invited she sat beside him and said, 'I've never seen you dressed in anything other than a suit. You look different.'

Glancing down at his hooded waterproof jacket and faded jeans, he said, 'I feel different without one and not in a good way.'

'You know we could have met somewhere that was easier for you to reach,' she said, pointing to his stick.

'I need to build up muscle mass in my leg again. It won't get any better if I sit around all day.'

'And it won't get any better if you run before you can walk, if you'll excuse my choice of words. I'm starting to wonder if you might have masochistic tendencies.'

'Hold that thought until my next annual psychiatric review. That is, if I ever have one again. Let's forget about that. Can we get down to brass tacks? What have you got for me? I brought a laptop as you suggested.'

Choosing not to comment on his evident

sensitivity about the bullet wound, she reached for the computer and asked, 'may I?'

'Be my guest. The password is Waterloo1815.'

'You boys and your military history,' she said as she tapped away at the keyboard.

She inserted a flash drive. While she highlighted various files on it, Kent said, 'any word on who Sir Anthony will be bringing in?'

Without taking her eyes from the screen, she said, 'not yet.'

'Aren't you curious?'

'Not very. It will be who it will be. There's nothing I can do about it.'

'How very fatalistic of you.'

'I prefer pragmatic. Okay, here we go. I've had all the surveillance tapes re-run for the flights from Edinburgh to Gran Canaria and from there back to London. Alan is apparently travelling alone. The people sitting with him on the flights have no connection whatsoever with him. That's the bad news. The good news is that we spotted someone following him. He's clever, that's for sure. He does a great job of concealing himself most of the time, but he's there alright and nobody can hide from every camera angle. I've pieced together here what we've got. The pictures have returned a 'no match' on facial recognition databases. We can't read too much into that given the relatively poor quality of the images. Even with enhancement software they may simply not be good enough.'

'Or he's not on any databases,' Kent said, taking the laptop from her. He watched intently as the grainy images played out in front of him.

'Before you ask,' she said, 'that is as clear we can get them.'

'Is there any indication that Alan knows this joker is watching him?'

'Not one. Then again, Alan is clever too.'

'You're sure it's not a coincidence?'

Amy Bishop was now in charge of ET1. Even if it was only temporary, she couldn't completely subdue the resentment that rose like bile in her at the way he was firing questions at her. She didn't work for him anymore and it was unlikely that she ever would again. She was taking a big risk by being there and it rankled that he had so readily forgotten what a big favour she was doing for him. She said, 'I would not have wasted my time or yours if it was a mere coincidence.'

That brought him up short. He said, 'I know you wouldn't Amy. It was a foolish of me to ask. I'm, you know, on a ledge here. I might leap, but it feels like someone will push me before I can make my mind up. My one chance to get safely back in the building is to pull something out of the fire.'

'If that's your attempt at mixing metaphors as an apology, then it's accepted.'

'Seeing Alan being stalked like this has

upset you, hasn't it?'

She pretended not to hear him and said, 'this character, whoever he is, has been watching and following Alan. When you analyse the footage, you will see that he goes to great lengths to always be behind Alan and never in front of him. He can always see Alan, but never the other way around. You will also observe that he's always wearing a baseball cap whenever he nears a camera but removes it when he's moving away from one.'

After watching the clips over and over again, Kent could see that she was right. There was also something about the figure which seemed familiar.

'Unless he's an expert on airport security, how could he know about the cameras?'

Amy stared out at the fields and took in some fresh country air through her nose. She let it out slowly and said, 'I'd put the probability of him being an Ascendant at about 95%.'

'Did data analysis give you that figure? Kent said.

'No, I made it up. I thought it sounded impressive, but I doubt that it's far from the truth.'

Kent grinned wryly. Although Amy Bishop wasn't an Ascendant, it felt like she was evolving every day. He said, 'was there anybody else around those flights?'

'Some, mainly airport staff. Some

passengers. We're slowly working our way through to identify them all. It will take a few days.'

'And this was the one keeping eyes on Alan?'

'It is and was.'

Kent brought the screen close to his face. He ran and re-ran the clips. Sometimes he paused them to interrogate the man's looks. Other times he rewound them to see if there was anything about the man's gait or mannerisms that might ring a bell. There was something there. He was sure of it. A snippet of recognition. He was like a customer at an optician's who was waiting for the right lens to be slid into place so that the blurry images would become clear enough for him to recite the letters on the optometry chart.

Amy Bishop was fast reaching the conclusion that her visit had been wasted. She had breached so many security protocols merely by the act of meeting her suspended ex-boss, let alone sharing highly confidential information with him. If it was all for nothing, then she would not have helped Kent or Harman. She would have succeeded in doing nothing except harm her own prospects. It had been a gamble, and she was very aware that the Bible had little good to say about gambling. What was the greater sin though? To take such a chance or to abandon her friends? And how could she be sure of that when she wasn't sure whether either of the men was truly a friend to her? She needed the wisdom of Jesus to resolve that conundrum and at the moment he wasn't speaking to her. He would listen though. She would pray for guidance.

However, before she could decide exactly what form that prayer should take, her attention was completely stolen away by Kent.

He put the laptop on the bench and, in little more than a whisper, said, 'oh shit, I think I know who that is.'

*

Harman was dipping a slice of bread into the last remnants of his fried egg when his pay-as-you-go cell phone rang. Charles Hope was the only person who had its number and Harman was not going to identify either of them over an open line. He put the bread on the side of his plate, answered the call and said, 'all, ok?'

'Hagihara phoned here first thing this morning. Osterfeld told him he was safe and sound. Hagihara said he would call again in two days.'

'No more? Nothing about our deceased friends in Gran Canaria and California?'

'He was checking in, that was all. What more did you expect?'

'I don't know, really. How is your host?'

'He's not exactly happy. He's pleading claustrophobia. Says he can't bear being down there all this time.'

'Don't fall for that.'

'I won't,' Hope said, managing a small laugh, 'and I'm still being intimidating.'

'You've done well, Charles. If you get out of there now, we should be able to meet up late tonight. Call me when you get to Spain, and I'll tell you exactly where you can find me.'

'What about Osterfeld? Shall I leave him where he is?'

'You don't see him, and you don't speak to him again. All you do is get out immediately. I told him I would arrange for him to be released and I will, but not until I'm sure you are well clear first. He can stew in his own sweat until then. We don't owe him anything more than that.'

'Whatever you say, Alan.'

'Good man. I'll see you tonight,' Harman said and terminated the call. He had kept the strain out of his voice. Charles Hope was never more than a wrongly placed word from getting the jitters. Harman was determined that all he should have on his mind was getting out of Israel. Sharing his doubts would have scrambled Hope's brain and so he had held them tight to himself. With the call over, he could give those doubts free rein. It wasn't his enhanced Ascendant nerve ends that were unsettling him, it was the old detective ones. They were telling him that something was very wrong. What they weren't telling him was what it was.

He went to pick up the bread again.

*

Virginia Brightwell broke up the remains of a baguette and cast the crumbs out to her gathering audience of ducks. She was glad to have found some moments to be with them again. She knew it was probably for the last time. Behind them the waters of Lake Geneva barely moved. Only the slight lapping of tiny waves against the banks betrayed its stillness. The innocent hunger of the birds and the serenity of the inland waterway helped to settle her thoughts.

The earlier call from Yukio Hagihara had been unwelcome, if not unsurprising. He had informed her that Hans Osterfeld had been compromised. Hagihara did not know how or by whom, but when he had phoned Osterfeld their man had used the phrase *safe and sound.* It was a simple code that he and Hagihara had adopted. It meant that he was being coerced and needed help. Hagihara had sought her permission to go to Osterfeld's aid. She had denied it. If a wolf was hunting sheep, it would be madness to send another one into the field. Osterfeld had always been loyal, and she in turn admired Hagihara's loyalty to him. It was why she had conceded to his second request. It was to dispatch a team of contractors to the address where Osterfeld was staying. He said contractors. She heard mercenaries. Their use was a small price to pay to keep the Old Man happy.

It is also meant that he did not resist when she ordered him to join her. The necessary funds were in place. The necessary arrangements had been made. There was no reason for him to remain any longer in Gibraltar. The prospect of having him again by her side warmed her more than the ski jacket she was wearing.

Of all her loyalists, he above any of them deserved to be there to witness at first hand the culmination of their years of struggle. There could be no better way to thank him. He had always said that time was their friend, well their time was fast approaching, and he should be able to glory in it alongside her.

That, at least, was what she had told him. What she had left unsaid was that the wolf was proving to be relentless and if it got their scent, she wanted Hagihara with her so that she could protect him. She believed she knew the name of the wolf. She believed it was Alan Harman. He was haunting her waking dreams.

She chastised herself for succumbing to the distraction that was Alan Harman. Nothing could be more important than initiating the Ascent. The weapon was ready and in less than twenty-four fours so too would be the means to deploy it. When that was done, she would turn every inch of her being towards hunting the wolf. Until then she could not, would not, permit herself to have any doubts.

She kicked the ducks out of the way. She needed to continue her work at the hotel. Tomorrow she and the Mir submersible would transfer to the support ship, the *Duttweiller,* which even now was steaming towards them.

*

Hans Osterfeld had lost track of time. The windowless bathroom had become his prison, and he was starting to believe that he would never get the smell of soap out of his nose. He had not noticed it when bathing down there, but prolonged exposure to it was driving him to distraction. For a long while he had felt like nothing could be worse than the cramp in his shoulders or the chaffing of the cord on his red-raw wrists, but how wrong he had been. He cursed his finely tuned Ascendant olfactory system. It had got so bad that he had tried in vain to bury his nostrils into the collar of his shirt, but he was no contortionist, and his neck would not bend enough to give his nose the respite that it craved.

His sole consolation was that he had been able to speak with Yukio and slip their code words into the brief conversation. Yukio would not forsake him. Help would be coming. All that was required of him was to remain patient. That, and to bear the bathroom odours that were driving him to distraction.

How long had it been since the call? Half an hour? An hour? It couldn't have been more than that. Hagihara wasn't a miracle worker. If he was coming himself, it might not be until the next day. If he hired help, it could be sooner. Hagihara certainly had the contacts for that. As much as he wanted to see Hagihara's assuring presence, he desperately wanted to be out of there. He didn't care who came for him as long as they were quick about it. He didn't worry about what would happen after that. Virginia Brightwell valued loyalty above all else, and he had never wavered in his support for her and her work. She would look after him.

Quite unexpectedly, the lights in the bathroom went out. Osterfeld wasn't a superstitious man, but everyone, both Normal and Ascendant, had a primeval fear of being underground and in total darkness. It was too like the endless sleep of death for it not to be unnerving. He was tied up. He was blind. He was helpless.

Osterfeld's heartbeat became faster. His breath came in shallow gulps.

The door creaked open like something from a cheap horror film. A thin beam of light crept across the floor.

'Is that you, Hope?' Osterfeld said.

'He is gone,' said a cheery voice from the other side. 'Little Charles will never be coming back.'

'Who are you? Did Yukio send you? I'm alone in here. It's perfectly safe. Come and get me out of these things,' Osterfeld spoke more quickly as relief infused his words. Whoever was outside had surely come to help him. Maybe Hagihara was a miracle worker after all?

'Oh dear,' the man outside huffed.

'What's wrong?' Osterfeld called out, 'I've told you it's safe to come in here.'

'I was trying a little experiment. I have to say, this is a bit of a let-down.'

'What are you talking about? Why won't you show yourself?'

'I'd been told that the light of the devil shines from their eyes. That's what it says in the Bible. Now, you're in the dark I can see there is no light shining from your eyes. Still, not to worry, metaphorical can be as important as literal, can't it?'

The hairs on Osterfeld's body stood to attention. He managed to control himself and said, 'I'm sorry, I don't know what you are referring to.'

'That's lovely. How polite you are,' said the man outside. 'I know what will be fun. Let's play a little game.'

Osterfeld's head was swimming. From nowhere he had found himself in an alien world where he did not understand the rules or even know if rules existed.

The man outside said, 'knock, knock.'

Osterfeld said, 'what? What do you mean?'

'Come on Hans, be a sport, play the game. You need to say, who's there.'

Osterfeld found himself saying uncertainly, 'who is there?'

There was delight in the laughter outside. The stranger said, 'the authority.'

Osterfeld could somehow not stop from saying, 'the authority who?'

There was the sound of hand clapping from outside, followed by the response, 'the authority to drive out demons that's who.'

The door sprang open. Silhouetted against the light from the landing a figure stepped into the doorway. His head turned towards the electric toaster and kitchen implements that were still where Charles Hope had put them.

Ernst Mannson looked at the still tightly bound Osterfeld and said, excitedly, 'Hans, my boy, are we going to have a good time with those.'

Then Mannson slowly tilted his head from side to side as if he was having an afterthought.

After that, he said, 'well maybe not such a good time for you...'

CHAPTER SEVEN

Harman walked up the ramp of the *Sunborn* in the centre of the marina. It was advertised as the world's first five-star super yacht hotel and had long since become a focal point for the enclave's social scene. All of which was irrelevant to him. All that mattered was that, according to Osterfeld, Hagihara was staying at *that floating hotel.* As this was the only one of those in Gibraltar, it was where Harman had come.

He reached the reception desk, waited while the couple ahead of him checked out and said to the smiling woman who greeted him, 'Hi, I've got a meeting with Mr Hagihara, and I was wondering if you could tell him that I'm here.'

She asked him to bear with her while she checked a computer console. She said, 'I'm sorry. He checked out this morning. Was he expecting you?'

'Yes, he was,' Harman said, looking crestfallen. 'Something must have come up.'

'Is there anything else I can help you with?' she said breezily, like an AI programme that knew communication but not empathy.

'I don't suppose you could tell me where he was going and when he left?'

'I'm afraid we don't have that

information, sir, and, if we did, it would be confidential. You will appreciate that we must protect the privacy of our clientele.'

His voice deepened and his eyes locked on hers. He said, 'is there anything you can tell me about where he was going?'

For her, the world condensed into the man in front of her. All she wanted to do was help him if she could. There was no protesting inner voice to remind her about the importance of confidentiality. Her answer slipped out as smoothly as honey from a pot, 'he did ask us to book a taxi to take him to the airport. He left about two hours ago.'

'You've been most helpful,' Harman said. 'You have a good day.'

Something about the way he spoke, left her sure that she would indeed have a good day. The next customer approached her before she could think about it any further.

Harman left the comfort of the hotel and hurried outside. Despite the proximity of the airport, he got into the first of two taxis that were waiting at the nearby rank and told the driver to get him there. Hagihara had at least two hours start on him, and he couldn't risk that gap getting any bigger.

He struck lucky on the short journey because the barrier across the runway was up, and they went straight through. The full title of the small but perfectly formed airport was

Gibraltar International, but as soon as he was through the glass doors and inside all he could see on the departures board were flights to London. Two airlines were represented. The booth for British Airways was closest. He went to that one to begin with.

It was pretty much a re-run of his conversation with the hotel receptionist. For the second time in a few minutes, he struck lucky. This time his helper was a smartly turned-out young man who carried the whiff of freshly applied deodorant. After initial resistance, he too told Harman what he needed to know. Mr Yukio Hagihara had booked a one-way ticket to Geneva, Switzerland. He had already departed on the first leg of the trip to London Heathrow. He would have a brief lay over there, before his flight to Geneva. He was scheduled to arrive there at 17.50 local time.

As he was already standing in an airport terminal, Harman was sorely tempted to get on the next flight. He thought better of it. Sebastian Kent was forever banging on about the arrogance of Ascendants. If he was right, Harman did not want to fall into that trap. They had captured him once and it would be beyond arrogance to offer himself up for the same treatment again. It would constitute unforgiveable stupidity. Only the fear of losing Hagihara, and by association Virginia Brightwell, had prompted such a reckless notion in the first place.

He found a quite spot outside and phoned Charles Hope. It was short and to the point. After assuring Hope that all was well, Harman told him to forget about Gibraltar and get on the first flight he could to Geneva. They would meet up there.

Harman had already spotted that there was one lonely taxi waiting by the airport. It was the one that had dropped him off. He tossed his barely used umbrella into a trash can and crossed over. On seeing him the driver did a double take.

'Malaga Airport please,' Harman said brusquely.

'Are you sure?' The man said glancing back at the terminal. 'Has your plane been cancelled or something?'

'No, I was due to meet a colleague, but he's been re-routed to Malaga. What you gonna do?' Harman made sure to sound suitably exasperated so that his hastily constructed lie would bear some hallmark of credibility.

It was not until they had crossed the border and were in Spain that it occurred to Harman that he did not have to lie. He could have influenced the driver to get what he wanted without constructing a deception. It was in that instant that he truly understood why Ascendants like Brightwell treated Normals with disdain. If they could readily be turned to your will, then why engage with them at any human level if you did not need to? Maybe

Kent has been right all along. Arrogance would be a ready by-product of such thinking. He had been an Ascendant for no time at all compared to Brightwell. And yet, he was already being tempted down that same contemptuous path.

The famous quote about the tendency of power to corrupt sprang to mind. He struggled to recall the quote in full. Using the search engine on his phone he looked it up. Something told him it was from George Orwell because he had read both *1984* and *Animal Farm* when he was at school, and it sounded Orwellian. He was surprised to find he was wrong. It came from Lord Acton, whoever he was, and included, *'Power tends to corrupt and absolute power corrupts absolutely. Great men are almost always bad men, even when they exercise influence and not authority...'*

The phrase 'even when they exercise influence' blazed out at him like a searchlight acquiring its target. The coincidence didn't just speak to him, it screamed aloud. Maybe Lord Acton had been an Ascendant, and this was a hidden message to those faced with the same moral conundrum? He shut down that line of thought. It would get him no further than a hamster on a wheel. He could not afford to be distracted from the challenge that was right in front of him. If he could get to Hagihara, he could get to Brightwell. After that, he would hopefully have many years to muse about the abuse of power.

*

A khaki Toyota Land Cruiser pulled up outside the house where Hans Osterfeld had been hiding. A small Israeli flag hung limp from a radio antenna that was mounted at the rear. Four men in drab olive-green overalls sprang out. Three carried assault rifles at the ready. One had a shotgun. They all wore body armour. They all had Jericho semi-automatic pistols in holsters hanging from tactical belts. It was only the lack of insignia on their uniforms that hinted that they were anything other than members of the Israeli Defence Force.

Without a word being said they ran up the stairs to the front door. The one with the shotgun braced his feet and rapidly fired door breaching cartridges into the upper and lower hinges. He stepped back allowing one of the others to kick at the door until the loosened and partially destroyed hinges gave way. The door crashed back. They filed in. Like the professionals they were, they efficiently cleared each room, moving on to the next when sure there were no threats and no sign of Osterfeld. They had each studied pictures of the German before arriving. They knew who they were there to save. If they encountered anyone else, they would take them down before moving on.

With the perfect mix of caution and speed they flowed down to the kitchen. After repeating the clearance process on that level, they went to the basement. It was after checking that the sauna was unoccupied did one of them kneel beside the body of Osterfeld and check for a pulse. Having seen the amount of blood on the floor, the mercenary did not expect to find any sign of life. However, the effects of extreme violence were sometimes unpredictable, and he had learned to make sure.

He turned to his companions and made a cutting gesture across his throat to indicate that they were too late to rescue their target. They wheeled away and headed back to their vehicle.

The man who had checked on Osterfeld rose smoothly to his feet. In the course of his profession, he had committed and witnessed torture. As he stood over what was left of Osterfeld, he reflected that he had still not seen anything like that before. He stared at the bloodied sockets and wondered what had happened to the dead man's eyes. Whoever had done that had gone far beyond what was required to extract information. He did not dwell on it. It was none of his business. And any residual interest he might have would dissolve as soon as he had reported their findings to their paymaster and the agreed funds were in their accounts.

*

Ernst Mannson arrived at Ben Gurion International Airport about five minutes before the mercenaries hired by Yukio Hagihara stormed the house in Komemiyut. With his head lowered he went to the gift shop. He acquired an I-love-Tel Aviv baseball cap. After pulling it down so that it hid half of his face, he made his way to the departures area. In locations where the risk of terrorist attacks was high, security and surveillance were of a commensurate standard. No more so than in Israel. As well as he could predict the location of CCTV cameras, it would be impossible to hide his features from all of them. That didn't mean he would make their work easier. Under the cover of the cap and by making subtle adjustments to the angle of his head, he was sure that he could avoid any instantaneous matches on facial recognition databases. That was all he wanted. If subsequent diligent examination of the data identified him then good luck to them. He would already be far away.

He was fired up. It was always that way after extinguishing the light from a demon. He struggled to contain the release of energy. He did not have the luxury of revelling in it. Not this time around. Airports were dangerous places. Even for the likes of him, their security systems provided a challenge. He had to concentrate On combating that challenge. He could revel in his success once he was staring out of an aeroplane window at the Mediterranean Sea thousands of feet below. Until then, he refused to be distracted.

Ideally, he would not be there at all. There were less high-profile methods of travel, but where Charles Hope went, he went. If he was to complete the mission that God had entrusted to him, then the pathetic figure of Hope, that snivelling excuse for an Ascendant, was essential in leading him to his prey. That task was made even easier when Alan Harman was not around to complicate matters. Whenever Hope was left to his own devices, it made Mannson's life simpler and so today was a good day. Hope should have got there about an hour earlier. It would be easy to ride on his coat tails again.

Mannson had much to thank Hope for, not that his gratitude would save the gawky, stuttering idiot. When the time came, Hope would have to go. The little man was such an irritant that Mannson had been tempted on many occasions to get rid of him, but while he served a purpose he would be allowed to exist.

*

Sebastian Kent was sleeping on the green leather Chesterfield sofa that faced the open fireplace of his Victorian home. A combination of painkillers and malt scotch whisky had helped to numb the ache in his leg and the pain of his suspension from ET1. They hadn't stopped him having the familiar stress dream that visited him regularly. He was running. He didn't know what from. All that mattered was that he had to get home, but he couldn't remember where it was. A procession of people flickered through his fantasy. He knew them all. In his dream they all denied any knowledge of him. They couldn't tell him where his home was.

He was still deep in the unsettling vision when his phone rang. He blearily came to wakefulness. Apart from the glowing embers in the grate, the room was grey and shadowy. With part of his mind still latching on to the dream, he rubbed his eyes. He tried to sit up. It was a mistake. Pain radiated from the hole in his thigh. He checked the call identifier, saw that it was Amy Bishop, and accepted it.

'I don't remember ordering a wake-up call,' he muttered.

'Is everything alright, Sebastian?' she said, defaulting to her doctor's tone.

He coughed. It set off the pain in his leg again. He tenderly rubbed the muscles in his upper leg as he said, 'forget it, I was in the middle of something. You have my complete attention. What have you got for me?'

'How do you know I have anything at all?'

'Come on, Amy, don't play games. You wouldn't call just to enquire about the state of my health.'

'I did when you were in hospital in Denver.'

'Yes, I suppose you did. I'm grateful for that.'

'Gosh, such sincerity.'

'Are you being sarcastic?'

'Were you?'

Kent's scarred face puckered with impatience. He said, 'as much as I enjoy sparring with you, I'm sure there is a purpose behind your call. If that's the case, then why are you suddenly reluctant to tell me what it is?'

'I'm not one of life's natural rule breakers.'

'It's too late for cold feet, Amy.'

'Cold? It is worse than that. They're feeling positively frost bitten.'

'And yet you still picked up your phone and dialled my number...'

'Maybe I'm the one who needs therapy.'

'Amy, stop beating around this very tangled bush, and tell me what you've got,' Kent said, concealing the urgency he was feeling.

The ensuing silence went on for so long that Kent checked the phone's screen to make sure the connection had not been lost.

When she did speak, the hesitancy was gone. She was a professional transmitting hard information to another professional.

'The man that you believe you recognised may have been seen at Ben Gurion International Airport. The match is far from perfect. If we weren't actively searching it wouldn't have been picked up, but I am confident it is him.'

'Why so sure?'

'The use of a baseball cap and the way he moves. If I hadn't had the previous shots to compare it with, I would never have noticed. Any behaviourist can tell they are not natural ticks or mannerisms. They are small, yet deliberate, movements to obscure his face whenever he knows he's near a camera. Nobody would give it a second thought unless they were specifically looking for them.'

They were once more on an open line and so Kent knew why she wasn't using the man's name, even though he had given it to her. They were both aware of who it was, and so naming him didn't matter. As Bishop was never one to jump to conclusions, he readily took her at her word. If she believed that the man he had recognised and the man at Ben Gurion airport were one and the same, it was enough for him.

Kent said, 'How old is the information?'

'I called you as soon as I was satisfied, but the timestamp on the film is from over six hours ago.'

'Damn, why so long?'

'If I'd put a priority flag on the request, it would have set alarm bells blaring at every intelligence organisation around the world. As it is, I'm amazed we got anything this quickly. You can thank whatever god you hold dear that he happened to be in Israel where their efficiency is a glory to behold. Anywhere else and it could have been weeks rather than hours.'

'I will happily count my blessings if you can tell me where he is now.'

'All I can tell you is that he boarded an easyJet flight to Geneva. It's non-stop. Flight time is 4 hours, 40 minutes.'

'So, he reached Switzerland before we'd even heard he was in Israel. That trail is going even colder than your feet.'

'You will be wanting to get on your way then. I've booked you on the 20.15 flight from Heathrow. Don't forget your passport.'

'Any update on Alan's whereabouts?' Kent said while simultaneously calculating how long it would take him to get to the airport.

'Not a word. Do you want me to contact Interpol, Europol, the Swiss…'

'Absolutely not. That would raise more questions than we've got answers for. From here on in we consume our own smoke as much as we can. This is a long shot, but at least it's a shot.'

'What about the Embassy? They might be able to furnish you with local support if you need it.'

'Scratch that. I can get what I need from people who will be much less inquisitive.'

'Like whom?'

'Best you don't know. The more plausible deniability you have the better. If things go wrong again, there's no need for us both to go down with the ship. That's the captain's role, not the medical officer. Unless there's anything else, I'd best get on with a quick bit of packing.'

'Do your best not to get shot again, won't you?'

'If there's any shooting, I intend to be the one doing it.'

'Brave words, Sebastian. It's always riveting to observe men when they are being macho.'

'You know you would be easier to work with if you didn't make the rest of us feel like we were part of some big psychiatric experiment for you?'

She laughed. He could tell it was genuine and that pleased him.

She said, 'I will try to do better.'

'Don't worry about that. All I need you to do is keep ET1 in good shape until I can take control of it again.'

'After all that's happened, do you genuinely think you will?'

'It's that or I will die trying,' he said, and unlike her he was not laughing.

CHAPTER EIGHT

From where Harman was standing on the concourse, he could see everyone exiting the arrivals area at Geneva Airport. He sipped a coffee. He seemed to have bought it more out of habit than desire. One downside of becoming an Ascendant was that his taste buds now refused to take any pleasure from coffee. The bitterness of the drink had been multiplied. It was like an acrid flavour bomb exploding in his mouth. Despite that, he still found himself going to places like the fast food stand a few feet away and to Koko's Koffee Kafe. He wasn't sure why he did it. Maybe it was more than habitual behaviour. Maybe it was because it was a familiar comforting anchor that tethered him to his old life. His reflections on the subject were cut short by the sight of Charles Hope's arrival.

Above his heavily tinted spectacles, Hope's forehead was deeply creased by a frown. His head was down, and his shoulders were drawn in. It was as if he was already braced against an attack. While passengers broke around him like a rushing stream around a rock, he gazed about the cathedral of transport. Aeroplanes were behind him. Ahead was the railway station, a caravan of buses, and a lengthy queue for taxis. A parade of drivers holding up signs partly obscured his view. He momentarily thought to see if his name was on any of them. He immediately dismissed the notion. Only one man knew he was coming and his new brother in arms would hardly have advertised their presence.

When his eyes eventually alighted on Harman, his face lit up. If he had a tail, it would have been wagging.

Harman tossed what was left of his coffee into a trash can and backed away to the rear of a news stand. It was as remote a spot as he could find in the congested travel hotspot.

A panting Hope followed him there and said, 'I can't tell you what a relief it is to catch up with you.'

'I told you it would be alright, didn't I?'

'And that sounded fine until you had gone. Please don't ever leave me in a situation like that again.'

'Deep breaths, Charles, always remember to keep taking deep breaths. You are here now and you're all in one piece. You can relax.'

'I've been so tense that I ache all over. That can't be good.'

Harman was glad that he hadn't bought a coffee for Hope. His ally was jittery enough already. Before he could concentrate on calming him down there was a lose end that he had to tie up. He said, 'how was Mr Osterfeld when you left him?'

Hope said, 'he still wasn't happy. I wish you had gagged him before you left. He was saying such horrible things.'

'You could have gagged him if it was bothering you that much.'

Hope looked as if Harman had just suggested that he amputate his own toes. He said, 'you've got another thing coming if you think I'd get that close to him.'

'He's suffered enough,' Harman said. 'It is time to get him out of there.'

'What if he warns Brightwell or Hagihara?'

'They already know I'm coming, Charles, you can bet your last dollar on that.'

Harman held up a finger to stop Hope talking and took out the new payphone he had acquired less than an hour ago. *Acquired* was the word he had adopted for himself when thinking about items that he had influenced somebody to give him. It sat more easily than constantly reminding himself that what he was actually doing was stealing. He dialled in the international code for Israel and then the 7 digits of the police authority that covered the town of Komemiyut. The call handler tried to keep him in conversation, but Harman kept his message short and to the point. He told the man at the other end that Osterfeld was being held prisoner, he gave the address, pleaded for urgent help and then cut the call short.

'Will that work?' Hope said. 'I don't like the thought of him being left down there to starve.'

'They're good at their job. It won't take much for them to see that the garden door was recently forced open. They'll have him out in no time.'

'If you're sure…'

'He's not your responsibility, Charles. If you've got any doubts, then remember what he's been part of. I'd say he's got off lightly, wouldn't you?'

'More lightly than Thibault Blanc and Daiyu Chen,' Hope mumbled.

'Hey, their deaths are not our fault.'

'We led somebody to them, didn't we?'

'Maybe we did and maybe we didn't. We can't let that put us off our stride.'

Hope's voice wavered as he said, 'but what if we led that man Mannson or somebody else to Osterfeld as well?'

Harman grabbed Hope's bicep. He squeezed it more than he had intended to as he said harshly, 'did you see anyone before you left the house? Was anyone outside? Could you have been followed? Think carefully.'

'No, I took every precaution, just like you told me.'

'But? You were going to say but, weren't you?'

Hope's head turned sharply in different directions like a bird making sure it was safe before dipping down to pick crumbs off the ground. He said, 'I didn't see anyone, I promise. It's...well...I've had this feeling. You will think I'm being childish...'

Harman released Hope and smoothed down his ruffled sleeve. He said, 'I'm sorry, Charles. I must be getting nervous in my old age. The closer I get to Virginia Brightwell, the more I worry that she will get away from me again. Tell me what's on your mind and I give you my solemn word that I won't think it's childish.'

Hope inspected Harman's face for any sign that it could be concealing a snigger. When he was sure that Harman had meant what he said did Hope's resolve collapse. He said, 'it's like there's a dark cloud that's getting closer. I can't see it and I can't touch it. I couldn't even describe it to you properly. All I know is that when it reaches me, I will die. There will be no more Charles Hope. I will disappear as if I've never existed.'

He spoke with such conviction and with an absence of high drama that Harman was sure that Hope believed what he was saying. If it had been a child speaking, Harman would have been moved to hug him close. As it was, it was one man expressing his inner fears to another man. Hope's frankness and vulnerability left Harman at a loss for words. He wanted to reassure him but wasn't sure how. Whether it was the best response or not, his brain defaulted to cheery bravado. He said, 'not on my watch, Charles. If that cloud ever shows up, I will be the biggest umbrella ever. I give you my word on that, ok?'

'I believe you will do your best to keep me safe.'

Harman heard the doubt that infected every syllable of that sentence. The doubt was not whether Harman would do his best, it was rather that his best would not be enough.

'Good, let's get after Hagihara then.'

'How? He could have gone anywhere from here.'

'It's not so much where he went, it's how. This is someone who enjoys living well. In Gibraltar, he could have stayed somewhere low key. He chose the best hotel. He could have walked to the airport. Instead, he caught a cab. He raises money for Brightwell, and I'd say he enjoys spending it as well.'

'And how does that help us?'

'Easy. Assuming he didn't choose Switzerland at random, he's not someone who'd get on a crowded bus or train to take him to his next stop. If it's Geneva itself then maybe a taxi, although I don't imagine him wanting to stand in line with a crowd of Normals.'

'What about self-drive?'

'Come on, Charles, try to get inside the head of this man. He knows he's better than the Normals and almost certainly believes he's better than most Ascendants. He's used to and expects others to do things for him. So why do something as grubby as driving yourself when you can have somebody do it for you? My money is on him arranging for a limousine to pick him up.'

'What if you're wrong?'

'Then we will have a lot more leg work to do. What do you say to us trusting my hypothesis first?' Harman said, pointing back at the long line of drivers still holding up placards.

Hope stared at the line of mainly male chauffeurs. He said, 'if that's what you think, why haven't you spoken to them already?'

'I wanted to wait for you first, Charles. We're a team, aren't we?'

'A team?' Hope brightened as if the cloud he feared had been blown away by a gale, 'yes, I suppose we are. I'd get nowhere without you.'

'That's the spirit, Charles. This team is closing in for the kill and you've earned the right to be there. Come on.'

Harman used the airport wi-fi to access the website of the Genomic Sciences Centre in Yokohama. Sure enough, Yukio Hagihara still appeared on the list of academics complete with a photograph and potted biography. He expanded the picture so that it filled the screen of his cell phone and then approached the line of drivers. A few were in uniform. Most were in business suits. Only the older men wore ties. He quickly concocted a story that would encourage them to give him a few seconds and view the photograph.

He began with a man at the end of the line who was checking his watch and had yet to raise the card in his hands. Harman apologised for bothering him, said he was working for the man in the picture, Mr Hagihara, and explained that the Japanese visitor had lost his wallet, and he was seeking to retrieve it. Unfortunately, nothing had so far been handed in to the police. He was therefore asking around to see if it might have slipped down the back of the seat of the car that had collected him from the airport. Unfortunately, again, Mr Hagihara was an elderly gentleman who could not recall which limo company he had used or anything of note about the car or driver. There would, naturally, be a sizeable reward for the wallet's return. It was this hook at the end that made the difference.

The first driver shook his head sadly. He looked like someone who had lost a winning lottery ticket. He did not recognise the man in the picture. Harman went down the line, sounding increasingly apologetic and aware of Hope's faith in him draining away. None of them remembered picking Hagihara up. Harman consoled himself with the thought that different drivers must be coming in and out all the time. It was too soon to give up hope. He waited for the line to freshen up and an hour later tried again.

This time the fourth person he approached, a woman in her thirties, said she remembered the old man.

Harman kept his sense of relief under wraps as he said, 'and where did you take him?'

The woman's expectancy changed to suspicion. She said in a strong French accent, 'if you are working for this gentleman, then you must know where he is.'

Harman inwardly winced at his foolish mistake. He recovered by saying, 'of course I do, but how else can I know if you were the driver who took him there?'

She mulled that over, shrugged, and said, 'the Lausanne Palace Hotel, but our cars are cleaned every night, and a wallet would have been found.'

'That is disappointing,' Harman said, keeping up the pretext, 'he really can't imagine where he might have lost it.'

The woman leaned closer to him. Her nostrils went up like a puppet on a string. She said as if it left a bad taste in her mouth, 'pickpockets. Gypsies. They are like a plague.'

'You really think so? Here in Geneva?' Harman made it sound like the most preposterous statement he had ever heard.

She said, conspiratorially, 'they try to cover it up, but we know, we know.'

Acting as if it was nothing short of a biblical revelation, Harman said, 'it's a scandal.'

He thanked her and shared his gem of information with Hope.

They contacted Hertz rentals and an hour later were experiencing the scenic drive from Geneva to Lausanne. Once out of the city the road hugged Lake Geneva. To their left it was mainly farmland and beyond that the soaring mountains of the snow-capped Alps. The light had faded before they arrived. Harman used the built-in Satnav to guide them to the hotel. Not wanting to park immediately outside for all to see he kept going up the hill, past shops and bars. There were plenty of people about, although the prevalence of coats and scarves was an indicator of how quickly the temperature had fallen after dark.

They left the car in the first residential street they came to and walked back. Hope shivered more than once. He didn't complain. He knew it was best to let Harman concentrate and get on with it, whatever it might be.

A row of columns guarded the hotel entrance. Above them flew the flags of the hotel, Switzerland, and the Olympics. There was even a red carpet that led up the few small steps and into the hotel itself. They followed along it, past the doorman, past expensive furniture, past glass-paned doors, and chandeliers hanging from the high ceiling.

Harman said, 'they weren't kidding when they called it a palace, were they?'

Hope said, 'I'm not accustomed to such opulence.'

'I told you, Charles, Yukio Hagihara likes his luxury comforts.'

Waiters in white shirts and black waistcoats were serving drinks in one of the lounge areas. Casually dressed people in expensive clothes sauntered around. Nobody seemed to be in a rush, and nothing seemed to be hurried.

The hotel reception was more functional, but it and its staff were immaculate. Harman knew that the Swiss were jealous of their privacy and extended that tendency to their guests. Swiss banks were internationally famous for it and the top hotels held themselves to that same high standard. Harman wouldn't waste his breath on the kind of ruse he had used at the airport. He would have to acquire the information he wanted, and he would have to do it where the conversation could not be heard.

There were sufficient staff behind the counter that he did not have to wait. He caught the eye of a young woman, also in white shirt and black waistcoat, who smiled professionally at him and asked if she could help.

Harman said, 'it's a rather delicate matter regarding one of your guests. I wonder if I could speak to the manager?'

She eyed him as she might if he had asked for a personal introduction to God and said, 'perhaps it is something that I can assist you with?'

Harman admired the way that she had switched to flawless English as soon as he had spoken. He was less happy with the doubt in her voice. It was time to use the influence. He wished he had an alternative. A voice in his head apologised to her before he said, 'tell me who is in charge here and then get him for me.'

'It is Monsieur Marin. I will get him for you.'

As she slipped through a door behind the counter, Harman was struck by how easy it had been. He had not had to try, let alone concentrate hard. It was like realising that your car could do 120mph, when all you wanted from it was to stay inside the speed limit.

Seemingly able to read Harman's thoughts, Hope said quietly, 'very impressive. I don't think I've seen any Ascendant evolve so quickly.'

Harman didn't know if that was a rare attempt at sarcasm from Charles Hope or genuine appreciation. Either way, the look that he shot him served to shut the other man up again.

The door reopened and a dapper middle-aged man appeared followed by the receptionist. She was downcast and Harman could picture her boss being irritated by her unwarranted intrusion on his time.

The man approached. His smile was

welcoming, his eyes less so. His golden tie pin glittered in the light from the chandeliers. He said, 'good evening, sir, my name is Jacques Marin. I am the duty manager. How can I be of service?'

Harman saw there was no prospect of sweet talking this one and for some reason felt much less guilty about influencing him than he had his younger and subordinate colleague. While holding Marin's gaze as if it was in a vice, Harman said, 'you will take me and my friend to your office and you will tell your staff that you are not to be disturbed? Do you understand me?'

There was the merest flicker of his eyelashes before Marin invited Harman to follow him. First, he opened the side door that gave Harman and Hope access to the sanctity of the staff-only space. Oblivious to the shocked glances from the four staff who were working there, he told them he was not to be bothered. He took Harman and Hope into his office. As soon as the door was closed behind them, the reception team began to gossip about his unprecedented behaviour.

Harman said, 'Jacques, I would like you to access the guest records from the terminal on your desk and tell me which room Yukio Hagihara is staying in.'

Marin said, 'of course, sir, please give me a moment while I do that for you.'

While Marin's fingers flew across the

keyboard with the precision and speed of a concert pianist, Hope said, 'even under influence, he likes to provide a top-quality service.'

'Maybe I just bring the best out of people, Charles.'

'Umm, I wonder if you could bring the worst out of them as well?'

There was something about the cryptic remark that rankled, and it caused Harman to snap back at him as he said, 'what is that supposed to mean?'

'Nothing, Alan, nothing at all. I was merely thinking out aloud.'

Before Harman could stoke the minor spat, Marin looked up from his screen and said, 'I'm afraid we have no record of a Mr Hagihara.'

Harman chastised himself. For a career policeman there was no excuse for ignoring one of the golden rules: if you ask the wrong question, you will inevitably get the wrong answer. If Hagihara was the last link to Brightwell, she would never have let him register under his own name. He asked Marin to check again to see if anyone with a Japanese name had checked in during the last twenty-four hours.

Marin checked again. He said, 'two. Mr and Mrs Matimo. A lovely couple. They are here on their honeymoon.'

Harman said, 'is there any chance that they are an elderly couple?'

'Definitely not, sir.'

Staring down a dead end, Harman threw the dice one more time and said, 'okay, Jacques, I know that a car service dropped Mr Hagihara off here. Do you have any record at all of him, or someone Japanese who wasn't the Matimo family, on any of your systems?'

'Yes, a Mr Kobayashi. He had made a reservation, but it was cancelled yesterday. Ah, that's unusual.'

'What is?' Harman said more calmly than he was feeling.

'No payment method is recorded. It's something that we of course require for any booking. I can't understand why it is absent.'

'Does anything on there say when the booking was cancelled, and whether it was done online, by phone or in person?'

Marin smiled obsequiously and checked again. After a swish of the mouse and a few keyboard clicks, he said, 'oh, I am not happy with that. There is a footnote here to say that one of our other guests cancelled on his behalf.'

'And who was that, Jacques?'

'Madame Beauchamp.'

'Would it be possible for me to speak to her?'

'Unfortunately, not, she checked out earlier today.'

Harman ignored Hope's groan of frustration and said, 'Would Madame Beauchamp by any chance be around sixty years of age, blonde, with blue eyes?'

A look of bliss fixed itself on Marin's face and he said, 'yes, a lovely lady.'

Harman said to Hope, 'that's Virginia Brightwell alright. If you ask any member of staff here who's had any dealings with her, they will say the same thing, using the exact same four words.'

'Are you sure? Are we that close to her?'

'There's no need to sound so nervous all the time, Charles. This is what we've been working towards. Feel free to give yourself a pat on the back.'

'It is really her, isn't it?'

'Peter Salt did the same thing. When Carol and I first investigated him, everyone we spoke to said he was a lovely man. It didn't mean they remembered nothing else about him, but it was the bedrock of how they felt. He instilled it in them as part of his social camouflage. It's no surprise that his sister has it in her game book as well. I suppose it's something they developed when growing up together and it stayed with them. Take it from me, that Virginia Brightwell is so close that we are almost treading on her toes.'

Hope shivered again and this time it wasn't caused by the cold.

Harman said, 'thank you, Jacques, that is very helpful. I'm sure that Madame Beauchamp will not have left a forwarding address, but is there anything else at all that you can tell me about her?'

Marin rested his chin in his hands while he thought about it. He could not have explained why, but he felt an irresistible need to help the Englishman as much as he possibly could. Eventually, he said, 'I recall her saying once that she had enjoyed a lovely walk down by the lake. She used to go out a lot. Mainly she ate in her room. Occasionally she would dine in one of our restaurants. She is a lovely lady.'

'Could you see if she dined here today?' Harman's said, his question sounding like a command.

Marin accessed the booking records and said, 'yes, a table for two at the Brasserie. 6.00pm'

Harman checked his watch. It was 8.45pm. He quickly told Marin to go back to his normal business and then he hustled Hope outside. Ignoring the curious faces of the reception staff, Harman and Hope followed the hotel signs to the Brasserie. Harman had no idea what he would do if forced to confront her in such a public setting, but he would worry about that if he found her there.

Bursting into the open eating area, Harman scurried past the tables. His eyes hungrily devoured each for any sign of Brightwell and Hagihara. Mouths drooped down and noses tilted up as diners resented the disturbance to their dining experience. When his tour had proved fruitless, he swore and said to Hope, 'just for a second I really thought we might catch them here.'

'Even if we had, what could you have done?'

'Done? I would have done whatever it takes to stop her,' Harman said angrily. 'It doesn't matter what happens to me after that.'

'Are you saying you would have killed her, right here, in front of all these people,' Hope said, managing to sound simultaneously both mesmerised and horrified.

'Forget that. Wherever she is, we can't be far behind her. She's been here for a while, and it won't have been to hide. That's not her style. Something around here has held her in place. We find that. We find her.'

As they came back into the main part of the hotel, Hope said, 'but it could be anything.'

'Keep the faith, Charles. You'd be surprised how far leg work can get you.'

'It's a bit late in the night for marching aimlessly up and down the streets of Lausanne, isn't it?'

'We can't afford to be despondent. Come on.'

Harman led them back to the grand entrance. The doorman that they had ignored on their way in, now drew them like pins to a magnet. Harman showed him the photograph of

Hagihara and asked if he remembered the man leaving.

The doorman confirmed that the Japanese gentleman and Madame Beauchamp, who was a lovely lady, had got into a taxi not half an hour before. He was sure it was from a local cab company but had not paid much attention to it and so could not say which one. Harman thanked him and trudged back to the reception. Without the need to exert any influence, he asked whether they might have a list of local taxi firms. A helpful young man, clearly well-schooled in his duties by Jacques Marin, printed out a list for him, placed it in a hotel-branded envelope and passed it over to him.

The night air bit into them as they left the hotel and returned to their hire car. Hope complained that he was dressed for the Middle East and not for the mountains. Harman corrected him by pointing out that they might be surrounded by the mountains, but he wasn't asking Hope to climb them. Nevertheless, he took partial pity on him by pausing at a Turkish café to pick up a couple of coffees and two kebabs.

Only when they were back outside that Harman silently ask himself why he had again bought coffee to go with his food. When they were settled in the car, Harman put the heating on and entered the first address in the Satnav. Hope stopped hugging his cardboard coffee cup just long enough to tear the paper from around his kebab and scoff the hot meat down. Harman stared at his own kebab. He had lost his appetite. He lowered his window and dropped it into the kerb outside. The full coffee container followed it. What to do next wasn't complicated. Like he had said to Hope, it was just more legwork.

And so, he got on with it.

One by one he drove to the taxi offices on his list. They struck out at the first three companies. It was after 10.00pm when they reached the fourth and it was closed. There was one more at the smart end of the market. It seemingly had little interest in call outs from late night revellers because it was already shut. The fifth, in contrast, was like an ant's nest with drivers and cars coming and going in a whirl. The busy dispatcher was in no mood for nosey enquiries from non-paying customers, but in between calls assured Harman that they had had no pick-ups from the Lausanne Palace since mid-afternoon. The last stop was on the edge of town. As they drove through the quieter streets of the suburb, Harman's already limited optimism deserted him. Sure enough, when they pulled up outside an unlit shop front, he knew that his optimism had made the smart choice.

Hope said, 'four down and two no shows. What now?'

Harman bit back on an impulse to vent his spleen on Hope. It wouldn't have been fair, and it wouldn't have been right. Hope didn't have to be there.   He could have left at any time. Harman had made that clear to him. But he had stayed as they had travelled half-way across the world and the bodies of Ascendants and others had piled up behind them. Hope had said when they first met that he was there as a favour to Peter Salt. To Harman, Hope had already gone above and beyond whatever Salt had wanted or expected of him. He had earned Harman's gratitude and not his scorn.

And so, instead of letting a black mood blind him, Harman chortled and said, 'what is that line from *Gone With The Wind?* Tomorrow is another day?'

'No offence meant,' Hope said, 'but you're too ugly to play Scarlett O'Hara.'

'I can't argue with that, Charles. We've done all we can tonight. We can come back to the two outstanding companies tomorrow. Until then I think you've earned a good night's sleep in an opulent hotel.'

'The Lausanne Palace?   That would be great.'

Harman smiled and said, 'I happen to know the duty manager there. I'm sure he could be persuaded to find us a couple of rooms....'

*

Yukio Hagihara used his handkerchief to brush away the dust from the seat before warily sitting down on it. The naked bulb that lit the storeroom at the boatyard was not strong enough to reach every corner and Hagihara did not want to think about what might be there. He did not try to hide his disdain for the three camping beds, even though each had been placed against a different wall to provide some semblance of order. The rolled up sleeping bags that lay on the beds were shop bought and still in their plastic wrappings.

'I ask you again, Ginny, is this necessary? I would have been much happier at that rather pleasant hotel.'

'We both would, Old Man, but when we are so close it would be foolish to take any unnecessary chances, wouldn't it?'

'Pah, there isn't an Ascendant in the world who could stand against us when we are together. This woman who is made nervous by some child is not the woman I know.'

Brightwell did not want to discuss Alan Harman. The Ascendant she had awoken in the caves of Colorado was a very different proposition to when she had originally met him as a plodding Normal back at Marston Creek in England. He had frightened her. It was an emotion she was unaccustomed to and one she despised in herself and in others. That had not stopped it erupting inside of her as word came in of the atrocities he had committed. If he would do that to other Ascendants in order to reach her, what might he be capable of if she was to fall into his hands? She could control that fear as long as she concentrated on what was most important. She was about to usher in the Ascendancy which would lead to her people, her kind, inheriting the Earth as evolution demanded that they should.

She replied to Hagihara, 'tomorrow we change the world forever. Is one short night in this hovel too high a price to pay for that?'

'You have avoided my question about whether all of this cloak and dagger routine is necessary, Ginny. However, your riposte contains a wisdom that I cannot challenge. In my own wisdom, I will pose another question and I would ask that you answer it with complete honesty.'

'Ask away, old friend.'

'Why am I here, Ginny? It is not part of our plan, and my presence adds nothing.'

There was no point in trying to lie to him. He of all people would see through it if she even tried. Brightwell said, 'there is no mystery, Yukio. I want you with me at the moment of our triumph. Over many long years, you above all others have helped me get here. You gave me clarity of purpose when I was a young woman drowning in a sea of anger and confusion.'

The troughs of old age on Hagihara's face deepened as he said, 'that may be true, but I suspect it is only a half truth.'

Brightwell made a clucking noise with her

tongue. There was no deceiving him and it had been a doomed task to try. She said, 'you really do know me well. The whole truth then. Whatever you believe about how strong we are, I have lost everyone else who was in our inner circle. First it was Arnie Jaekal. Most recently it was Hans Osterfeld. They are all gone. You are the last and the most precious to me. It is only if you are with me that I can know with certainty that you are safe. It is no more simple and no more complicated than that.'

Hagihara closed his eyes. His fingers rubbed at his temples. The liver spots on the back of his hands showed that even Ascendants could grow old. He said, 'to fear the monster, is to lose to the monster.'

'If Harman is the monster that he seems to be then I am the one responsible for creating him. I am his Dr Frankenstein.'

'Then the monster must be killed.'

Brightwell was not surprised that he had reached the same conclusion as her. She said, 'we deploy the weapon tomorrow. It cannot be stopped. After that I will turn all my energies to exactly that purpose.'

A key turned in the lock. Brightwell's speech and thought froze. The door swung open. A man in a heavy coat and woollen hat entered. He quickly closed and locked the door behind him.

Brightwell inhaled deeply and relaxed. It

was the man who had kitted out the room as a makeshift barracks. The man for whom the third camp bed was reserved. She said, 'welcome, Zarif, is everything in hand?'

The dark-eyed Moroccan peeled off his tight-fitting hat and ran a hand through his thick, curly hair. He said, 'I've just spoken to the *Duttweiller.* She is on schedule to be here at 7.00am. The submersible is ready to be loaded. The dockhands we hired will be here at 6.00am to begin the preparations. As far as anyone knows, we are scientists undertaking another water testing project on behalf of the government. It's not unheard of on the lake and so nobody outside of the contractors has shown any interest.'

Hagihara said, 'it helps that we pay them so well for their services. Wouldn't you agree Dr Tobji?'

'And that was made possible through your tireless fundraising,' Tobji said.

Brightwell was pleased by Tobji's diplomatic response. The two men had met for the first time that evening and Hagihara with an adept passive aggressive performance had made it clear that he did not appreciate Tobji's involvement. The Moroccan was not and never had been part of her inner circle. To Hagihara he was a scavenger, a jackal who was feeding on the carcass that the lions had worked hard to bring down. For her part, she had no need to explain herself to anyone. That included her oldest and dearest confidante. Ever since she had fled from Harman in Colorado, she had known that the chain made from her circle of key Ascendants could be compromised. She had needed someone that they did know to be her new adjutant. Someone that they could not name because they did not know of his existence. He was already scoping out the planned test in Amekoura, so who better to call upon? He might be a wild card as far as Hagihara was concerned, but he was her wild card to play as she saw fit.

Brightwell said, 'thank you, Zarif. Only someone who has witnessed your efforts could truly appreciate what you have done to get us to this point.'

Hagihara grunted. It could have been with irritation or humour. He was hard to read. He said, 'your meaning is deafening if not subtle, Ginny. I will take it from here that my precious breath would be wasted if doubting the good doctor in any way. It seems you are to be commended Zarif.'

Tobji shrugged off his coat and dropped it on to the camp bed. He bowed from the shoulders and said, 'such a compliment from you means a lot to me.'

Hagihara's eyes narrowed to slits as he tried to divine whether there was some hidden intent behind the other Ascendant's words. Brightwell coughed daintily behind her hand like some well brought up young lady in an Emily Bronte novel. It was a reminder to Hagihara not to press Tobji any further.

Hajihara tilted his head fractionally. It was not quite a nod of acquiescence. It was more an acknowledgement. He said, 'as we are all here and will not be subject to additional interruption, might I beg your indulgence, Ginny?'

'Your wish is mine, you know that to be true,' Brightwell said.

'May I see them?'

'You will not be impressed. They are unremarkable.'

'Even so…'

'Zarif, would you be so kind as to show them to Yukio?'

Tobji reacted to her voice like a well-trained dog to a whistle of command. He opened an old cabinet next to his bed. Inside it was a new top of the range biometric safe. He placed his thumb on the fingerprint reader and then inputted an eight number sequence. There was a momentary hum as the bolts slid back. He pulled it ajar. He drew out a metal case and placed it on his bed. He flipped the latches and raised the lid.

Hagihara did not wait for an invitation before walking to the case. He raised a hand to touch the case's contents and then thought better of it. Set deep in black foam were the phials. Their contents were clear like spring water. There were no labels on the phials. What was inside them had no name. To Brightwell and the two men with her it was simply the weapon. It needed no other identifier.

Unsteadily he got to his knees. He moved closer until his nose was barely two inches from the case. Tears came to his eyes. He eased away before any of the droplets could fall on the phials. It was nothing short of a marvel. When released there would be a fraction of a gram of the toxic material. Once in the water supply it would infest the DNA of every non-Ascendant that it came in to contact with. The changes it would trigger were irreversible and deadly. The scale and genius of Brightwell's endeavour threatened to overwhelm him. A father could not have been prouder of his daughter. Unashamed by his unique display of emotion he stood on aching legs and went to Brightwell.

With a tenderness that neither of them would have believed him capable, he grasped her hand, kissed it, and said simply, 'thank you.'

CHAPTER NINE

The white hull of the *RV Duttweiller* towered over the grey concrete quayside. Its Greek flag drooped at the stern in the dull windless morning. The four-hundred-foot-long research vessel had been built in Finland thirty years ago. Its best days were behind it, but it still had many more to look forward to as long as there were enough scientific projects and film production companies who needed its specialist services. There was accommodation on board for up to ninety people, but for this charter it was down to a bare crew of forty-two.

Six of those, overseen by a deck officer, with the ship's master, Captain Tomasis, watching on from the bridge, were working one of the two cranes that stood near the stern. On the quay, Zarif Tobji was making sure that the dockhands he had hired were handling the Mir submersible with the care they would give to their own children. It was unthinkable to him that after so much planning and sacrifice, Brightwell could be stymied by damage to the Mir that was so critical to her plans. He would not allow it to happen.

His stomach tightened as the Mir was lifted on its cradle. The higher it rose, the more it swayed in its harnesses. Watching eighteen tons of mini submarine floating through the sky was not for the weak hearted. The clanking of the crane mixed with the shouts of men. Tobji's tension eased as he saw the bored expressions of the handlers who were manipulating the submersible. For them this was a basic chore of the sort they undertook regularly. Despite that, Tobji held his breath as the submersible swung over the ship's deck. Its rocking increased. Again, this was met with nothing more than quiet application by the crew. The Mir was lowered out of his sight. There was a sharp thud of metal on metal. The deck officer leaned over the rail and give a thumbs up. Tobji let his breath out.

As the straps and chains were released from the Mir's cradle, Tobji strode back through the boatyard to the office where Brightwell and Hagihara were waiting.

Apart from the idle chatter of workmen, the only sounds came from the screeching birds who were hovering and swooping around the ship in search of discarded scraps.

Before he could get there, they came out to meet him. They did not want to take a single second longer than they had to. Tucked under Brightwell's arm was a non-descript leather bag. Inside it was the metal case that until ten minutes before had been in the hidden safe in the storeroom. Tobji fell into step behind her as she walked to the gangway that had been lowered for them.

The new cargo would be secured before the perfunctory, yet obligatory, welcome was offered to them by Captain Tomasis. The four diesel engines would soon turn. They were capable of driving the ship to a speed of over twelve knots. They would not be required to stretch themselves so far on this trip. They would cruise at half speed. Lake Geneva might have many aspects of the sea, but it was no ocean. At that rate of knots the ship would take a bare fifteen minutes to reach the co-ordinates given by Brightwell to its captain.

Brightwell could not stop herself from looking out across the lake. In her mind's eye she could see exactly where the ship would anchor. She could see the Mir being lowered. She could see it being freed and her piloting it to the precise spot that her extensive modelling had identified. She pictured her hand as it flicked the switch that would release the phials' contents into the underwater stream that coursed through the waterway.

In less than two hours she would make history.

*

Harman strummed his thumbs impatiently on the steering wheel. They had been sitting outside of the office of *Lac Taxis* for half an hour. It felt longer. Much longer.

Harman sighed and said, 'what sort of Mickey Mouse business are they running here? Why aren't they open yet?'

Hope said, 'we could try the other place and then come back here?'

'That one's right across town. I gambled on coming here first. We might as well give it a bit longer.'

'I'm sure you're right, Alan. Good things come to those who wait.'

Harman was about to say that gems of sagacity that were straight out of Christmas Crackers were not what he needed. He stopped himself. It wasn't Hope's fault that he had chosen the wrong place that morning to resume their search. It was his call. His responsibility.

A saloon car pulled up. It had no branding on it, but Harman saw that it carried a taxi licence. He was out of the hire car before the newly arrived driver had reached the shop door.

The man heard Harman approaching. He turned to him and said gruffly, 'we are not open yet, come back later.'

'So much for customer service,' Harman said.

'Go get a taxi somewhere else if you don't like it.'

Harman was in no mood to mess about, and the man's rudeness removed any uncertainty about influencing him. Harman took him by the arm, swung him around, and raised the picture on his phone of Hagihara. He said, 'have you seen this man? He would have been picked up early yesterday-night from the Lausanne Palace.'

The man found it hard to avert his eyes from Harman's gaze. When he did, he scrutinised the picture. He found himself eager to help the stranger. He said, 'yes, he was my last pick up of the day. He was with a woman.'

Harman kept his elation in check. It was too soon to be thinking of success. He had learned that you never had Brightwell until you could feel your fingers pressing into her. He said, 'that's very good, thank you. Please tell me where you dropped them off.'

'The Montaine boatyard. It's on the lake, east of here.'

'How do I get there?'

'Follow the lake road. It stands alone. You will not miss it.'

Harman was not inclined to thank the man again. After all, he had not helped willingly. Hope had barely reached him when Harman turned him around and took him back to their car.

They left the taxi owner scratching his head and wondering what had just happened.

Harman smiled, even though he knew it was premature. He said, 'we are so close, Charles, so close.'

'Excellent, I only hope you know what to do when we get there.'

'It will come to me, don't fret about that. I'm getting the feeling that's what being an Ascendant lets you do.'

Hope coughed like he had swallowed a fly, and said, 'no, it's what it lets you do. It's not the same for us lesser mortals.'

'Surely no Ascendant is a lesser mortal?'

Hope gave him a side eye and said, 'you can tease me all you want, Alan, but you know what I mean.'

Harman wasn't exactly sure what he had meant. It would have to be a discussion for another day. Unbidden, he heard Peter Salt talking about laying down breadcrumbs to be followed. All that Harman wanted to do right then was get on to the next of those. He put the car in gear and headed south towards the lake.

If his mind had not been so preoccupied with getting to the Montaine boatyard and the promise that it held of closing in on Brightwell, he might have noticed the car that followed them and the single passenger within it. As it was, he remained oblivious to the man who was tracking them.

*

The information had been right. The boatyard

was beyond the city's limits and away from the leisure boats and commercial shipping that were more commonly seen around the marina closer to the centre of Lausanne. Harman slowed a couple of times to read the signs for turn-offs from the lake road before seeing on a fading red board in both French and English, *'Montaine: ship maintenance, repairs, and services'*.

Not sure what they might be walking in to, he switched off the engine and let the car roll to a halt on a grass verge before the gates. He was just in time to see them dragged open by an elderly man in dirty overalls. A van pulled out. The two men in front were in denims. One of them called out something good-naturedly to the old man as they drove past him. He responded with an obscene hand gesture and closed the gates behind them.

Once the van had passed them and turned away up on to the main road, Harman and Hope went to the chain link fence that surrounded most of the boatyard. Apart from the caretaker or whatever he was in overalls it was deserted. What took their attention was the ship that was steaming away from them. Its Greek flag was now rippling half-heartedly as the lake air tugged at its threads.

There was a separate gate set into the fence. There was a buzzer next to it. Harman pressed it hard and kept doing so until the boatyard worker reappeared. He was audibly grumbling to himself. After getting rid of the dockhands and seeing the ship depart, he had expected a quiet day. He had not wanted to see anyone else. He scowled at them through the mesh of the gate.

He did not get to express his displeasure at seeing them. Harman told him to open the gate. His grumpiness dissipated. He found himself pleased to help the man. After they were inside, Harman repeated the routine of showing Hagihara's photograph. It reminded him of going to door-to-door on an army base many years before. It was his first posting with the Ministry of Defence police force and a child had gone missing. He soon lost count of how many times he had shown the picture of her to soldiers and their families. Some things never changed. The girl then had turned up safe and well. No harm had been done. He was desperate for the same outcome now. The stakes then had been high. How could they not be when the safety of a child was at stake? The weight of responsibility on his shoulders suddenly felt like it would crush him. If he failed that day, it was not one child who might suffer. It was hundreds of thousands, possibly millions, who would die.

Hope sidled closer to him and said, 'Alan, Alan, are you listening?'

'What?' Harman said, as if suddenly being catapulted back from the past.

'The watchman or whatever he is. He

recognised Hagihara from the picture.'

'Yes, sorry, Charles. Ascendant memories can be very vivid, can't they?'

'For good or bad, Alan. They're something else that you will learn to control.'

Harman nodded as if he understood, but he didn't. As much as Hope had helped him, becoming an Ascendant felt like being abandoned in a maze where something new, and often daunting, lay in wait around every corner.

He shook his head like a drunk who was trying to stop the room from spinning and said to the caretaker, 'the man in the picture, where is he now?'

In place of words the man jabbed a hooked finger in the air. It pointed at the *Duttweiller.*

'Where is she going?'

The man, even under Harman's influence, sounded like he was talking to a simpleton when he said, 'the lake, where else?'

Harman said, as quick and hard as nails from a nail gun, 'how can we get to it?'

'You will need a boat.'

'Yes, I rather assumed that. Do you have a boat we can use?'

'There are many. This is a boatyard.'

The man's literal answers to the questions left Harman wanting to punch him. Since that would not help their cause, he opted to phrase his next question with more precision.

'Please take us to the fastest boat you

have, which is in working order, and for which you have the keys.'

The watchman beamed at him and went to the office. He came straight back, handed a ring with two keys on it to Harman, and waved for them to follow him. On a short wooden quay on the far side of the dockyard, several smaller craft bobbed gently in the slight swell of the lake. The second one in was padlocked to a steel mooring post.

Harman took one look at the Seago inflatable rubber boat and its two-stroke outboard motor, and said, 'Is this thing the fastest you have?'

It sounded like he was pleading. He didn't know that much about boats, but he knew this one wouldn't be overtaking that ship any time soon.

'Or that one,' the man pointed his stubby finger to the one furthest from them.

'You're saying it's faster?'

'No, same boat, same speed,' the man said like it was blindingly obvious.

Harman turned to Hope and said, 'I can't stand any more of him. Let's get in this one and get going.'

While Harman opened the padlock with one of the keys given to him by the caretaker, Hope reluctantly and unsteadily stepped into the small boat.

Harman unhitched the blue nylon rope

that secured the boat at the other end and jumped in. He put the second key into the motor's ignition.

Hope said, 'shouldn't we have life jackets on?'

Harman turned on the engine and slowly steered the boat out. He said, 'forget about that, just hold tight.'

As soon as they were clear of the low dock, he turned the handle of the outboard motor and got it up to full speed. Hope rocked back, let out a yelp, and latched his arms around the bench seat. Harman sat down beside the motor. He did not need any complex navigation. He simply pointed the boat at the *Duttweiller* and kept going. He prayed that the ship would stop before his little motor ran out of juice.

He could not take his eyes off the white ship that must already be half a mile ahead of them.

Had he done so and looked back, he might have seen a dark figure carefully scaling the boatyard's fence before slipping into the office where the boat keys were kept.

*

A walkie talkie squawked in Tobji's hand. Even though he couldn't see the bridge from where he was standing, Tobji threw a glance in its direction. He was expecting it to be Captain

Tomasis. He was wrong. An anonymous seaman, his voice sounding rasping and robotic over the functional device, said, 'we are approaching the launch co-ordinates, sir.'

As Tobji acknowledged the message, he felt the plates of the ship shudder as Tomasis reduced its speed. Taking a step closer to the Mir, he called up towards the open hatch, 'Virginia, we will be there shortly.'

Inside the cramped compartment, Brightwell was completing her checks. The specialist support staff assured her that the Mir submersible was in perfect shape. They were only Normals though, and she would not rely solely on their promises. Fitting tightly between her seat and the wall of the vessel was the leather bag. She would not unpack the metal case or load the phials until she was underwater and ready to deploy the liquid death that waited within them. She contorted herself around the chairs and equipment so she could push herself up through the tight hatch.

She flashed a smile at Tobji. It was a poor reflection of her growing euphoria. She stared forward past the funnel and the rest of the ship's infrastructure. There were some white-sailed yachts cutting back and forth in search of the slight wind on the lake. Further afield, looking like half-sunken building bricks, were a couple of freighters. One was moving east. One was moving west. She judged that one of them might eventually come within hailing distance, but none of the vessels would hinder the launch of the Mir or interfere with its task.

After spending so many weeks studying the lake, it felt like she knew it as well as any of the sailors who had grown up navigating their way around it. They coasted closer to the co-ordinates that she had painstakingly calculated. She stared into the water as the ship sliced through it and spewed out its own pale-topped waves. At its deepest the lake was 310 metres. She would be descending to 140 metres. As the Mir had a maximum operating depth of 6000 metres, the short dip would be as easy for the submersible as it would be for Brightwell to put her big toe in a bath.

A second voice called to her. She swivelled around in the hatch to see Hagihara at the stern. With an effort he turned away from whatever he had been looking at and yelled, 'Ginny, come here please.'

If it had been anyone else, she would have cut them short. Nothing could be as important as the preparations for launch, but this was Yukio Hagihara and he deserved to be heard. He was also someone who did not make frivolous requests. She nimbly hoisted herself out of the hatch and used the steel step ladder that had temporarily been affixed to the Mir to get down to the deck.

Standing at the rail that framed the ship,

she said, 'what is it, old friend?'

'If you look back through our wake and towards the coast you will see a small craft. I have been observing it for several minutes. I have no doubt that it is following us.'

She watched for a few seconds and then agreed. It might be a coincidence, but there was no profit in complacency. Taking her lead from Hagihara, she called to Tobji in a way that was archly measured, 'Zarif, would you be so kind as to ask our hosts if they could provide me with a pair of binoculars?'

He did not have to be told twice. Getting any questions of his own answered was less important than following her commands. He ran across the gently lilting deck. Sailors shook their heads as he passed them. Except in emergency, they all knew better than to be running around topside. It was a bad habit to get into and one that frequently led to accidents. Tobji did not notice and would not have cared even if he had. He found the deck officer who had managed the loading of the Mir. After politely, yet forcibly demanding to borrow the man's binoculars, Tobji took them and returned to Brightwell. He handed them over. It reminded him of when he had given her a different set of binoculars in Amekoura. The test there had been a failure. He could not bear for there to be another. With an anger heated by fear, he rushed to the rail. He needed to see for himself what this new threat was and why she was so anxious to get a better look at.

Her Ascendant eyesight would have been the envy of any Normal, but it still had its limitations. She found the small boat in the binocular's sights and adjusted the focus until the image was as sharp as it could be. Her mouth moved. No words come out. She kept looking until she could be sure that her imagination was not playing her false.

She whispered, 'I don't believe it.'

Hagihara sensed her disquiet and said, 'do you recognise them, Ginny?'

She lowered the binoculars and handed them to Hagihara. She said simply, 'one is Harman. The other one, the one in glasses, I do not know.'

Tobji looked from Hagihara to Brightwell and said, 'how is that possible?'

Brightwell said, 'the how is unimportant now. We know what he is coming for. That is all that should concern us. We need to shorten the timescale and do what we can to prevent his interference. I need you to speak to Captain Tomasis and tell him that we want preparations made for the Mir to be launched the second that we reach our destination.'

Although Hagihara was listening to them, he had already raised the binoculars so that he could monitor the boat that was skimming across the water in their direction. As the ship decelerated, the boat was for the first time making up ground on them.

The ship began to curve gently on its approach to the launching point. The manoeuvre would further slow the ship as the captain took steps to ensure that the ship did not overshoot the target area. Crew members came aft to prepare the stern anchor. Others replicated the task for the anchor at the fore of the ship.

As the ship turned, the deck tilted. It momentarily caused Hagihara to lose sight of the boat that was pursuing them. What he saw because of that caused him to give thanks to the Japanese Seven Gods of Fortune.

He said, 'Ginny, at the risk of repeating myself, would you please take a look at this?'

Brightwell too quickly said, 'we won't stop Harman by looking at him through those things.'

Pushing the binoculars towards her, he said, 'when you are ready, perhaps you would care to take a look behind them?'

Snatching the binoculars out of his hand she raised them to her eyes. First, she saw the boat with Harman in it. It was getting closer. Harman's face was as fixed and unyielding as those of the former US presidents on Mount Rushmore. Every tiny hair on her neck and shoulders prickled. She lifted the binoculars slightly and scanned the waters behind Harman. Sure enough, she saw what Hagihara was trying to alert her to. There was a second boat. It looked identical to the first and was on an identical course. A sole figure was on board that one.

Hagihara said, 'another uninvited guest to our party. Do you know who this one is?'

All she could make out was a man whose windcheater was flapping about like a sail on one of the yachts she was just looking at. The nylon jacket had a hood, and it was tied tight about the man's head. It completely concealed his face from her.

'It could be anyone, Yukio,' she said and returned the binoculars to him. 'Please watch them for me while I seek to bring our timetable forward.'

Tobji was still awaiting her final orders. She gave him what she thought was a reassuring grin, and said, 'please do instil Tomasis with an appropriate degree of urgency, won't you?'

'Of course. Nothing can be allowed to stop us.'

'By the way, are there any weapons on this ship?'

Tobji frowned and said, 'this is a research vessel, so I would think it unlikely.'

'Improvise then, Zarif. If any of those men board this ship, use whatever you can find to stop them. If necessary, permanently. They cannot be allowed to stop the launch of the submersible. Everything depends on that.'

With the zealous glee of a kamikaze pilot, Tobji said, 'my life is yours,'

*

Hope was being tossed about in the bottom of the inflatable as it lurched violently whenever it met the smallest disturbance in the water. Like Harman he had been concentrating on the ship. The watchman had called it the *Duttweiller.* As it came to a gradual halt, Hope turned to ask Harman what they were meant to do when they reached it.

The question froze on his lips. He had seen that there was another boat following in their wake. He didn't wait to consider if it was a coincidence or not. Cupping his hands around his mouth he shouted so that Harman could hear him over the revving of the engine that was beside him, 'there's a boat following us.'

Harman struggled to make out what he was saying. He touched the lobe of his ear to indicate the problem. Hope growled to himself and then waved manically. Harman got the message and screwed around to see for himself. As the wind pricked at his eyes, he squinted to get a better look. The boat was another Seago. It was safe to assume it was the one from the Montaine boatyard. Which meant they were being followed, or was chased a better description? There was one man in it. He was sitting in the identical spot as Harman was on his boat. The tightly drawn hood around his head obscured the man's face. It could have been anyone.

It was a complication that Harman didn't need, but that boat was behind him, and it was more important to focus on the ship ahead of him. He turned back to it. Hope was crawling towards him.

When he was close enough to be heard clearly, Hope said, 'what do we do now?'

Harman said, 'nothing's changed. I came for Brightwell. She's on that ship so that's where we're going.'

'I've got a bad feeling about that boat behind us.'

'We'll be on the ship before he can reach us. If he gets in my way, then he'd be wise to be more worried about us than we are about him.'

With the ship steady in the water, its mighty anchors were released. Harman was close enough to hear the heavy chains running out and for the man-sized stern anchor to hit the water. White-plumed water splashed high before spattering back into the lake. With the *Duttweiller* left to bob in its place, Harman's boat closed on it quickly.

Hope said, 'how are we ever getting on that thing? If we try to influence the crew to drop us a line, Brightwell will stop them.'

'Don't give in so easily, Charles. Sit tight and do what I tell you.'

As they approached the ship, they craned

their necks towards the deck. It was high above them and seemed even more distant as they came level with the ship. Harman kept the throttle of the outboard motor fully on. The Seago bounced past the ship's stern. A line of faces gawped back at them. Apart from one, they were all dark-haired men. In the centre, standing out like a white swan among a murder of crows, was a blonde-haired woman.

Harman recognised Brightwell immediately and knew that she had recognised him too. He threw a mocking salute in her direction. She pushed back a lock of hair from her forehead and gave him the sort of wave that a queen would once have given to her peasant subjects.

Leaving her to watch on, the inflatable sped by. As soon as they neared the *Duttweiller's* prow, Harman slewed the boat about and cut the engine. He grabbed the mooring line from under his seat and attached it to the ship's anchor cable.

'Right, let's get up there quick as you can', he said to Hope.

Hope stared up in disbelief. He said, 'I'm not a monkey. How am I supposed to climb up that chain?'

Harman got a grip on the cable and began to climb. Over his shoulder, he called, 'Charles, you're an Ascendant for God's sake. For once, try to act like one.'

Hope was not about to stay on the boat

alone. He rubbed his palms on his legs, put his fingers around the first of the fist-sized cable links, said a small prayer, and began to drag himself upward. Although he couldn't match Harman's aggressive ascent, he did his best.

Up ahead, Harman was moving with the grace and purpose of the best climbers in the monkey kingdom. He put a foot in the hole that the anchor had been lowered from and thrust himself up. He grabbed the wooden-topped rail. He pulled himself up until he was able to throw a leg over the top. In one motion he rolled on to the deck. Quickly getting his feet under him, he got his bearings. High above him was the ship's bridge and main infrastructure. Behind that was the ship's funnel. A fine wisp of smoke was barrelling from it. The deck ran down both sides of the ship from prow to stern. To the port side of the ship men were running towards him.

A gasping Hope flopped on to the deck next to him. He looked like he was ready to sleep for a week.

'Charles, there's no time for that. There's a gangway over there. It will take you below decks. Find a way up to the bridge and influence whoever you must. Make sure they won't let Brightwell off this ship.'

Hope did not want to be separated again from Harman, but his protest died in his throat as soon as he heard the thump of running feet on the deck. As he reached the gangway, he saw four men burst out from the shadow of the upper deck. Two carried axes. Two carried long-bladed kitchen knives. Hope didn't hang around to see what would happen next. His feet clanged down the metal stairs as fast as a chef tenderising meat.

As Harman squared up to the unwelcome, welcoming committee, he enjoyed a moment of relief as he saw Hope scrabbling to safety with the speed of a rabbit diving into its burrow.

The four men formed an arc around him. They held their collection of weapons at the ready but, like apprentice pirates, their postures were not those of experienced killers.

Harman kept his arms loose at his sides and said, 'would you like to surrender?'

One of them stepped forward. He was darker skinned than the rest and was not dressed as a seaman. He had broad cheekbones. His hair and moustache would not have looked out of place on a male model. He said, 'whatever you think you might do, you can forget it, Mr Harman.'

'I don't remember us being introduced. Did Virginia give you my name?' Harman said. He was in no mood for conversation when Brightwell was back there and temptingly close to being in his hands, but he wanted to buy Hope enough time to get to the bridge.

Tobji said, 'sit down by the capstan. We will secure you there until she is ready to deal with you.'

'The capstan? You mean that thing the anchor cable is attached to? I don't think I'd be very comfortable there. How about instead if you drop that axe and get out of my way?'

Tobji said, 'one word from me and these men will chop you into small pieces.'

Harman said, 'are you sure of that? I'm guessing she will have told you more about me than just my name. From the way you talk and the fact that Brightwell said anything at all to you, you must be an Ascendant just like me, but if I try to influence those men can you be sure they won't chop you to pieces instead?'

The flick of Tobji's eyes towards the sailors betrayed his doubts.

Harman said, 'let them go. They're not toys for you to play with.'

The doubt on Tobji's face transformed into malice. He said, 'they will all be dead soon, so what does it matter?'

'It matters if they fall under my influence first and they toss you overboard.'

Zarif Tobji glared at Harman. The thought of having his numerical advantage turned on him was draining his reservoir of bravery. He switched his attention to the three sailors and said, 'store away your weapons and return to your normal duties.'

They dutifully drifted away.

'Good choice,' Harman said, 'what are you

going to do now?'

Without a hint of indecision, Tobji raised the axe above his head and charged at Harman.

*

While Brightwell, Hagihara, and Tobji were being distracted by Harman's arrival on the ship, the second Seago boat floated alongside. Unlike Harman, its passenger had given more forethought about how he was going to get onboard. He had brought with him from the boatyard a grappling hook. With practised ease he swung it underarm several times and then released it to fly upward. It hooked itself on to the railing. He tugged the line that was attached to it. Satisfied that it was secure, and with what he needed tied over his shoulder, he climbed arm over arm up the rope.

He stepped softly on to the deck. His limbs ached from the exertion of climbing. Doing his best to ignore the discomfort he squatted and looked around. He was near the middle of the ship. Those at the stern were busy with a submersible of some kind. To the fore, three men were heading towards him. He ducked down below a lifeboat before they could see him. For what he had to do, he did not want anyone to know he was coming. Death was on his mind. That was his secret and he intended to keep it that way until it was time to act.

Feeling too exposed on the main deck, he waited for the three crewmen to pass, and then entered a doorway directly below the bridge. There was a passageway that went through to the port side of the ship. There were stairs up to the living quarters and laboratories above. There were stairs down towards the engines. Reasoning that there would be fewer people to see him if he went that way, he took those.

*

The axe flashed towards Harman. He swayed to one side. The blade passed close enough for him to see the grain in the steel. He hopped back before Tobji could swing again. Darting behind the capstan so that he could keep some space between him and his attacker, Harman realised he had made a mistake. Even worse, so did Tobji.

When Harman should have been seeking the freedom of the broadest part of the deck, he had retreated towards the prow where it was at its narrowest. He darted to one side to try and get around Tobji, but the Moroccan mirrored his move. He swung the axe, this time from the waist. Harman jumped back, his body shaping like the letter C, as the heavy blade whooshed through the space near his midriff.

Tobji widened his grip on the shaft of the axe. He weaved left and right like a sparring boxer.

Harman took another step back. With a nonchalance that he did not feel, he said, 'any chance we can discuss the surrender option again?'

Tobji's whole face was lit by the thrill of the hunt. He said, barely managing to suppress adrenaline-prompted laughter, 'it's too late for that, Mr Harman. You are running out of ship.'

He swiped again with the axe. Harman ducked. The blade went over his head, but instead of pulling it back to strike again, Tobji reversed the swing. Harman had not expected it. The blunt end of the axe head battered into his shoulder. It sent him tumbling. The end of the anchor cable tripped him. He went down hard. Without waiting, Harman braced one of his feet against the capstan and pushed off from it. As his body was thrust forward, he heard the axe strike the deck where an instant before his head had been. The clash of metal on metal sent a vibration through his entire body.

With movement his sole means of defence, he staggered up. He didn't care where he went as long as it kept him out of Tobji's reach. He stumbled and was brought up short by the rail. Instinctively his hands shot out to stop him falling again. Independently they grasped the rail that ran around the entire length of the ship. It was then that he realised one hand was on the rail to his left and one on the rail to his right. He had reached the foremost part of the ship. All that lay ahead of him was the grey water of the lake. There was nowhere else to run.

Pulling himself up straight he faced Tobji.

His foe stepped in closer. He was no longer in a rush. He wanted to enjoy his moment of triumph against this man who somehow had made the great Virginia Brightwell apprehensive. She would be so pleased with him.

While Tobji gloated prematurely, Harman made his move. Crouching low, he charged. If he could grab Tobji's legs and tip him on to the deck their fight would immediately become more equal.

Tobji anticipated the move. He brought the shaft of the axe down and moved to the side. He caught Harman with a glancing blow to the head. Harman went down like a charging bull shot in the legs. He clattered into the railings. Spinning around he saw Tobji hoisting the axe high above his head. Tobji's bulging eyes told their own story. He was putting everything into it like an executioner taking aim at someone whose head was on the chopping block.

The axe descended with the speed and power of a guillotine. Harman dropped to the ground. He heard Tobji roar. The axe scythed through the Swiss air. The shriek of cracking wood sparked in Harman's ears. The axe head was buried in the Ash wood atop the railings. Tobji was leaning over Harman. He tugged maniacally at the axe to free it. He raged at the railing for it to release the axe.

Harman couldn't wait. With all his strength he pushed upwards. His shoulder pummelled into Tobji's stomach. His legs protested, but they found the resolve to keep pushing. Tobji's feet came off the ground. A cry that was a mixed recipe of fear, anger, and disbelief, erupted from the Moroccan. With his arms and legs flaying wildly, Tobji was hurled over the railing. For short moments, he dropped helplessly through the air. His head cracked off the hull. He became a dead weight. He hit the water.

Harman dragged himself to the rail and looked down in time to see the splash. Tobji's body disappeared below the surface. Harman panted as he waited. When Tobji bobbed back up again, the air pockets that had been trapped in his clothing gave his corpse a grotesque, misshapen appearance.

The body floated face down.

Harman rested his hands on his knees while he caught his breath. The axe was still firmly wedged where it had struck. It crossed his mind to retrieve it. He thought better of it. Whatever else he might have to do, bloody butchery would not be part of it.

*

Ernst Mannson was delighted that nobody knew

he was on the *Duttweiller*. The inevitable surprise of his Ascendant victims would add an enjoyable frisson to the act of removing them from God's earthly realm.

The ruckus up on deck was an unwelcome distraction, but one that he was compelled to witness. Tiptoeing up the stairs from the lower deck, he stopped as soon as his eyes were level with the lip of the entrance way. He wanted to see but not be seen.

The fight between Harman and the other man was wildly entertaining. He bit his lip to suppress a cheer as the axe swung this way and that. He knew Harman well enough. The other Ascendant was a stranger. It was always more fun to support someone in a clash of arms, and Mannson found himself wanting Harman to prevail.

When Tobji eventually took an enforced dive overboard, Mannson whispered to himself in a faux posh-English accent, 'well played, sir.'

Then he slipped back into the bowels of the ship. Fun time was over. It was time for work. The unknown Ascendant who was now sipping on lake water would have made a nice hors d'oeuvre, but there was still plenty more meat on the table for him to sink his teeth into.

*

Brightwell was perched on the hatch of the Mir.

It was ready to be lowered into the water. The larger of the two cranes would be needed for that and it was controlled from the bridge.

Glaring towards the bridge, she said, 'why is it taking so long?'

Hagihara stared up at her from the deck and said, 'everything is in hand, Ginny, nothing can go wrong now.'

'Yukio,' she said, her voice straining, 'Harman could be here at any second.'

'Then, we will deal with him.'

'What if your confidence is misplaced?'

Hagihara made a dismissive gesture with his hand and said, 'I wish you would let me come with you. I would like to be present at the instant when our destiny becomes manifest. There will be two empty seats in there when you descend. Is it too much to ask that I occupy one of them?'

'There is nobody that I would rather have with me, Old Man, but good plans can be spoiled by amending them at the last minute. You know that. Besides, you will be safer here and that will free me to concentrate.'

A deckhand called from the upper deck, 'one minute to launch'.

A light on the crane bloomed red.

Brightwell and Hagihara shared a long glance before she slid inside the submersible. She locked the hatch. She buckled herself into a seat. She checked the controls were all good to go and then watched from a porthole as

Hagihara retreated to the edge of the loading area. He stepped towards the heavily shaded covered walkway that linked the fore and aft parts of the ship on the starboard side. His face was expressionless and yet it carried so much meaning for her.

The smile that was forming on her lips wilted into shock as she saw someone slink up behind Hagihara. She couldn't see who it was, but she saw the shine of a knife. Brightwell jerked rigid in her chair. She screamed for Hagihara to turn, to run. The reinforced hull of the Mir stopped her pleas from escaping.

She saw a look of confusion on Hagihara's face before a hand cupped his chin and yanked it back. As if part of the same fluid choreographed routine, a knife cut smooth and deep across his throat. As the blood pulsed from the wound, Hagihara's face contorted in terror.

Brightwell watched impotently as Hagihara's eyes rolled in his head and his legs crumpled. His precious blood surged across the deck. Streams of it trickled towards the Mir.

As Hagihara died, the crane's winch came to life. The slack in the harness was quickly taken up and the Mir began to rise.

Brightwell could not move her eyes from Hagihara's pale body. She had not seen the killer, but it could only have been Alan Harman. She cursed his name and swore vengeance on him.

Telling herself to get a grip, she

concentrated on the controls. There would be time for Harman later. What mattered more than anything and any life was completing her mission. Part of her revenge would be seeing Harman as the Normals that he so wanted to protect began to fall all around him. It would be a sweet moment. It would be one to revel in before she killed him.

The Mir rose above the height of the railings. The crane slowly moved it away from the deck. As soon as it was clear of the ship, its descent would begin. The harnesses would be released, it would submerge and sail away under the power of its own 9-kilowatt electric motor.

Brightwell extracted the phials from their metal case. She slotted them into the modified dispenser from where they would soon be released into the water that quenched the thirst of thousands who lived around the lake and beyond.

She would not be stopped now.

*

Ernst Mannson was elated. He had extinguished the light from another demon. It had been quicker than he would have preferred, but if that was God's will then so be it. He was the hand of God to be used as the Almighty saw fit. He ducked back inside the ship. Out of sight, he found a washroom and thoroughly washed his hands. He found not even a spec of blood anywhere else on him. Given how much had been sprayed around that was some achievement. Verging on committing the sin of pride, Mannson complimented himself on his expertise. He really was quite good at delivering justice to Ascendants.

He hid the knife behind a cistern. He would come back for it when it was needed again. In the meantime, it would be easier to do what he had to do without having it on him.

Mannson stared back at himself in the wall mirror. He said, 'right then, Ernst, it's too soon for you to be feeling so pleased with yourself. Do not be so naughty. God, bless his name, will not be happy with you.'

The face in the mirror said, 'whatever you say, Ernst, you're the boss.'

'Quite right too. One down and two to go. Let's get on with it.'

*

Harman sprinted down the port side of the ship to the aft deck. He skidded to a halt as he saw the raised submersible traverse the ship and be borne out over the side. There was nobody manning the crane, nobody for him to influence to stop it. In the time it would take him to get to the bridge, the Mir and Brightwell would be gone.

Through one of the Mir's portholes, he

saw Brightwell's profile. It was dimly lit by the control board inside the submersible. The urge to stop her deafened him to every rational thought that was yelling to be heard. Without knowing exactly what he was going to do, he ran towards the Mir. His concentration was so focussed that he did not notice Hagihara's still draining body.

The humming tone of the crane changed as it began to lower the vessel towards the water. Harman measured his run like a triple jumper. His feet slapped against the deck. He skipped up onto the railing and hurled himself at the red roof of the Mir. For an instant all he was aware of was flying through open space with the gap between ship and submersible gaping below him.

Then he slammed into the Mir. His weight and impetus caused it to weave a lazy pattern as it dangled in mid-air. As he slid from its smooth surface, he thrust a hand towards the harness that was secured to the top of the tiny craft. Gripping it like the lifeline it was, he steadied himself. Knowing it would be released as soon as the submersible was settled on the lake, his eyes darted about for something else to cling on to.

To the rear was the broad horizontal fin. Behind that was the round black propeller. Getting near to that was far from inviting. To the front there was little except the main viewing glass. It might be gratifying to eyeball Brightwell through that, but it would be like trying to cling to ice. The one place to get a good grip was on a metal bar below him. Affixed to it were some underwater lights, a mechanical grip, and what looked like two lidded dustpans. With some reluctance he let go of the harness and slide the few feet down to the bar. With the Mir still swaying, he lost his balance. His arms wheeled as tried to stop himself. He reached the tipping point and fell.

As he flew past the Mir's hull, he grabbed frenziedly at it. The flawless metal offered no help. He was bracing himself to hit the water when his arm clattered into the metal bar. The burst of pain invigorated him. He managed to grab the grabber. In the heat of his struggle, the irony of that was lost on him. He levered himself up until he was astride the steel beam. With his body at a 45-degree angle, he held the grabber tightly and reached up with his other hand to latch his fingers on to the rim of the porthole through which he had just seen Brightwell. The colour drained from his fingers and knuckles as he clutched to it and pulled himself up.

There was no time to be thankful for his escape. The submersible was moving inexorably towards the lake, and he had no way of getting inside.

*

Charles Hope blinked. He finished cleaning his

tinted spectacles on the tail of his shirt and slid them back on. He blinked again. His eyes always needed to adjust to the effect they had on his sight. Below decks had been more of a labyrinth than he had expected. It had taken him longer to get there than it should have done. Navigating the narrow corridors and gangways was oppressive. He had disliked that. It was something he would grin and bear. What was most important was that they had kept him out of harms' way and almost completely unseen.

There was a sign on the wall next to the stairway in front of him. It was in Greek, but he hoped it pointed towards the bridge. Up he went.

*

A sharp chill rippled through Harman's body as his feet slipped below the bitterly cold water of Lake Geneva. He looked down to watch his knees and thighs join them as the beam he was standing on led the Mir's descent. Without knowing why, his gaze was drawn back to the small porthole.

Virginia Brightwell's face was on the other side. He had not expected anything other than anger from her. He was taken aback to see more than that. He saw pure, baking hot, hatred. It was as if every molecule in her body hungered to tear him to pieces. This was not the coldly calculating woman he had encountered twice before.

The creeping rise of the water up his body wrenched him back to his immediate problem. It was up to his chest. Questions for which he had no answer jostled for his attention. How long could he survive in that temperature? How long could he hold his breath for underwater? When should he let go and save himself? What damage could he still do that would screw her up?

As his neck felt the icy tickle of the lake's surface, he wondered if this was destiny exerting justice for what he had just done to Zarif Tobji.

He took two deep breaths and then a third to fill his lungs as the Mir moved from the world of air to the world of water. He kicked at the equipment on the bar. Maybe it wasn't too late to dislodge something that Brightwell needed to drop her deadly payload.

It crossed his mind that if he could break something free then he could swim around and ram it into the submersible's propeller. Brightwell wouldn't get far if that was broken.

But no matter how hard he tried, nothing moved in the slightest.

Bubbles slipped in a garland from his mouth. The Mir would surely be released from the ship soon. How much longer could he hang on for once it was fully submerged and being steered to its underwater destination? He guessed, not nearly long enough.

He couldn't let her succeed. The Mir had

to be halted. It had to be disabled. He managed to keep his eyes open, but the murky inland sea refused to let in much light from the surface. His world was reduced to the submerging boat that he was clinging to.

A final question, a final challenge, burst forward from his subconscious: was he willing to make the sacrifice it demanded of him?

He had known the answer to that for a long time. Did he have any family? No. Did he have any friends left? Charles Hope maybe. Amy Bishop at a push. And how could he look them in the eye again if he faltered now? All he had was a single purpose and that was to stop Virginia Brightwell. There was nothing else.

And so, he shoved off from the beam that had been supporting him and breast-stroked towards the rear of the Mir. If something had to be shoved into the propeller to break it, then his arms and legs would have to do the job.

He had barely begun his short swim when the water whirled like a shoal of piranha had been dropped into it. The Mir thrummed with energy. Brightwell had turned on the propeller in readiness for the harness to be released.

*

Charles Hope nudged his glasses back up on the bridge of his nose. Apart from the captain, there were five other men in the control room.

Assuming the man in charge was the one with the most braid, he went straight to him and said, 'you will bring that submarine thing back on board immediately.'

Captain Tomasis felt unusually relaxed as he gave the order to the crane operator. The woman looked uncertainly to the man sitting next to her. He shrugged. It wasn't for them to query any of the skipper's commands.

Hope positioned himself behind the captain's shoulder and said, 'excellent. Once it's back on board, I'd be grateful if you could cruise around for a bit, or whatever you sailors call it, until you're asked to return to shore. Have you got that?'

Tomasis replied, 'yes, sir, of course.'

It was then that Hope scared himself with a troubling thought. What would he have done if the captain and crew only spoke Greek?

Maybe some saint was watching over him? Whatever had delivered the smattering of good luck, he was grateful for it.

*

With water spewing out all around it, Harman clung limpet-like to the black metal covering that encircled the propeller. If he had any breath left, he would have taken some in as he made the ugly choice of whether to thrust an arm or leg into the fast-spinning machinery. With a detachment that he had not expected, he chose his leg. It was thicker and stronger than his arm. It stood to reason that it would cause the most damage to the spinning mechanism.

Adjusting his body, he readied to shove it in as hard and far as he could.

The submersible jerked. It had to be the harness release. Inside the Mir, Brightwell would be preparing to steer it away and down. Lights came on behind him. Here we go, he thought. He didn't mean the Mir moving off. He meant the sacrifice of his leg.

Against the resistance of the water, he swung it wide and aimed for the propeller. At least in the darkness, he would not see it happen.

With his leg in motion, he sensed the submersible rise rather than fall. His foot halted an inch from the whirling blades of the propellor. It was the drag of the water that saved him. It wasn't wishful thinking. The Mir was gradually ascending. With his lungs close to collapse and his heart beating like a miner hammering to get out of a mine fall, he released himself from the Mir and kicked for the surface.

He was still gulping in that beautiful and life-affirming lake air as the submersible rose like some bulbous mono-eyed sea monster. As it was painstakingly cranked up, he again took hold of the beam. If the Mir was being returned to the deck, he deserved to be given a free ride on it.

Swinging back across and being lowered

to the aft deck, water poured from every inch of the Mir. It pooled and then most of it ran away down the ship's gunwales. Some of the remainder meandered down the deck to wash away Hagihara's congealing blood.

Harman jumped down and waited for the Mir to settle on the deck. He expected crewmen to come and secure it. That was unless Hope stopped them. He was sure that it could only have been Charles Hope who had caused the Mir to be retrieved. Whatever fears haunted Hope, he had conquered them. He had come through when it counted. Harman pledged that he would never forget that.

His deep thanks to Hope would, however, need to wait a bit longer. He still had the biggest fish of all to fry, and a crazy notion was forming about a very special oil to cook her in. He skipped up again on to the Mir. There was a whirr as the hatch was unlocked. Like Brightwell, he knew she had to try and escape from there quickly or risk getting trapped inside while lesser others prepared to deal with her. The vessel that should have paved the course to Ascendancy would be reduced to her personal prison.

Her shoulders appeared and she put her hands out to lift herself up.

Harman was face to face with her. He registered again that detestation in her features. It meant nothing to him. With an ungentlemanly force, he shoved her back inside the Mir. Off balance, she dropped like an ice block from an aeroplane. Her back hit one of the three chairs and she cried out. Before she could right herself, Harman lowered himself down and closed the hatch.

As Brightwell untangled herself, he settled himself in a chair and said, 'I think we're due a bit of private quality time, don't you?'

Strands of blonde hair draped over her forehead. Her clothing, until now always ladylike, was stretched in all directions as if she had thrown it on in the middle of an alcohol-fuelled binge.

Despite that he expected her to be demure, her words carefully selected and biting. What he did not expect was for her to lunge at him. His head snapped back as painted fingernails scratched at his face and pawed at his eyes. The very limited space in the Mir didn't allow for anything clever. He kicked out. His foot hit her in the hip. She spun and shot backwards. Before she could recover her feet, he towered over her and punched her hard in the side of the head.

He inwardly cringed at his action. It didn't matter what she might be guilty of, it would never feel anything other than completely wrong to strike a woman. He swallowed down his distaste and while she was still groggy, he dragged her into one of the chairs. He pulled the belt and buckle tight around her. There was little else to use in the sparsely furnished craft, so he ripped open one of the panels and tore out some wiring. What did he care if the thing never worked again? He hastily tied her hands behind her back and then sagged back into the chair next to her.

While she regained her senses, he took the chance to scan the craft that he had so far only seen from the outside. He saw the metal case, pulled it on to his lap, and opened it. The phials in their black foam surround were still sitting there. He didn't have to be told what was in them. It was almost incomprehensible that something so small and so intangible could be the worst weapon ever devised in the planet's history, especially given some of the competition for that most dubious of honours.

He turned from the phials to Brightwell. It was a much-needed reminder that she was not a woman, she was a monster in human form. She had concocted this devil's brew. She had tested variations of it on live subjects in that hellish mine in Colorado. The thought of the immeasurable suffering that she had inflicted on those men turned his hot anger into an ice-covered pool righteous revenge. The fact that the men she had as human test tubes were convicts, did not lessen her awful crime. In those same caverns he had also watched Peter Salt be killed by her command. At the Marston Creek research facility, she influenced one of the armed guards to kill him. Instead, Inspector Carol King had taken the bullet for him and died in his arms. She was his friend and mentor. Since the death of his ex-wife, Francesca, nobody had been closer to him.

The more that those thoughts swirled around in his head, the more certain he was that the sentence he had passed on her was the most fitting. Giving her a physical beating was nothing compared to what he had planned. In the sleep free nights of recent weeks, he had spent hour after hour thinking of how to punish her.

Prison maybe? How could he be sure she wouldn't escape, with or without the help of the followers that she must still have. There were more than just those on the list that Peter Salt had given him. The attacker with the axe was proof of that.

Execution then? Who would do that? Him? He wasn't sure, despite everything, that he was capable of it. ET1, Homeland Security, some other government agency? He wouldn't trust any of them. Her value to them was alive as a source of information, and not as a dead martyr to the Ascendant cause.

What then was the most appropriate sentence to hand down. What punishment could possibly fit her crimes? What was it that she would dread more than anything? Short of killing her, how could he be sure that she would never again pose a threat?

That broth of ideas had bubbled in his brain as they cooked. Like a Michelin-starred chef he had kept coming back to taste it until the flavour was perfect. Finally, if he truly had it in him, he was ready to serve the dish up to Virginia Brightwell.

He watched as she slowly raised her head. The brief nap had done nothing for her temperament. As soon as she was again aware of her surroundings, she tried to get at him. Tying her hands had been the smart thing to do.

When she accepted that further struggle was useless, she sagged back into the chair. Through tightly clenched teeth, she said, 'why did you have to kill him? He was harmless.'

Misunderstanding who she was referring to, he said, 'I'm not sure you're in any place to make accusations, but he came at me with an axe. What did you expect me to do?'

If she was confused, she did not show it. She said, 'not Tobji, you know that I mean Yukio. He was an old man, the Old Man, and you left him out there like a slaughtered pig. I will kill you for that. And then I will kill everyone who has ever shown you the smallest kindness.'

'If you mean Yukio Hagihara, then I can't say I'm sad to hear he's dead, but it wasn't by my hand. As for what you might do, to me or anyone else, I think I'm about to put those days behind you.'

For the first time, her anger was diluted by

uncertainty. She said, 'you're a fool if you think you can halt the Ascendancy.'

'Peter Salt told me that the Ascent was an evolutionary inevitability. It should be left alone to take effect in its own time. Let nature take its course, eh? I'm happy to wait. It's a shame you and your friends aren't.'

'Then you are not just a fool, you are a naïve fool.'

Harman closed his eyes and rolled his neck. There were clicks as the vertebrae aligned. He gathered himself and said, 'much as I'd like to debate this with you, which is not at all, it's time to do what must be done.'

'Stop wasting your breath,' she spat,' and hand me over to whoever pulls your strings at ET1.'

'I am happily string-free and what comes next is solely between you and me. Do you remember when we were alone in that Colorado cave? Like now, the two of us and nobody else. You tried to influence me to kill myself. I recollect you found it amusing at the time. The pain I went through was anything but that. Instead of getting me to shoot myself, with my own gun, you inadvertently triggered the dormant Ascendant genes in me.'

Brightwell made a pretend yawn and said, 'arrest me, kill me, I don't care but if you have any heart don't bleat on with any more of your pathetic life story.'

Harman continued as if he hadn't heard her. He said, 'Peter Salt told me that you were scared by what happened. I've pondered on that a lot. I can't say that I've known a lot of Ascendants, but all of them so far have either feared or respected your power. That made me wonder why, if you're so fearsome, did you feel the need to disband your circle of closest supporters. I mean, why bother? With Peter Salt finally out of the picture, what could you possibly be afraid of? What could have happened to make the high and mighty Virginia Brightwell take such a drastic step? It took a while for me to realise it was me. I was what happened. I think you made that change because you knew I would come after you. And that scared you, didn't it?'

'No, I did it to protect them from you. To make it harder to reach them. I failed and your blood is on their hands.'

'Believe it or not, I didn't really hurt any of them. Maybe one day I will find out who did. The point, which I am labouring to get to, is that you, the great Ginny Brightwell would surely have found it quicker and easier to hunt me down rather than wait for me to get to you? So, why didn't you? I've thought about it a lot. There's only one credible conclusion. Peter was right, you are scared by me. Why would that be though? What could there possibly be about me, someone who is still learning day by day what it means to be an Ascendant, that would make you fearful of coming face to face with me again?'

'You poor man, you are delusional,' Brightwell did her best to sound dismissive. She was belied by her inability to meet his eye.

'I can't claim to be great at self-reflection, particularly when I've been running from pillar to post around the world after you, but something has been bugging me. You see, I think that when you recruited your little clique to bring forward the Ascendant revolution, you would have chosen carefully. You would have picked not just the most useful, but the best. I know Thibault Blanc was scared, that Daiyu Chen wanted to co-operate, and that Hans Osterfeld was sure you would destroy me. And yet, even so, looking back why did each of them speak so readily? Then there's your dear friend, Yukio Hagihara. I never got to speak to him. You pulled him out before I could reach him. Whatever reasons you gave to him, I think you did that to prevent me speaking to him. He really did know too much didn't he, and you knew he would tell me all about it if I caught up with him.'

'No, I didn't want him murdered like the others. I wanted to keep him safe,' Brightwell said, with the fire returning to her belly.

'That might have been a fringe benefit. It wasn't the true reason. I believe it was this. My friend, Charles Hope, who you have yet to meet and who is by far a better model of what an Ascendant should be than you are, told me that he had never encountered one of us who could influence another. He had no reason to lie about it, but his knowledge is limited to his experience. You do know where I'm going with this, don't you?'

Brightwell struggled to free herself. Her actions were frenzied. Panic gave her strength. Before she could break free, Harman got from his chair and held her arms firmly until she stopped.

'You will hurt yourself if you keep doing that, Virginia. I've already told you that I didn't hurt your people, and I won't hurt you either. I don't have to because, apparently, I have the ability to influence other Ascendants. Somehow you saw that in me and that's what terrified you. It's why you knew I would eventually reach you. It's why you have rushed to get here and deploy whatever filth is in those phials of yours.'

'Please don't,' her voice came out as little more than a whimper, 'I'm begging you.'

'I don't suppose you have shown mercy to anyone in your life. You had your own brother murdered. You had my friend killed right in front of me. How many others have you destroyed, and how many were you planning to massacre with that bioweapon of yours?' Harman said, with a complete absence of malice. A heavy shroud of sadness unexpectedly descended on him.

Her scream did not escape the small space she was trapped in. Through tears her muffled words sounded like they came from a child as she said, 'please kill me, anything but that, please... please...'

It was obvious that she knew his intentions. He hardened his heart to her pleas. He took her head in his hands and forced it towards him until their noses were almost touching. In a slow low voice where he precisely enunciated each word and syllable, he said, 'Virginia Brightwell, from this moment on, you will forget and never remember that you are an Ascendant. Whatever abilities you had as an Ascendant will be lost to you forever. From now on you will consider yourself to be a Normal and you will be unable to act in any other way. Do you understand?'

Her face reddened as the blood vessels swelled. Her eyes screwed up in pain. Her jaw worked, but she could not speak. Her body convulsed. Harman held her tighter so that she did not damage herself. The change was violent. He had not known what to expect. It was impossible to know if she was fighting it. He was in the unknown. He didn't want to think about his options if it did not work as planned.

When she went limp in his arms, his first thought was that he had killed her, that, despite what he had tried to do, he had still ended up being her executioner.

Relief flooded through him as she slowly sat up straight.

He held her cheeks in his hands. He said,

'are you ok? How do you feel?'

Even to him it sounded feeble and out of place. They were words for an elderly woman who had suddenly fainted in a grocery store. They were not words for someone who had been eager to unleash death on every continent.

'I feel...' she licked her lips and tried again. 'I feel...peaceful.'

'Do you remember your name, who you are?'

'I, er...my name is Ginny Brightwell. I'm a scientist. Forgive me, I'm feeling a little confused. Where are we, it's hard to breathe in here.'

Harman undid the hatch. The inrush of cooler air helped her. Taking her by the hand, he said, 'come on. Let's get you out of here.'

He didn't know how much she would remember or how quickly it might come back to her, but he watched every nuance of her movement and speech for anything that might hint at the Ascendant in her still being alive.

The tear stains were still tracks through her make-up as he helped her down the side of the Mir. He saw Hagihara's body and steered her to the other side of the ship before she could see it. He sat her on a wooden box that held life jackets. He said, 'sit there for a little while. I will get us off this ship soon. First, I just need to find my friend, Charles.'

A quizzical expression came over her. She

said, 'a friend? I was with a friend, wasn't I?'

'Don't worry about that. There will be time for all your questions later. Take a while for your head to clear,' Harman said, although he had no clue about whether it ever would.

Leaving her alone with her addled memories, Harman moved up the deck towards the bridge. It was where he expected Charles to be. Harman's hair was heavy with lake water. He brushed aside the trickles that were running into his eyes. Pelts of water flicked off him to merge on the deck with the heavy droplets that were streaming from his clothes.

He was already judging how he could possibly express his thanks adequately, when Charles Hope came out of a door amidships. Harman could see the glee on Hope's face. He had never seen him so carefree and happy.

Out on the lake, one of the freighter's that Brightwell had spotted earlier was cutting across the bows of the *Duttweiller.* It was an old work horse whose red hull bore the taint of too much rust. It was unremarkable and Harman paid it no attention as he watched Hope walking towards him.

He would never know whether it was because he was exhausted from his treatment of Brightwell, or if he had simply relaxed too much after completing the arduous task that he had set himself. Whichever of those was to blame he did not hear the movement behind him until it was too late.

It was the clicks of wood on metal that caused him to turn.

Facing him with a walking stick in one hand and an automatic pistol in the other was Sebastian Kent.

His sudden appearance was as surprising to Harman as anything that had happened that day.

Hope was now close enough to Harman to easily hear him saying, 'Alan, we did it, we really did it.'

Harman was about to ask Kent what he was doing there, when the former head of ET1 raised the gun. It was at exactly the same time as the wash from the passing freighter caused the *Duttweiller* to roll slightly. Kent pulled the trigger. Harman was sure its bullet was destined for his head. He was wrong. He felt the heat from it as it slashed through the air near his throat. He heard a cry. Behind him, something soft and heavy staggered back across the deck before collapsing. Dread made Harman clench his jaw tight. He whipped about, not wanting to see what he was already sure was there.

Charles Hope lay on the ground. His chest was heaving, and a circle of blood was expanding around the bullet hole below his shoulder. Harman rushed to his new-found friend. Tearing off his jacket, he pressed it against the wound.

At the sound of the shot, Virginia Brightwell had snapped to her feet. She already seemed much sharper than when Harman had told her to sit down. He called her to him, took hold of her hand and told her to keep pressing down on his jacket. He was torn between tending to Hope and exacting retribution on Kent. The lure of the latter was too strong.

He spun to face Sebastian Kent.

Recognising the look in Harman's eyes, Kent threw the pistol as far as he could into the lake. The murderous intent in Harman was reason enough to get rid of it. Harman had made Cornel Culpepper turn a gun on himself in Colorado. Kent was not going to make it easy for him to repeat that particular trick.

He said, mustering as much calm as he could, 'Alan, let me speak before you do anything rash.'

Taking no heed of Kent's plea, Harman said, 'you're a cold bastard, Kent. You tried to kill me, and you hit him instead. That was a mistake, a big mistake that you will regret.'

'Just do one thing,' Kent barked with the unfettered passion of someone whose life was swaying in the wind, knowing that one single gust would blow it over, 'look in his hand.'

Unwilling to give Kent the slightest invitation to evade him, Harman kept staring at him as he said, 'Virginia, how is he?'

'I'm not sure. I feel like I should know, but

I do not.'

Kent shouted over both of them, 'Mrs Brightwell, is he holding anything?'

She went to each of his hands in turn and replied, 'no.'

Harman glowered at Kent and said, 'whatever game you're playing, Sebastian, it's over. I will make you forget to swim and then tell you to jump in the lake. Drowning was on my mind not so long ago. It was hard to imagine what it would be like, but you won't have to imagine it. You are going to experience it. It will be your last ever memory.'

Kent stood tall as he had been trained to do when on parade drill. He said, 'if you think I will beg for my life then you do not know me.'

'Beg or not it makes no difference to me.'

Harman readied himself to influence Kent to leap into the water. Something happened then that neither of them could ever have predicted. Virginia Brightwell saved Kent's life.

She said, 'look, this was under his arm.'

Kent and Harman's attention was drawn to the knife she was holding up. The reddish-brown stains on its blade and handle were unmistakeable.

Harman muttered, 'I don't understand.'

Kent, using the sort of tone that was normally reserved for talking down suicidal jumpers from tall buildings, said, 'listen, Alan, I don't know who you think that is, but I know it's

Ernst Mannson. Despite the phoney glasses and shaved head, I recognised him from surveillance footage. That was when I figured out that it must have been him and not you who was killing all those Ascendants. Once we knew who we were looking for it was much easier to track back. We found him travelling with you or close behind you. I couldn't be sure what was going on, but when I saw him coming up behind you with that blade, I knew he planned for you to be next on his list. And I'm sorry for speaking so quickly, but I wanted to get it all out before you could make me go over the side.'

Harman's head felt like it would spin clean off. He didn't know who to believe. Easing Brightwell away, he knelt at Hope's side. Brightwell was staring at the knife as if it held some mystery for her. Harman did not fear her any longer. He had eyes and ears for Hope alone.

Harman said, 'he's lying, isn't he, Charles?'

The man lying there coughed and winced. He said, 'pretending to be that runt turned my stomach, but he served his purpose. I might be dying, but I have darkened the light of many devils and have served my God well. My solitary regret is that you escaped me. I have the authority to drive out demons and the evil in you shines out more than in any other Ascendant I have encountered.'

The words stung Harman. He drew back. Reaching out he pulled away Hope's tinted glasses. The eyes that stared back at him were not Charles Hope's. Harman said 'you really are Ernst Mannson. How could I not have seen it?'

Harman wasn't sure if he was asking himself or Mannson the question.

'Shut up, Harman, self-pity does not suit you and I do not want to hear it in my last seconds,' Mannson's outpouring of hate was interrupted by a further bout of coughing. When he continued, he was wheezing more, and he could taste the iron of blood on his teeth, 'I never expected to be stopped by a dumb Normal with a gun. I don't understand that, but if it is part of the Almighty's great plan then I will accept it with grace. I sent Thibault Blanc, Daiyu Chen, Hans Osterfeld, and Hagihara to face God's judgement. You killed one of the demons yourself on this ship. Now I will join them. That is six Ascendants and their pestilence less. It is a cause for rejoicing.'

Harman pulled away the jacket that had been used to staunch the blood. It made Mannson gasp, but Harman didn't care about that. He tore open Mannson's shirt and carefully inspected the wound. Less blood was seeping out. Ships normally had pretty good medical facilities even when they didn't carry a dedicated medical officer. He would make use of them soon.

Letting the shirt drop back into place, Harman said, 'I hate to disappoint you, but you're not dying. Sebastian over there can tell you how much bullets hurt and how long it takes to recover from being hit by one, but no arteries or vital organs have been damaged. We'll get you to a hospital, probably one run by the military so that you can more easily be handed back to Homeland Security. I hear they're not happy about you taking them for fools. They're never letting you escape again.'

A grin that would have terrified the stoutest of men and women fixed itself on Mannson's face. He said, 'God will not give up his war on the Ascendant demons, and he will not give up on me. He has spared me to continue my work. I will see all of you again, even that bitch over there, although I don't know what sort of abomination you have turned her into.'

Brightwell said as if awaking from a dream, 'Hagihara...he mentioned Hagihara.'

Mannson sneered and said to Harman, 'you really did a number on her. She doesn't know what day of the week it is. Good work.'

Brightwell was saying under her breath, 'Hagihara, Yukio Hagihara. Yukio Hagihara.'

Something told her that the name and the man with that name had some special meaning for her. If only she could tear away the cotton wool that clogged her mind she would remember why.

The clip-step-clip-step gave notice that Kent was hobbling closer. He said, 'I've really overdone it with this bloody leg of mine. My doctor would have a fit if he knew I'd been climbing up fences and ships.'

Oblivious to him or what he said, Brightwell turned her ear to the sky as if hearing somebody call her from a distance. She nodded to herself and whispered, 'I know now. Yukio was my friend.'

She went from quiet self-absorption to uncontrolled rage in the time it took Mannson to blink. Like a rabid she-wolf she descended on him. The knife that she had picked up from its resting place on the deck plunged up and down into his chest. His body jerked like a punch bag being pummelled by a heavyweight boxer. With each thrust, more blood spurted out.

Harman grabbed her in a bear hug and lifted her off the ground. Kent squeezed her wrist until the gore-covered knife clattered to the deck. Brightwell went still in his arms while he told Kent to see if Mannson was still alive.

Brightwell, her voice devoid of any emotion, said, 'he is dead. I remember that I am a doctor. I remember where the heart is.'

Kent looked at her like she was some strange animal in a zoo that he had never seen before, before bending down on his good leg. He said, 'she's right, he's dead.'

'Are you absolutely sure?' Harman said. Part of him, the part that could still see Charles Hope lying on the deck, wanted Kent to be wrong.

'Trust me, if you'll excuse the phrase given the circumstances, he's dead. I've seen enough dead men to be sure of that.'

*

While Harman influenced Captain Tomasis to instruct his crew to stay away from the aft deck, Kent was making calls. The key one involved persuading Sir Anthony Wildman to pull as many strings as he could to get a clean-up team to the ship as soon as possible. He took some persuading, but eventually he was willing to take Kent at his word. If Kent had truly captured Virginia Brightwell and her damned bioweapon it was more than enough to buy Kent a seat back at the table. Kent going full Rambo, as Wildman described it, was not easily overlooked. He conceded however that good battles could save bad generals. On top of bringing Brightwell to book, the death of Mannson was a commendable bonus. If not the perfect outcome for their American allies, it still served to clear up the mess they had contributed to by losing him in the first place.

Kent always felt that some of Wildman's metaphors were left deliberately open to multiple interpretations. That way the master string-puller always left himself a plausible excuse if something went wrong. Despite that,

Kent was left satisfied that he had pulled his feet out of the fire. Results were what counted, and he had delivered a fine result.

When Harman returned, he found Kent sitting next to Brightwell on the lifebelt box. She was staring unwaveringly across the lake to the mountains on the Swiss side.

'Did you get it done?' Harman said.

'The cogs are greased, and the wheels are turning.' Kent said, realising straight away that he was sounding like Wildman.

'How has she been?'

'Hasn't moved a muscle. Quiet as a mouse and as docile as a lamb.'

Harman said, 'we need to watch her. She was like that before she turned into Norman Bates from Psycho.'

'Who from what?'

'He's a character from a Hitchcock film. Are you telling me that you've never seen it or heard of it?'

Kent massaged his leg as he said, 'if it will make you happy, I will add it to my to-do list. Putting that to one side, would you care to explain what you've done to her?'

'Another time maybe, when I'm less tired.'

'I have to admit that my money was on you killing her at the earliest opportunity,' Kent said, as if it was the type of conversation that two men would have in a bar.

'She was prepared to die. She always was.

She's a zealot. Giving her martyrdom would have been a gift, not a punishment. What I've done to her, as you put it, is worse than death to her. Can we leave it at that?'

'It still sounds to me suspiciously like naked revenge.'

'One man's revenge is another man's justice,' Harman said with the certainty of someone who had recently been giving the subject a great deal of thought, and who was not minded to be convinced otherwise.

Kent accepted that it was the wrong place to be debating the subject. Not that it would have been much of a debate because he agreed with Harman.

Moments of quiet reflection passed when the only sounds were the screeching of gulls and the whistle of the wind as it blew through the ship. Both men had things to say to one another. Neither was sure how to go about it.

It was Kent who first broached the awkward subject of Harman's immediate future. He said, 'you know you will have to come back with me.'

'I can't do that. Maybe sometime, when I've got my head straight. Not before then.'

'There's still work for you at ET1.'

'You say that now, and you probably believe it, but you will never be able to trust Ascendants and with all that's happened you surely won't be able to trust me anymore. You've got enough here to make everyone happy. You don't need me as well.'

'What will you do? Where can you go?' Kent protested.

'You know what, I've been a policeman for most of my life. Some people used to think I was a pretty good detective. I will carry on with that. Maybe it's what the Ascendants need. Someone to protect them from the Mannsons of this world. Someone to stop another Brightwell rising to the top.'

Kent sniffed the air and said, 'that's not being a detective, that's being a Sheriff in the Old West.'

'I suppose it could be wild, but it is what it is, and I am what I am.'

'Listen to me, Alan. If you're really plan to make a difference you need resources. How many times have I told you that? You got lucky this time by playing the Lone Ranger. Hell, we both did, but it can't last. I'm asking you again to come back with me.'

'My mind is made up, Sebastian. One way or another I will do what I've said. As for the best way to go about it, I reckon I've earned some thinking time.'

Kent shook his head in sad disagreement. When he looked up, he saw a motor launch powering towards them at a high rate of knots. He went across the deck to see better. His phone rang. It was Wildman. He said the help that Kent had requested should be with him soon. Kent said he could see them. Wildman said good and ended the call. Kent smiled to himself. Whatever anyone might think of Sir Anthony Wildman, when he pulled strings, things happened fast. Never this fast though, surely? That boat and whoever was on it must have been waiting in the wings. Kent realised that he had not been as clever as he thought he had. Either Amy Bishop, or Wildman, or the two of them in partnership had been keeping their own close eye on him.

He turned around to tell Harman about the call, but he was nowhere to be seen. Kent called out for him. There was no answer. He searched for Harman as best he could. Standing on the deck, he swivelled awkwardly with the aid of his walking stick. His injured leg pulsed. It emitted a warmth that had not been there before. Without looking he knew that the wound had opened, and fresh blood was infusing the bandages that were wrapped around it.

His ungainly pirouette came to a halt when he saw one of the Seago inflatable boats bounce at full speed past the prow of the *Duttweiller.* It was heading south towards the French coast of the lake. The man in it had no jacket on. He had left that garment to cover the dead face of Ernst Mannson, or, as he still thought of him, Charles Hope.

CHAPTER TEN

Although they were in Sebastian Kent's office at ET1, it was Sir Anthony Wildman that was holding court. Kent and Amy Bishop were his two courtiers.

'As you know I don't enjoy being this far from civilisation, so I will keep the meeting short.'

'Your rare visits are always welcome, sir,' Kent said quickly. They were no more than a few miles from Whitehall, the centre of British Government, and it irked him to be treated as if they were hidden away in the backwoods somewhere. However, following his still recent suspension, he had tried to suck up to his superiors and play the game of bureaucratic politics with more skill. Before it would have stuck in his throat, but together with his pride he had learned to swallow it.

'Thank you, Sebastian. You've been back in the big chair for what, two months? How are you enjoying it?'

'Never better, sir.'

'To the victor the spoils. You earned it. It's fortunate that we couldn't identify a suitable replacement for you while you were suspended. That's by the by. Thanks to you, we have

Brightwell and her infernal bioweapon. It would have been nice to have Ernst Mannson to tie a bow on and hand over to Homeland security, but they are happy enough. For them his death is like having a painful tooth extracted. Not to put too fine a point on it, we are for the present the prettiest girl at the Ball and every agency with an interest in Ascendants wishes to dance with us. Nevertheless...'

That one word made the contents of Kent's stomach curdle. When using it Wildman always sounded like a surgeon who was cheerily telling you he had saved your thumb, before going on to say that unfortunately he had been forced to take your leg off.

'...Nevertheless, it had been decided that the emergence of Ascendants can no longer be treated alongside other emerging threats. It warrants a department of its own. We will therefore be moving swiftly to establish ET:A. Assuming that she is happy to accept, it will be led by Dr Bishop. You do accept, don't you?'

Bishop said, 'I would be honoured, sir.'

Wildman smiled benevolently at her, and said, 'and so you should be. By the by, how is your work proceeding with Mrs Brightwell?'

'An updated report will be with you by the end of the day, but there is little change. Whatever happened to her, she seems incapable of accessing any of her Ascendant talents. Any drive or even tiny inclination to harm people such as us has disappeared. That is rational because she believes herself to be completely normal, as in the same as you or I. Every psychological test we have run confirms that to be her true belief. On the downside, her memory is unreliable, and she suffers extended bouts of confusion. I would describe it as some form of dissociative fugue state.'

'Beyond being your guinea pig, Dr Bishop, how much of an asset will she be to us?'

'It's too early to say, sir. With extensive psychiatric and psychological treatment her memories may return. In which case she could be a treasure trove of information about other Ascendants.'

'And you are sure this is not some act she is putting on? It would be unforgivable if she ever posed a threat to us again.'

Bishop said, 'I believe it to be genuine, Sir Anthony. However, we can never take the chance that she might…relapse. The new facility will be ready before the week is out and she will be transferred there. After that she will never meet a single human being in person for the rest of her life. Escape will be impossible. Ingress by anyone else to reach her will also be impossible. She will remain heavily sedated until the transfer is completed. I can assure you that valuable lessons have been learned as a result of Alan Harman's escape from the prototype facility in Surrey. Those mistakes will not be made again.'

In response, Wildman smiled benignly at her.

Kent listened attentively to the charade that was being played out in front of him. It was an insult to his intelligence, albeit one he could live with. Surely, they didn't expect him to believe that this was the first that Amy had heard about this new department? It could not be more obvious to Kent that she had already jumped at the chance to lead it, and that she had been directly briefing Wildman behind his back. He could only guess at how long that had been going on for.

While his face revealed none of those calculations, under the table his fists were gripped tight around his walking stick. He was imagining it to be Wildman's scrawny neck.

He did not know how Bishop had wangled the secession from ET1, but he had to give her credit for playing the gambit so well.

Wildman said, 'keep up the good work.'

Kent, forcing himself to do the right thing as they would see it, said, 'many congratulations, Amy, your promotion is well-earned.'

Part of him genuinely meant it, the other part was worrying about how much meat would be torn from the body of ET1 to feed this new department of hers.

As if reading Kent's mind, Wildman said, 'our masters, quite rightly, have recognised the need to make the overall resources cake bigger so that the wider efforts of ET1 are not undermined. Rest assured, Sebastian, your budget and staffing levels will not suffer because of this change. If we have learnt anything from our recent experiences, it is that we cannot take any emerging threat lightly. The problem this creates for you is that you will have to search for an able deputy to replace Dr Bishop. That's not so bad, is it?'

Kent marvelled at how Wildman had managed to make the question so threatening. There was always much to learn from him. He said, 'thank you, sir, that's very reassuring. I was merely wondering, as this is the first that I've heard of this, whether an alternative might be to expand ET1 so it could adequately continue with both roles as before? After all, wasn't it ET1 that made us the prettiest girl at the Ball?'

Wildman laced his fingers together. On his face was the same expression that a cat might have towards a mouse held in its claws. He said, 'it isn't worth dwelling on, but one might argue, indeed some have argued, that it was ET1 under your leadership that almost got us thrown out of the Ball completely with the Americans pulling down the pretty girl's knickers and spanking her arse. What would you have me tell those who think that?'

Kent had always believed that death before dishonour was one of the worst rules for a soldier to live by. Honour could always be earned again. Death was permanent and he was not about to commit professional suicide. He said, 'I would have you tell them that, when all things are considered, their choice is a wise one.'

'Excellent, back to business then. As Dr Bishop has accepted our offer, please relieve her of any tasks that are currently allocated to her, except for those that are Ascendant related. She will need all her time to get ET:A off the ground. Her new base of operations will be ready in a week or so. She will have a small specialist team to begin with. Now, I must get back to civilisation.'

Wildman shook their hands, told them to keep up the good work, and was gone.

There was an odd emptiness about the office once he had left, like a field after a tornado had ripped through it.

Kent prised his fingers from the walking stick. He counted himself lucky to still have his beloved job and the office they were in. There was nothing any of them could do to stop him keeping a secretive eye on Ascendants, but there was plenty of other work to get his teeth into.

He shook his head in mock disbelief and said, 'congratulations again, Amy. Tell me though, how did you swing it? I really don't get it. One minute we're being threatened with complete closure, the next we have not one, but two, ET departments. Talk about coming back from the dead.'

Her innocent eyes glowed under her innocent bob of hair, but he now knew as well as she did, that they were merely effective and convincing camouflage that concealed the true Amy Bishop. She said, 'why so surprised, Sebastian? After all, you are the hero of the hour. A couple of months ago, you averted a global catastrophe. I expect that you are in line for a gong or two next year. Sebastian Kent, OBE, sounds good, doesn't it?'

'Order of the British Empire? You know what they call that in the army? To me OBE will always stand for Other Blokes Efforts.'

She shrugged and said, 'maybe something else then.'

'Besides, if I'm the hero, how come you are the one getting the reward?'

'Come off it, Sebastian, ET1 will always be your baby. They will have to drag you out of here kicking and screaming. Hanging on to this department is all you ever really wanted from this.'

Kent shrugged back at her and said, 'maybe you're right. It still doesn't explain how you pulled this off. Your own base of operations, Wildman called it. Staff and funding as well? I've been trying to get those Shylocks at the Treasury to open their purses for years. Somehow, in no time flat you've got them handing over the whole purse. Have you got friends in high places that you've never told me about?'

Amy Bishop smiled like a siren calling sailors to the rocks as she moved to the door. She said, 'if you will excuse me, I really do have a lot to be getting on with.'

'That's it then, you're really not going to tell me?'

She paused in the doorway and said, 'no, I don't have friends in high places. Let's just say that I have a friend who can exert influence in those high places.'

Kent's eyes widened. Before he could put his thoughts into words she had gone and closed the door behind her.

Amy Bishop had told the truth. As a born-again Christian it was what she was always driven to do. She really did have a lot to be getting on with. It was time to begin recruiting for ET:A.

Back in her own office, with every security protocol in operation, she called a single-use phone number. The call was picked up by someone in Paris.

Alan Harman said to her, 'did everything go as planned?'

'Like clockwork. Welcome to ET:A. It's time for you to get back to work, Alan.' As she spoke, she could only hope that she would do a better job of keeping Alan Harman in line than Sebastian Kent had done.

AUTHOR'S NOTE

If this is the first of the Ascent Trilogy that you have read, then I hope it has piqued your interest sufficiently to go back and read the preceding two books in the series. On the other hand, if you have already read the first two, then my thanks to you for sticking with it. I can only hope you enjoyed the journey and that you found the conclusion satisfying.

In each of the books, I have included an author's note. As I mentioned in both *Status Green* and *Status Amber,* I did not want to bog the story down with too much repetition of the science stuff. There is, hopefully, enough to give the underlying premise enough credibility. However, the author's note does provide an opportunity to share some of the source material that did not make the cut.

First though, a small confession. The naming of characters always deserves to be done with some care. People's names often provide an insight into their culture and background. For readers they can provide a short-cut to understanding those characters and to differentiate them. Beyond that, they can also provide hidden clues about characters. In the Ascent Trilogy, I could not resist using the names of a couple of characters to do exactly that. They were hidden in the open, but even so give yourself a pat on the back if you spotted each of them. For any of you who identified them early on as glaringly obvious, I can only promise to try harder next time.

So, what were they? Well, quite rightly given his prominence in the story, the first involves Alan Harman. At various places it is mentioned that his middle name is Patrick. Hidden in his full name is Alpha Man, as in **Al**an **P**atrick **Har**man. More than a hint perhaps of what he was to become by the end of the third book.

Then there was Ernst Mannson, the Ascendant who believes that God has appointed him to be an Ascendant hunter. He makes his debut in the second book and becomes a major character in the third. Faced with how to latch on to Harman, and in so doing be led to his prey, he constructs the persona of the inoffensive Charles Hope. The clue to this crazed killer and Harman's assistant being one and the same, was that if you put the first name of one with the surname of the other, you get Charles Mannson. Which to many will conjure up images of Charles Manson, the American cult leader, whose *Family* committed at least nine murders in 1969.

Coming back to the factual basis for the story and doing my best not to simply rehash what was in previous author's notes, I have set out below some relevant and, I believe interesting, snippets of information.

Evolution – theory of saltation

More about this theory is contained in *Status Green* when Alan Harman and his colleagues are grappling to understand what they are dealing with, but the Encyclopaedia Brittanica states that the theory argues, "that new species are produced rapidly through discontinuous transformations. Saltationist theory contradicted Darwinism, which held that species evolved through the gradual accumulation of variation over vast epochs."

The Ascent Trilogy is based on this notion that mankind might evolve rapidly over a handful of generations rather than over millions of years. There is evidence, albeit limited, of such rapid change taking place in other organisms.

The two questions that are prompted by this, and which recur throughout the trilogy, are: (i) how would this more quickly evolving strand of humanity differ from the rest of us; and (ii) how would they react to us Normals?

For the purposes of these three books, the answers are: (i) although there would be some variation between the evolved, as there is within the general population, they would share many facets such as living longer, having fewer genetic health defects, benefiting from heightened senses, needing less sleep and, most notable of all, the ability to influence people; and (ii) some would inevitably be threatened by the sea of lesser, yet still dangerous, mortals that surround them,

Bioweapons

There are countless books and learned works about this subject, and no doubt many more will emerge in the future. It is a dark area of research. Its sole role here is to demonstrate that the principle of DNA weaponisation is science fact and not science fiction. Depressing as this may be, the potential existence of such a targeted method of mass destruction explains why Virginia Brightwell would choose it to clear and hasten the Ascent of her people in this story.

To illustrate very briefly the reality of this threat:

a)   The US Department of Homeland Security states that "A biological attack is the intentional release of a pathogen (disease causing agent) or biotoxin (poisonous substance produced by a living organism." See Communicating in a Crisis: Biological Attack (dhs.gov)

b) In July 2022, at the Aspen Security Forum, US Representative Jason Crow warned that bioweapons are being made that use a target's DNA to kill that particular person.

c)   In August 2021 the Genetic Literacy project stated that: "The most alarming use of biotechnology is in developing 'genetic weapons'. The integration of biology with AI computation has facilitated scientists' understanding of how different population groups have differing susceptibility to diseases and disorders, and their responses to medicines. It has now become possible to design and develop precise genetic weapons that could be deployed stealthily over wide areas, and such weapons would affect only targeted people, of specific ethnic group or race." See **Genetic warfare: Is China on the path to developing a biological superweapon?** - Genetic Literacy Project

d) "Many pathogenic bacteria contain multiple plasmids (small circular extrachromosomal DNA fragments) that code for virulence or other special functions. The virulence of anthrax, plague, dysentery, and other diseases is enhanced by these plasmids. What occurs naturally in nature can be artificially conducted with basic biotechnology techniques in the laboratory. Virulent plasmids can be transferred among different kinds of bacteria and often across species barriers. To produce a binary biological weapon a host bacteria and a virulent plasmid could be independently isolated and produced in the required quantities." US Air Force Counter Proliferation Center. See 14NEXTGENBIOWEAPONS.PDF (defense.gov)

e)   In September 2015, Mikhail Kovalchuk, president of the Russian National Research Centre Kurchatov Institute, said in a speech that it would soon be possible to develop targeted medicine, but also genetic weapons that could strike specific ethnic groups as a weapon of mass destruction. See Fear and Loathing in Moscow: The Russian biological weapons program in 2022 - Bulletin of the Atomic Scientists (thebulletin.org)

f)   "The method through which a biological weapon is deployed depends on the agent itself, its preparation, its durability, and the route of infection. Attackers may disperse these agents through aerosols or food and water supplies." See Communicating in a Crisis: Biological Attack (dhs.gov)

Lake Geneva and Mir submersibles

Each of the locations in the book are real and as

described, but I chose Lausanne and Lake Geneva for the climax of *Status Red* because I have been there many times and, particularly, as a research vessel and two Mir submersibles were deployed there in 2011. Between June and August, the trusty Mirs made over sixty dives in support of various research projects. They were also used in numerous other scientific expeditions and in the making of multiple films and documentaries. The work on and under Lake Geneva was pretty much their swan song and both are currently on display in Russian museums. It felt nice to give one of them a final hurrah with a guest appearance in *Status Red*.

CLIVE HAWKSWOOD

ABOUT THE AUTHOR

Clive Hawkswood

Other Books By The Author:

ASCENDANT SERIES

Status Green
Status Amber
Status Red

QUINTRELL SERIES

Quintrell's Black
Churchill's Gold
Bismarck's Plague
Quintrell's White

STAND ALONE BOOKS

The Seventh Coffin
Incidentia MMX
The Last Traitor
Legs of the Spider